FATAL
REMAINS

Also by Eleanor Taylor Bland

Windy City Dying
Whispers in the Dark
Scream in Silence
Tell No Tales
See No Evil
Keep Still
Done Wrong
Gone Quiet
Slow Burn
Dead Time

F A T A L
REMAINS

E L E A N O R
T A Y L O R
B L A N D

ST. MARTIN'S MINOTAUR.......NEW YORK

www.minotaurbooks.com

Library of Congress Cataloging-in-Publication Data

Bland, Eleanor Taylor.
    Fatal remains / Eleanor Taylor Bland.—1st ed.
      p. cm.
    ISBN 0-312-30097-2
    1. MacAlister, Marti (Fictitious character)—Fiction.   2. Police—Illinois—Chicago—Fiction.   3. African American police—Fiction.   4. Real estate development—Fiction.   5. Chicago (Ill.)—Fiction.   6. Policewomen—Fiction.
I. Title.

PS3552.L36534F37 2003
813'.54—dc21

                        2003053049

First Edition: December 2003

10 9 8 7 6 5 4 3 2 1

Congratulations on their retirements to Andy Stimson, executive director, Waukegan Public Library, and Barbara Richardson, coroner, Lake County, Illinois.

A warm welcome to Owen Neely Harris
"Our children are not our children . . . they belong to a tomorrow that we cannot visit . . . not even in our dreams."

A very special happy eightieth birthday to Ed Gilbreth, a friend and supporter of Chicago mystery readers for many years.

This novel required a great deal of research. I would like to acknowledge the following sources:

Bennett, Jr., Lerone, *Before the Mayflower: A History of the Negro in America, 1619–1964.* Penguin Books.

Burroughs, Tony, *Black Roots, A Beginner's Guide to Tracing the African American Family Tree.* A Fireside Book, Simon and Schuster.

Clifton, James A., *The Potawatomi.* Chelsea House Publishers.

Turner, Glennette Tilley, *The Underground Railroad in Illinois.* Newman Educational Publishing, Glen Ellyn, Illinois.

I would also like to express my appreciation to Nanette C. Boryc, researcher extraordinaire, for her professional research skills as well as the time she so generously provided when I became totally overwhelmed by what was "out there" on the Internet. Nanette also "rescued" this manuscript when my computer crashed.

As always, I must express my deep and continuing appreciation to my agent, Ted Chichak, who is always there for me; to Kelley Ragland, my editor, and to Ben Sevier, assistant editor. I would also like to thank Erika Schmid, the copy editor of this book, for doing such a professional job.

I would also like to thank my family for their patience and support with all of my endeavors.

Many thanks to super fans Rhonda Pope, Washington, D.C., and in Illinois, Mark Dobrzycki, Keith Corbin, Augie at Centuries and Sleuths, John Doggett, Wendy Beshel, and June Zaragoza.

A special thank you to Jack Cody, retired professor, Southern Illinois University, and to Camille Taylor, retired professor, College of Lake County. Over the years, so much of what they taught me has continued to resonate as I write.

For technical assistance I relied very heavily on the expertise of Professor Emeritus Dr. William Bass, University of Tennessee, and John Rorabeck, assistant coroner, Lake County, Illinois, Barbara D'Amato, author, and research librarians Lourdes Mordini, Yan Xu, Eva Gracia, Patricia McLaughlin, and Peter Sprinkle at the Waukegan Public Library.

I have discovered that in order to write as I do, I need to see good in the world. I would particularly like to thank the following individuals for providing me with that opportunity: my sister-in-law, Julia Anderson, age eighty-five, who, with selfless love and dedication, cared for her brother, Sterling, during his final illness, my church family at St. Anastasia Church, my family of lay Carmelites, Brother Benjamin, Dr. Charles V. Holmberg, Robert F. Reusche, and Phillip Carrigan.

THATCHER

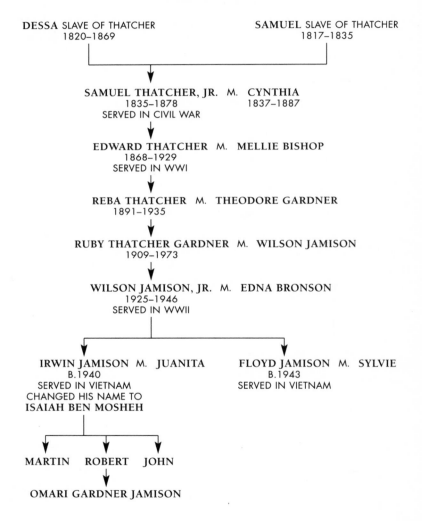

DESSA SLAVE OF THATCHER
1820–1869

SAMUEL SLAVE OF THATCHER
1817–1835

SAMUEL THATCHER, JR. M. CYNTHIA
1835–1878   1837–1887
SERVED IN CIVIL WAR

EDWARD THATCHER M. MELLIE BISHOP
1868–1929
SERVED IN WWI

REBA THATCHER M. THEODORE GARDNER
1891–1935

RUBY THATCHER GARDNER M. WILSON JAMISON
1909–1973

WILSON JAMISON, JR. M. EDNA BRONSON
1925–1946
SERVED IN WWII

IRWIN JAMISON M. JUANITA
B.1940
SERVED IN VIETNAM
CHANGED HIS NAME TO
ISAIAH BEN MOSHEH

FLOYD JAMISON M. SYLVIE
B.1943
SERVED IN VIETNAM

MARTIN   ROBERT   JOHN

OMARI GARDNER JAMISON

SMITH

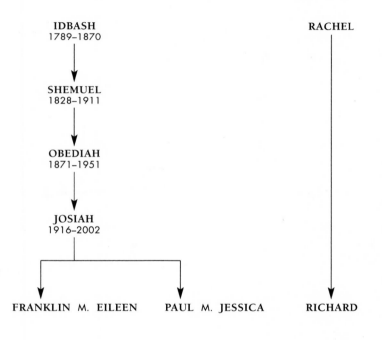

IDBASH
1789–1870

RACHEL

SHEMUEL
1828–1911

OBEDIAH
1871–1951

JOSIAH
1916–2002

FRANKLIN M. EILEEN   PAUL M. JESSICA   RICHARD

FATAL
REMAINS

Naawe could hear the screams of the wide-winged lake birds as she hurried up to the place where Dessa was hiding. The white birds moved swiftly, flying in wide circles. Naawe was high enough above the place where the water crashed against the rocks to look down at them. Some swooped down to the Mitchigami. Others walked or ran on long legs across the sand, seeking food. She looked for the boats of the Neshnabek, her people, but there were none. Nampizha was angry today. There were many places close to land where his breath could be seen breaking the water. Not even an offering of tobacco would calm him. Perhaps, as her grandmother had once told her, it was good that the "hairy faces" came, bringing horses.

Soon there would be no Neshnabek here, not in boats, not on horses. Already her people were traveling over land far from the waters where Nampizha lived. They would cross the great river to the land far beyond and never see this place again. The time for leaving had come, but she would not go with them. Soon she would be alone. She would have to stay away from the trails marked by her people, stay away from the kitchimokomon who said that Neshnabek land was now theirs. She would follow the lake north, to the place where it met the small river. There were other Neshnabek there whose land the kitchimokomon did not own.

Naawe stopped and closed her eyes. She listened to the sound of the water as Nampizha thrashed beneath the surface.

1

She listened to the screams of the wide-winged birds. She took one more look at Mitchigami, the great lake that went to where the sky began. Then she turned away, toward the tall trees that held back the sun. She stepped on the flowers that grew in the places the sun did not reach. Small flowers, green and white now, with thick, sharp leaves that were not crushed when she stepped on them.

Once she left here, she would not see this place again. She would be far from here now were it not for Dessa, whom she had found hiding two days ago. Dessa was also running away. She was also frightened and alone. The kitchimokomon was looking for Dessa, too. Not because he owned her land, but because he owned her.

Naawe heard Dessa before she saw her, heard soft cries and moans, then grunts and fast breathing. Naawe moved toward the sounds of pain, careful not to be heard or seen in case it was the kitchimokomon who were here and not the baby whose time it was to be born. When she reached a place of many bushes, the sounds were louder. Naawe crouched and listened. Then she heard the cries of a child, not the loud cries that she had heard before when Neshnabek women gave birth, but a quiet cry, as if the child had no strength. Naawe stood. She parted the bushes until she came to the place where Dessa lay. The baby, smeared and bloody, was on her belly. Dessa's blood flowed, soaking into the grass. Naawe took the pouch from her back, reached in and found the pitchkosan for childbirth. She opened the otter-skin bundle and took out the root for bleeding that would not stop.

Later, when it was the time before the stars, and the sun went to the place away from the lake and the sky became dark, Dessa put her boy child to her breast.

"What do you name him?" Naawe asked in the language of the kitchimokomon.

"Samuel, for his father," Dessa answered. She stroked the child's dark hair. "We leave here soon, so the white man cannot take him."

"You should come with me," Naawe said. "The child will grow strong with what I have in my pitchkosan."

Dessa shook her head.

"Dessa, you ran away from the kitchimokomon, who you call white man. When he caught you and your people, only you got away. He has taken the others to the dark place, the place of death. Come with me, before he finds you."

Dessa shook her head again. "North," she whispered. "We go north. Tonight I go to see if they have hung out the quilt that tells us when it is time to leave here."

The house with the quilt was the house of the kitchimokomon. Naawe did not trust any of them. She did not know why Dessa did.

Dessa held out her sleeping child. "I will not be gone long. Will you watch him?"

Clouds hid the moon when Dessa left. Naawe held the sleeping baby in her arms. She should go now, while the kitchimokomon expected her people to move west, but the child was not strong, nor was his mother. The medicines that would make them strong were in her pitchkosan. Perhaps if she gave them to Dessa and told her how to use them . . . the baby stirred, gave a few weak cries and went back to sleep.

Naawe listened to Nampizha, stirring up the waters of the great lake and making the water crash against the rocks below the bluffs. The god of the waters was angry. He was warning her away from this place. She listened to him speak and was afraid.

TUESDAY, JUNE 18

As Detective Marti MacAlister and her partner, Matthew "Vik" Jessenovik, walked across the wide expanse of grass toward the man who had found the skeletal remains, they could here his voice rising with hysteria.

". . . looking at me . . . he was looking at me . . . he . . . he . . . he was . . ."

"He didn't have any eyes," the uniform interrupted.

"And grinning . . . he was . . ."

"They all look like they're grinning."

Marti could see that the man was wearing a long overcoat despite the seventy-five-degree weather. Limp brown hair fell across his forehead and hung to his shoulders. He was clutching a fraying nylon duffel bag.

"What if I was sleeping on him? What if . . ."

"You probably were."

The man dropped the bag and began rubbing his arms through his coat sleeves.

"I just wanted a place to sleep." He sounded as if he was about to cry.

Close up, the man looked to be in his teens. Marti could smell him, just dirt and perspiration, not the sickening odor of rotting garbage or the sweet, acrid smell of marijuana.

The uniform looked at her and Vik with raised eyebrows. He shrugged.

"Okay, Brandon, here are the detectives who are going to

4

investigate this." He introduced them, then took a few steps back while they showed Brandon their badges.

"What happened?" Marti asked.

"Went to sleep and woke up with this head staring at me and grinning."

"A skull," the uniform said. "Just a skull."

"Just hell. Wasn't more than six inches from my face."

"What did you do?"

"Do? What do you think? Grabbed my stuff. Ran like hell. Woke up those people in that house." He pointed toward a large Georgian in the center of the lawn. "Sleeping on a dead body. Damn." He shook his head. "Middle of June and I still can't find a safe place to sleep."

"Nothing's safe when you're on the street," the uniform said.

Marti turned to him. He needed something to do. "Where did he find it?" she asked.

"Down in there." He pointed to a ridge of trees midway between the top of the bluff and the little-used four-lane roadway at the base of the bluff. From where they stood, Marti could not see the lake at all.

"Did you disturb anything?" she asked.

"No. Flashed my light in, saw the skull, called it in."

"Good. Go watch for the coroner's van and the evidence tech. Direct them down there."

She turned to Brandon. "Did you see anything else?"

He shook his head.

"Sleep here before?"

"Couple of times."

"Ever see anyone here?"

"No. If I wanted to see people I'd go someplace else."

She gave Vik a small nod. It was his turn.

"How old are you, son?"

"Nineteen."

At six-two, Vik towered over him. Vik's face was craggy, with a beaklike nose that was skewed to one side by a break. Wiry salt-and-pepper eyebrows almost met in a ferocious scowl. He seldom smiled. Now he struck what Marti called his vulture pose. Most adults were intimidated by this, kids weren't fazed at all. Brandon didn't seem to be afraid either.

"Where are you from?"

"Around."

"Around where?"

Brandon shrugged. "Wherever."

"Where are you headed?"

"No place in particular."

"Well, in that case, you won't mind if we detain you for twenty-four hours, make sure there aren't any warrants out on you."

Another shrug. "Think you could make it the hospital? Psych ward? Food's better."

Vik shook his head. "Sorry."

"Vagrants," Vik said as they walked away. "Strange way to live. Somebody will probably find his body someday. Or his bones."

Vik whistled as he led the way through the woods where the remains had been found. It was a tuneless whistle, not a song, something he did so seldom that Marti had to think for a minute before she realized that Brandon's age bothered him. As she followed him, she wondered what would bring anyone, especially a homeless teenager, to this place. Low bushes snagged her slacks. Tree branches scratched her arms. There was no path. The dirt was hard-packed and the undergrowth spiky and sharp. As they headed about thirty feet down to the base of the bluff, they pushed scrub and low tree branches aside, heard the scurrying of small animals, and flushed the occasional bird.

This was all that remained of the ancient bluffs that once descended to sandy beaches and the then unpolluted, fish-filled waters of Lake Michigan. For several hundred years the Potawatomi Indians had foraged here. According to Marti's eleven-year-old son Theo, they called themselves the Neshnabek, which meant The People. Then the French and the English brought civilization, or uncivilization, as Theo would say—and ultimately, relocation.

As Marti and Vik descended through the woods and toward "civilization," Marti could see the stacks of the "coker" plant, which still converted coal to electricity; the tops of concrete storage silos; gray mounds of gypsum waiting to be loaded onto ships; and the flat roofs of deserted buildings where fishing and boat-building industries once thrived. She couldn't see the lake at all. When they reached the base of the bluff, clumps of dandelions and clusters of prairie grasses took over. There wasn't much litter and not enough traffic to overcome the faint but unmistakable odor of a skunk.

"The Alzheimer's Expressway," Vik said.

"The Anstandt Expressway," she reminded him. Tufts of the tough, enduring grass had sprung up in concrete cracks along the little-used road.

"Depends on your perspective, MacAlister. It begins nowhere, ends nowhere, and goes nowhere. About the only thing it's good for is filming car chases and drag racing."

Marti could understand Vik's animosity. The roadway, two blocks long when it was built in the seventies and extended a few more blocks a couple of years ago, served no essential purpose that she could discern other than to divert some of the morning and evening commuter traffic. The Anstandt was supposed to go north, then west, and hook up with Route 173. It was also supposed to go south as far as Leebuck Road. Those links would have created a major bypass around the city. That never happened. There was a major manufacturing facility in the way, a cemetery with graves going back several hundred years, as well as churches and homes that had been built in the mid-to-late eighteen hundreds. For some reason none of that had initially been taken into consideration.

When Marti didn't say anything, Vik said, "Alzheimer's Expressway, like I said. This whole lakefront area should have been off-limits, just like they were smart enough to do in Chicago and Milwaukee."

Marti knew that was Vik's real complaint. "That would have been nice," she agreed, thinking of trips to the lakefront when she lived in Chicago; the beaches, the parks, museums and marinas. Here there was industrial pollution, an EPA asbestos cleanup in progress, mercury in the water, and miles of train track that could not be taken up.

Marti stood at the verge where grass met gravel and that yielded to asphalt. She turned and looked at a place among the trees. The medical examiner and the evidence technicians had arrived. Strips of yellow plastic marked the spot where the skeletal remains had been found. It was a peaceful place, quiet, a place where few people came, and none for any good reason. Someone had been buried there, perhaps died there. It was a lonely place to die. Most places were.

It was after eleven the following morning when Marti parked at the coroner's facility. Based on bits of clothing found with the remains, the medical examiner, Dr. Cyprian, estimated that the victim had been in a shallow grave for nine to twelve months. No ID had been found. Now somebody was going to read the bones. Marti wanted those bones to talk to her too, perhaps yield a few secrets that were less obvious than those a forensic anthropologist could have identified.

"Hurry up or we'll be late," Vik grouched. "Our expert from the big city has been here for half an hour."

"So? She arrived early."

Dr. Cyprian, a quiet-spoken East Indian, was waiting for them, along with Dr. Elaine Altenberg, who had driven up from Chicago. Marti and Vik had worked with her once before. Altenberg was good at what she did. She was a friendly, relaxed middle-aged woman who liked to talk. Marti had requested Meline Pickus, who had helped them when a mummy was found in the Geneva Theater, but Pickus was on vacation.

"Morning, Jessenovik," Altenberg said. "MacAlister."

The bones that had been recovered were arranged on a metal table in the autopsy room. The hands and feet were missing except for a few joints from the fingers.

"Animals," Altenberg said.

Most of the remaining bones had been gnawed. It was obvious from the damage to the rib cage that the victim had been shot.

The autopsy room was all concrete and stainless steel. Tools were assembled on carts and tables. The floor slanted toward a central drain. Marti tried to ignore the odor of the dead, a smell that reminded her of uncooked pig's feet at room temperature. The room was cold. She shivered and wished she had remembered to retrieve her jacket from the backseat of the car.

"I'm going to consult with Professor William Bass down in Knoxville to determine an approximate time of death," Dr. Altenberg said. "We found some blowfly pupa cases near the body. Dr. Bass is the expert on seasonal dating based on the presence of fly pupae. We also have some soft tissue on the arms and legs and Dr. Bass is more familiar than I am with decay rates when the body is buried in a shallow grave."

"Will that take long?" Vik asked.

"No. A day or two at the most," Dr. Altenberg said. "Now"— she pointed to the pelvic area—"there is no question that this is a male."

Before she could continue, Marti said, "Confirmed by the pubic shape, sub-pubic angle and the ventral arc." She had only seen one partial female skeleton, but she had seen three male skeletons and remembered that.

Altenberg paused, then picked up the skull and pointed to the ridge of bone above the eye sockets. "The suborbital crest is prominent, and . . ." She rotated the skull. "The nuchal crest at the back of the skull is more pronounced than a female's would be. And, look at this." She pointed to a small bump on the bone above where the ear would have been, and at two more small bumps above the eye socket. "Very unusual. Symptoms of something called Gardner's Syndrome. It's genetic, passed on by the male. And something else." She turned the skull until it seemed to be grinning at them. "See how large the teeth are, and how the incisors have a shovel shape? Native American. Most unusual."

Surprised, Marti took a closer look. "But . . . these are not old bones."

"No, new bones, nothing ancient."

"Potawatomi?"

"I can't say yet. There are facial variations among the different tribes. Maybe we'll get lucky and have so much difficulty finding out who he is that we'll have to do a facial reconstruction." She went on for at least ten minutes, describing how they used to do reconstructions; then said, "Of course, now we use computers," and launched into an explanation of that.

"Smart woman," Vik said as they walked to their car. "Knows her stuff. Just talks too much."

"She was still going strong when we left," Marti agreed. "At least Dr. Cyprian seemed interested."

"Nice of her to tell us all the things that could have happened to the victim's hair."

"Kind of like listening to the migratory habits of the yellow-bellied sapsucker," Marti agreed.

"Maybe we should take her over to the Alzheimer's, let her find a few animal burrows and climb a few trees to check the birds'-nests. See if she could find some of his hair. Maybe that would get her out of our hair."

"Having a bad day, Jessenovik?"

"I wasn't," Vik said. "Until now."

"Interesting that it's an American Indian."

"Native American," Vik said.

"Not according to Theo," Marti told him. Theo, and her stepson Mike, who was also eleven, were working on a major Potawatomi project with their Boy Scout troop.

As soon as she got back to the office, Marti called the North American Indian Center in Chicago. The man she spoke with gave her some leads on whom to contact about missing Indians. He was not optimistic that she would identify the remains after this length of time unless there was an existing missing-persons report. She began scanning those as soon as she hung up.

By Thursday afternoon Dr. Altenberg had determined that the victim was five feet eight inches tall, weighed about one forty-five and was over twenty-one, but not older than twenty-five. None of that information matched up with the missing-persons reports they had targeted, but it did provide a minimal description. The odontologist Altenberg consulted had not made a tribal identification. As soon as he did, Altenberg would begin the computerized reconstruction.

On Friday, Marti scanned the forensic reports. "Nothing useful," she concluded. "And nobody seems to be looking for him either."

Dr. Altenberg called just before noon. "That was a lucky guess, MacAlister."

"What was?"

"Potawatomi. Sorry it took so long to confirm that."

Marti thanked her, hung up, and relayed the information to Vik. "We better start making inquiries about missing persons in Kansas, Wisconsin, and lower Michigan." The Potawatomi had reservations there. "And I'll put in another call to the Indian Center. They might be able to provide some additional leads now that we've identified the tribe."

It appeared that the victim was not from this area. But if not, where did he come from? And why come here? Was he just another homeless man seeking a place to bed down for the night? Just passing through? Or, like his ancestors, who had once lived east of Lake Michigan, in what was now Indiana, had he come here seeking refuge? Marti decided that making abstract assumptions was not the best way to proceed. She had been listening to too many of Theo's and Mike's Potawatomi stories. She went back to her notes and went over the list of people and agencies she had identified. Those she had contacted were checked off. It was a short list and she had almost reached the end.

2

SATURDAY, JUNE 22

Larissa Linski spread a blanket on the grass not far from where the Des Plaines River flowed. It was hot in the sun, but she preferred that to the shade. She had brought her lunch—cheddar and Monterey Jack cheese, bread that was home-baked this morning, apricots, and diet pop. The river was sluggish, the water shallow, with a smell that was less than pleasant but not overwhelming. There were a lot of weeds and thistles near the water's edge. She loved the tranquillity of this long-neglected place, and imagined it the way it might have been once and could be again—tall prairie grasses with feathery heads, flowering rush with clusters of rose-pink petals or stemlike yellow tips; high free-flowing water where turtles, toads, and newts spawned, and where fish swam, camouflaged with dark, dull backs and silvery bellies. Raccoons and woodchuck, opossums, and perhaps even beavers would return, along with the graceful long-legged waterbirds that now nested farther south. And, high in the trees, crane's nests. As a child she had learned to make cranes by folding shiny, bright-colored paper. They were still her favorite bird.

She had taken this assignment because of the money. It was more than she could make the entire summer working retail. She wasn't sure why they were paying her so much. The woman who had hired her said it was because of a dig she had worked in Australia last summer and also the necessity for confidentiality. She had come here with no expectations. Mr. Smith had explained that there was nothing to be found and they just needed to confirm that before they gave the land away. It was to become part of the historic trail that abutted it to the north and south.

Even though she had worked digs before, she had just been one of the many who sifted and sorted and occasionally found some shard of pottery that hinted at how life used to be. Being here was different. She wasn't just looking for some small bit of history. Here she was a part of something that was going to happen, and not just documenting the past. This land would be restored. Here, the past would become the future. For the first time, she knew what she wanted to do with her life. She did not just want to confirm or clarify what used to be. She wanted to make it relevant to the future. She had been seeking something without knowing what she was looking for. And here, where a prairie had become a well-kept lawn, and a forest had become little more than a park, and a river had become a stagnant bog, she had found it.

Larissa finished off the cheeses and then bit into one of the apricots. The pulp was soft and sweet. As she ate, she thought about the four metal tags she had dug up yesterday. She had found something here, although they said she would not. The tags were square, about as big as a quarter, and they had been buried for a long time. All four had "JCMO" engraved or stamped on them in raised letters, along with a number, and something else that was abbreviated, "smi" on two, "mec" on another, and "fld" on a third. She had never seen or read about anything like them and didn't know if they would mean anything to the Smiths either. She hoped they were as insignificant as she thought they were. She didn't want anything to delay the work that needed to be done to restore this land and the river.

She was tossing bread to a couple of ducks when she heard the car pull up and the door slam. She turned as footsteps came toward her, looked up and smiled.

"I'm glad you could come," she said. "I know you're busy. Let me get these . . ." She reached for her purse and took out three of the tags. She had kept one. They were all alike and just old metal, and certainly not important enough to delay what was going to happen here.

"I don't know what they are. I've never seen anything like this before. I am sure that they're not Indian artifacts. I'm not sure they're anything at all." She held them in her hand, palm open. "If you'd like, I can ask about them when I go back to the university."

She smiled as she held them up.

Josiah Smith was an early riser, although at eighty-five he had no compunction about taking an afternoon nap. Morning was his favorite time of day. His study faced east and sunlight streamed in through tall windows. Above each was a smaller hexagonal window with multicolored leaded glass. It was a little like being in church, he often thought, and wondered if that was why his father had added the windows. They made the room seem like a cathedral of sorts, not that any of them were, or ever had been, churchgoing people.

As he did so often now, Josiah unlocked a secret drawer in his desk and took out a metal box. Inside was his great-grandfather Idbash's journal. He seldom opened it. The paper was so fragile now that he was afraid it would crumble. Idbash had settled in this part of the country, which was now northern Illinois, in 1822. Idbash had never allowed anyone to paint his portrait. Nor was there any public record of anything he had ever said. No favorite quotes, biblical or otherwise, no wise or foolish sayings, no pioneer or family stories. There were documents that recorded some of what Idbash had done, but Idbash spoke through this journal. With either some concern for the future or some desire to be remembered, Idbash had entrusted his journal to his only son, Josiah's grandfather. It had been passed to his father, then to him.

Josiah touched the worn leather binding. The last entry in the journal was dated April 21, 1870, three days before Idbash died. The first was dated July 14, 1822, the day Idbash arrived here. He was thirty-three years old.

"I have no plans to stay," Idbash wrote, on July 27, 1831. "The land I have been able to lay claim to has not been cleared of trees, nor broken to the plow. It is part of a virgin forest with trees of vast size. I am on the east side of a wide river that feeds many smaller streams and has fish of great size and all manner of birds nesting along its shores. West of this river is a fertile prairie with many grasses and flowers of many colors. Much of this land is still inhabited by Indians, although it has belonged to the United States since 1829. There is a Pottawattommi village upstream as well as one on the land that I have staked for myself. Whites are forbidden by federal law and treaties to settle here until after the Indians go west in 1836. We pay no heed and take possession of the land by agreements with the Indians. They are trusting and witless and know no better. My land is not the choicest because the land to the west of the river is more hospitable for farming and the raising of animals. But there are many trees to be felled and sold as choice lumber. I will make what money is to be had here, sell my land holdings at good profit, and continue west."

If only he had, Josiah thought. Instead, Idbash remained here. Idbash purchased 350 acres of land for $1.25 an acre. His land was worth $35,000 an acre now. And now Josiah was being forced to sell it for half that.

Josiah closed the journal and returned it to the locked box. He looked at the only other contents, three metal tags. According to Idbash's journal, there should have been four.

3

After roll call, the desk sergeant handed Marti a fax. Eileen Altenberg had sent a computer-generated reconstruction of the skeletal remains. Marti thought of the skull with its empty eye sockets and toothy grin. Now the face was round, with a receding forehead. The nose was wide and prominent; eyes brown and deep-set; ears flat against the skull. This was not at all the way she had pictured him. He lacked the characteristics she thought of as American Indian. As she took out her list of contacts and began faxing his likeness, she wondered if she would ever know how accurate this reconstruction was.

It was nine o'clock by the time Marti and Vik left the precinct. It had already reached eighty-five degrees, too hot for the short-sleeved jacket she had on. She was considering removing her holster and putting her gun in her purse when her cell phone rang.

"Some kind of cave-in," she told Vik. "Old Smith place." Vik probably knew why three hundred and fifty acres of land with a mansion and a ten-car garage was called that.

"Why doesn't that surprise me?" he said.

"Meaning?"

"Unlucky place. Supposed to be haunted."

She decided to ignore "haunted," for now at least. "Why unlucky?"

"Odd things happen to members of the Smith family. A teenage boy drowned in a wading pool. A cousin fell off a balcony and was impaled on a marble statue. Nothing recent. Until now."

The Smith place had been in the local news a lot lately. The family wanted to sell to real estate developers, and every agency in the county involved with land preservation had identified a parcel they wanted the Smith family to donate. As Marti drove down a long narrow tree-shaded lane, she thought of the place where the bones had been found. Unlike the trees along the bluff, or what was left of it, these trees did not have to fight wind and sand, leeched clay and dirt, and pollution to survive. The oaks had thick trunks and leafy branches. Stands of evergreens had peaked tops thirty feet high and wide boughs that touched the ground.

"They're going to chop down all of this?" Marti asked.

"No, this is part of the land that's supposed to be given away when they sell."

"Then what kind of digging is going on that could cause a cave-in?" She hadn't read anything about any excavating in the *News-Times.*

"Good question."

The road curved to the right, then the left. The glare of sunlight was sudden as they emerged from the shade of the trees. Ahead, Marti could see three black-and-whites parked off the road in the grass. She parked in front, but kept clear of the Porta-Potty. The work site wasn't more than fifty feet square and was marked off by mounds of dark, rich soil. There were three holes, about ten by ten, with an equal distance between them. Each hole was shored up with planks. Marti estimated that they were about a hundred and fifty feet from the river.

A deputy coroner came toward them. "Deceased is female. Larissa Linski. She was working alone. Looks like she fell into an old root cellar. Two large rocks were dislodged, probably part of a wall, and fell on her. Guy who found her is the one who did the digging." He indicated the mounds of dirt. "Said she was checking for remains and artifacts. Lots of virgin land here. She might have found something."

Marti didn't know much about archaeological excavations or the preliminaries, but she did know that if and when something was found here, it would be a while before anyone developed anything, or the owner gave away any of the land.

"Looks pretty cut-and-dry," the deputy coroner said. "The employee who dug the holes stopped to see if she needed anything. Got her out. Too late. Okay to move the body?"

"Get an evidence tech out here," Marti told him. She didn't want to leave anything open to question, especially now that Vik had mentioned other accidents.

The deputy coroner shrugged. "Your call. Looks straightforward to me."

"How deep is the hole?" Vik asked.

"Nine feet—not including the root cellar."

"Where's the guy who found her?"

"That way."

A backhoe, with a man sitting atop it, was parked not far from the river. The man didn't look their way as they approached. He continued to stare off in the distance when they identified themselves as police officers, but did tell them his name, Harry Buckner.

"You found her," Marti said.

"Yeah."

She waited.

"Nice kid."

Buckner was an older man, stocky, with bulging muscles and a belly that overlapped his belt.

"I remember when my girl was her age." He didn't look at them as he spoke.

"How old is your daughter now, Mr. Buckner?" Marti asked.

"Zoe would have been thirty-six on November third. Drunk driver."

"I'm sorry to hear that. What can you tell me about Larissa?"

"Nothing much. I just dug the holes. I came out here two, three times a day to check on her, see if she needed anything.

She really liked what she was doing, not that it looked like much of anything to me."

His Adam's apple bobbed as he swallowed hard and then swallowed again. "Shouldn't have happened. If we had just known what was down there. Shouldn't have happened, not to her, not to anyone's little girl."

He turned away, but not before Marti could see the tears that came to his eyes.

The evidence tech didn't spend much time at the scene. "Autopsy," he said as he trudged back to his van. Marti knelt beside the victim. Larissa Linski's T-shirt was covered with blood, not unusual when the victim's chest had been crushed. Her face was streaked with blood, her blond ponytail caked with dirt. Her face . . . she looked to be about seventeen . . . her eyes, blue but filmy now, were filled with fluid. Marti resisted the impulse to brush dirt from around her mouth and close her eyes. Instead, she took out her camera. She shot a roll of black-and-white and one in color, and then okayed the removal of the body. That done, she ordered the site secured with an officer on duty pending the autopsy results.

"Unlucky," Vik repeated as they walked to their car.

"I thought you weren't superstitious."

"It's got nothing to do with superstition."

"Ancient curse on the Smith family," she teased. "Ghosts."

Vik didn't answer right away; when he did, all he said was, "Odd accidents. Josiah Smith's brother suffocated in a silo. Another family member was killed in a small-plane accident. One of those prop jobs with two seats."

As Marti drove back to the precinct, Vik said, "Nice way to begin the summer, MacAlister. It looks like it's going to take us a while to get anywhere with the skeletal remains, if we do. And this one, accidental death. Prominent family, with at least one politician in every generation since Little Fort became Lincoln Prairie, so it'll get a little attention in the media for a day or two and go away. As for our other cases—open-and-shut."

"Things will heat up soon enough," Marti said. "They always do."

There was a message from Lieutenant Dirkowitz when they got back to the precinct, so they headed for his office. The lieutenant had been known as Dirty Dirk ever since his days of playing football for the Southern Illinois Salukis. He still had the build of a linebacker. At thirty-six, his hairline was beginning to recede, and he had become a father for the first time. Angela Faith was three months old now.

As Marti and Vik sat down, the lieutenant took the last bite of an apple and threw the core in the wastebasket. "We need to talk about this morning's fatality—Larissa Linski."

"Are the Smiths calling you already?" Vik asked.

"They went a little higher up—called the governor."

"Of Illinois?"

"One and the same, Jessenovik."

"The current governor?"

Dirkowitz nodded, smiling.

"But the Smiths are Republicans."

"So is the President. Ever hear of Senator Richard Wagner?"

"He lives downstate, not around here."

"He's Josiah Smith's nephew."

"I know."

The lieutenant picked up a deactivated Vietnam-era hand grenade that he kept on his desk. It wasn't a memento but a reminder of his brother who had died there. "So, what have you got on this?"

"Looks like an accident," Vik said. "Seems straightforward enough. What's the problem?"

"Nobody's told me there is one. But I have been advised that a few phone calls were made." He weighed the grenade in one hand. "Why don't you fill me in on the rest of your caseload?"

After they discussed that, Dirkowitz dropped the hand grenade, a signal that the meeting was over.

*　*　*

"Well," Marti said, as they returned to their office. "Looks like we're not ready to file the Linski case. Think the lieutenant's holding out on us?"

"I think he told us as much as he could, or maybe even as much as he knows."

"Who is this Senator Wagner?" she asked.

"I don't know where the Smiths came from, but Idbash Smith settled here, his sister married a Wagner and settled somewhere in the southern part of the state. Her son became a politician, and there's been someone in politics on her side of the family ever since. One of them, Smith or Wagner, picked up the phone. Typical when you're well-connected."

Marti considered that. Whenever anyone involved in a case tried to interfere with or direct the focus of the investigation, she assumed they had a reason. In this case, it could be something as simple as trying to control adverse publicity. "Suppose this is not an accident, Vik? What if the Smiths have a reason to interfere?"

"I'm sure they do," Vik said. "That doesn't mean they had anything to do with Linski's death. With all that's happened there, they're probably just anxious to get things over with."

"We're going to have to ignore the history of unusual accidents, Vik."

"From the looks of this one, they could be worried about a civil case."

Marti wasn't sure why someone would call the governor because they were concerned about something like that.

After an hour of reading and rereading scanty notes, Marti had more questions than answers. The deceased was a twenty-year-old undergraduate studying archaeology. The land she was working was part of a fifteen-acre parcel along the path of the Des Plaines River, land that the Preservation Board wanted donated to the county.

"So, Jessenovik, why do you excavate a piece of land that is going to be set aside and not developed? Couldn't the county do that?"

"I don't know. I suppose it could have something to do with transferring the title."

"Why did they get a student in there instead of an expert?"

"Too cheap, probably. How else do you think they got to be so rich?"

Marti reached for the telephone several times without picking it up. She didn't want to call Dr. Altenberg, and Meline Pickus was still on vacation. She called Dr. Cyprian.

"Ah, yes," he said. "The autopsy is tomorrow at five A.M. There isn't much I can tell you now."

"How much do you know about archaeological excavations?"

He chuckled. "Very little."

Marti drummed her fingers on her desk. She didn't even know what questions to ask. Yet. She would have to get on the Internet. It was going to be a long night.

"The photographs have not yet been developed, MacAlister," Cyprian said. "Nor have I taken a look at the body. Perhaps then we will learn more. My colleague . . ."

"Not Dr. Altenberg?"

"No. No. We will talk in the morning."

She would have to be satisfied with that.

When Marti remembered to check her in-basket, she had five responses to the faxes of the facial reconstruction that she had sent out. She handed Vik two of the messages and they both got on the phone. An hour later, she had far too many useless details about three missing persons and no useful information at all.

"Nothing here either," Vik said. "An older man who has a cousin who's been missing for five or six years and thinks our guy looks like the cousin's brother. Explain that. And a female schizophrenic who fell in love with a male who is bipolar while they were committed to a pysch facility and hasn't seen him since he was released. This happened two years ago."

Marti didn't tell him that both stories made more sense than the three she had listened to.

"I knew this computer reconstruction was a bad idea, MacAlister. Too bad he doesn't look more like Sitting Bull," Vik said. "Or Geronimo. I bet if they used the real skull, you at least would have been able to tell he was an American Indian. This is just attracting the loonies."

Marti looked at the likeness again. What made someone look like an Indian? A prominent brow? Deep-set eyes? A long narrow nose? That was like asking what made an African-American look black. It sure wasn't skin color or hair texture or any one set of features. Why should things be any different for an American Indian?

"Maybe this does look like him, Vik. Maybe what we think he should look like is getting in the way."

Ethan Dana looked at the computerized likeness of his cousin, Tommy Strongwind, for a long time. One of the other grad students had seen it hanging on the bulletin board at the Indian Student Center, recognized Tommy, and brought him a copy. What had Tommy gotten himself into now? Tommy, always running, even when they were kids on the reservation. Always wandering, always returning to the place he kept trying to leave. Ethan put the Xeroxed sheet on his desk beside a stack of papers he had to grade. This either meant that someone had given the police a description of Tommy because he had finally gotten himself into serious trouble, or that Tommy had run away from himself for the last time.

There was a knock and his door opened. Solveig burst in, all belly, all smiles.

"Ethan, the baby comes in seven weeks now!"

Tall, blond, blue-eyed, and Norwegian, Solveig was everything that he had been running toward when he left the reservation. He went to her, stood behind her, touched her hair, and then wrapped his arms around her stomach. Their baby kicked him.

"Strong," he said. "He's strong. We have to decide what to name him."

"A big decision, Professor." She spoke with a slight accent.

"Grad student," he reminded her.

"We will name him for your grandfather," she said. "At least his middle name." Solveig had loved the old man. She was the one who had insisted that he be buried the old way, with a drumming ceremony. Ethan had put aside all things Potawatomi when he came here to the university.

"Maybe," he said. His grandfather had been called Topash.

Solveig sat behind his desk. She looked down at the picture without touching it. "Ethan, this is Tommy. Now what has he done? He would not get into serious trouble, would he? He is all right?"

"There's a number if you have information. I'll call," Ethan promised. He hoped she would forget about this for a while so that he could put off making that call for as long as possible. He did not want to know what Tommy had done, or, this time, if something had happened to him.

Josiah Smith could see the moon from his bedroom window. It was three quarters full, and waxing. He had lived here all of his life, walked every inch of this land, watched fish flash silver in the river, flushed pheasant from the tall grass, fed Canadian geese, picked apples and talked Cook into baking pies and making applesauce. This was home. But, as much as he loved it, he wanted to be rid of it now. There was a time for everything. Now it was time to let go of all that Idbash had bequeathed them.

He went to the table near the fireplace. Idbash's table, just as this had been Idbash's room. A heavy, hand-hewn table, and on it a heavy, hand-hewn legacy. Maps, treaties, government contracts, all of them Idbash's, signed and dated by Idbash's hand. All of it passed down to Idbash's heirs. Josiah sat in a chair as intricately carved as the table. He turned on the brass lamp that had sat on this desk for over a hundred and fifty years, a lamp that had been converted from kerosene to electricity. The lamp Josiah had used to draw the maps that were spread out now. For all of the years Josiah had been on this earth, the weight of these maps had been his. He was careful as he folded them. The paper seemed sturdier than that in Idbash's journal, but it was brown with age and almost as old, and worn thin where it was creased.

Josiah opened the wooden chest designed by some nameless artisan before he was born. He put the maps he had just folded inside. That done, he stood by the window. His bedroom faced the front of the house. There was a wide expanse of lawn, then a stand of red oak. The apple orchard was beyond the trees. In the moonlight he could see the woman walking. She did not walk there every night, nor were her appearances predictable. She came as a shadow, always pausing at the same places—the oak tree where the swing used to hang from the lowest branch, the place where the gate used to be when he was a child and there was a long, low, white picket fence, then toward the apple orchard as she vanished among the trees.

He knew nothing about her—who she was, why she came. Before him, his father Obediah had seen her, and before his father, his grandfather. Idbash didn't know what would become of her once the land was sold. He did not fear her, or believe that she meant him harm. Perhaps, when he left this place if he went to the spirit world where she was, he would understand her unrest.

4

Marti stifled a yawn as she followed Vik out of the autopsy room. It was ten past six in the morning. She had logged two hours on the Internet last night. Even though she woke up tired, she had decided against having coffee on an empty stomach before coming to work.

The findings during the autopsy were consistent with crush asphyxia—hemorrhaging from the head and chest and around the eyes, excess fluid in the eyeballs, cracked ribs.

Dr. Cyprian suggested that they wait in his office while he changed clothes. His secretary hadn't come in yet so there was no coffee, but Marti did find a tin of cookies. She took a handful and offered some to Vik. He shook his head.

"I'll wait for breakfast."

The only personal items in Dr. Cyprian's office were a philodendron with vines that cascaded from the top of the bookcase to the floor, and a nine-by-twelve family photo that hung on the wall. The chairs were padded but not comfortable. There were several stacks of folders on the desk, sorted by color: red, yellow, blue. Marti wanted to take a closer look and identify the categories but decided not to be nosy. She focused on the family photo instead. Dr. Cyprian and a woman who must be his wife, five other adults, and four young children. There was something timeless about Dr. Cyprian. His hair was as black as the day she met him, his face unlined. She realized with a start that the little ones must be his grandchildren.

The door opened.

"So," Dr. Cyprian said, "you remember Dr. McIntosh. Before he became focused on medicine, Gordon wandered through academia—philosophy, psychology, anthropology. He even worked a few digs in his youth. He might be able to assist you with your inquiries."

Vik scowled. "I hope not."

They had worked with Gordon McIntosh before, while Cyprian was out of town, and, as Marti recalled, Gordon tended to wander—away from the main focus of the investigation, preoccupied with details that contributed little or nothing.

"Jessenovik, MacAlister! This is great! We're working together again."

Vik had an expression on his face that suggested he had just swallowed vinegar.

Gordon rubbed his hands together and sat down. "So, how can I help you two this time? What do you want to know?"

"What can you tell us about the dig?" Marti asked. "Anything unusual?"

"For starters, you can forget the dig," Gordon said. "Forget just about anything that has to do with archaeology."

"Why?"

"I had a look at the evidence tech's photos and I'm not sure what was going on there. No telling why she was hired to poke around."

Vik rubbed his thumb and finger together. Speculation, no facts.

Marti replied with a slight shrug—we'll see.

"We need to see Linski's notes and work papers and the surveyor's report. You also want to know why they dug nine feet and stopped. I can't make out any strata in the photos—layers of dirt deposited over time. Nice, rich soil, stable. Silt or clay would be much more likely to shift."

He seemed to be getting focused, so Marti took out her notebook.

"There were no grids, no excavation units."

She began writing, just in case.

"Linski was working with a pick when she died. There were several trowels at the site . . . brushes, a dustpan . . ."

"Which suggests that she was just at the level where she would begin looking for something," Marti concluded, based on last night's research. "Was there anything about the sides of the excavation that would indicate instability?"

"Nothing that grabbed my attention. Unfortunately, she was right above that old root cellar."

Marti looked up from her notebook. Unlike the Dr. McIntosh who had been deputy coroner in charge the last time they worked together, as Dr. Cyprian's assistant, Gordon did not make assumptions or go off on tangents. Vik did not seem impressed.

"And oh," Gordon added. "JULIE had to be called in before they could dig."

"JULIE?" Marti asked. "The guys who put up those little orange flags?"

"Right. Joint Utility Locating Information for Excavators. They have to check for electrical wires, telephone lines, gas pipes, things like that. State law."

"There wasn't anything like that there," Vik said.

"It doesn't matter. JULIE has to be called in no matter where you dig."

Marti made a note to make sure the Smiths had complied. "What should Linski's work papers and reports tell us?"

"Why that location was chosen, for one. The dimensions of the dig are very specific. They must have had a reason for digging there. They brought in someone with a backhoe, and then called in Miss Linski. The digs I've been on were much more sophisticated."

Marti thought for a moment. "If something important were found there, would the way the dig was conducted give the find less credibility?"

"Probably not. A lot of things are found accidentally. It's not that difficult to authenticate them."

"But in terms of where it was found and not what it was?"

"That's possible. Or vice versa."

Or, she thought, if something wasn't found there but put there. One of the things she had found out last night was that there was a thriving black market for Indian and other artifacts. If someone had something they bought that way and wanted to authenticate it, all they had to do was put it in the right place and pretend to find it.

"Is there anything else we should know?" she asked.

Vik looked up at the ceiling.

"Nothing I can think of right now."

"Good. We'll probably get back to you on this."

"Is it okay if I go out there and take a look, MacAlister?"

"Sure. Wait until this afternoon. You can come with us."

Vik raised his eyebrows and gave her a look that implied disapproval, but she was impressed with what Gordon had been able to tell them. And, given the research she had done so far, she was certain that if she were a member of the Smith family, she would be concerned about a civil action.

Senator Richard Wagner smiled as he stroked the stocking-clad thigh of his legislative assistant. She was a lovely young woman, "young" being the operative word. Kat Malloy, his mistress, wasn't so young anymore. At least not young enough. He couldn't remember his wife ever being young, although she had been—before children, before sagging breasts and cellulite, before menopause. He couldn't respond to older women. It was becoming difficult to pretend with Kat, and impossible with his wife. Lori, at least, was content with being the senator's wife. But Kat, she was going to be difficult to deal with. That would have to wait until after the election. Meanwhile . . .

His legislative assistant touched the swelling in his groin. He moaned with pleasure, leaned against his desk. She kissed him, her tongue darting into his mouth as she unzipped his pants. The curtains had been drawn. The door was locked. As she knelt in front of him, the Seal of the State of Illinois and the flag of the United States came into view.

Josiah was completing the day's *New York Times* crossword puzzle when Richard called.

"Uncle Josiah! Damned shame about that accident you had up there, but I have good news for you!"

"And what might that be?" Even though Richard had finally returned his call, Richard was more concerned with protecting his own interests that anyone else's.

"I've seen to it that the detectives assigned to handle this are the best officers available. They come very highly recommended."

That was exactly what Josiah didn't want.

"This is such a minor incident, Richard. Let's not suggest any more importance than necessary, and certainly not with a couple of homicide detectives."

"This is an election year, Uncle Josiah, and unfortunately, this accident doesn't involve a member of the family. After the accidents we've had this wouldn't be more than footnote. As it is, we don't want any more media focus than necessary and I'm handling that. And I've contacted the girl's family. They know they have our full support and deepest condolences. Let's not upset the balance. If we call attention to this now by not allowing the police to follow standard procedure, the wolves will be knocking at my door."

The best detectives available. After Richard hung up, Josiah wondered just how good these two detectives were. He didn't want the wolves Richard was worrying about to knock at his door first.

Larissa Linski had been boarding at a home in Grayslake. It was a large house with a wraparound porch and a wide expanse of lawn bordered on one side by a grove of fruit trees.

"Apples," Vik said as Marti parked in the driveway.

"Granny Smith or Red Delicious?" she teased. She couldn't tell one fruit tree from another. Vik grunted.

Even though this was a well-populated area, Marti felt as if she were far beyond city limits. Two Irish setters played on the grass. Hostas lined the walkway. Birds sang. One whistled, then charooped. Marti didn't know if it was a blue jay or a cardinal.

A middle-aged woman met them at the door. She had an open book in her hand and was wearing glasses with a cord attached so that they could hang from her neck.

"Yes?" She was at least eight inches shorter than Marti's five feet ten.

"Are you the police officers who called?" Her expression was stern. Marti knew she was a college professor, but could envision her silencing noisy, playful kindergartners with a look. The woman held out her hand. "Mary Ellen Channon."

When she invited them inside, Marti suggested that they sit on the porch instead. A roof provided shade from the sun and there were wicker rocking chairs with thick cushions. Something about this place reminded her of paintings she had seen at the Art Institute—and made her think of the Smith property where the body had been found.

"I only knew Larissa for a little over a week." Ms. Channon began. Her voice sounded wistful. "When they're that age you never think of death. Yesterday morning she was sitting out back having breakfast. Yesterday afternoon I identified her body. Her mother . . . poor woman . . ." Her voice became brisk. "Her mother will be flying in as soon as the coroner says it's okay to take her home." She looked into the distance. "Such a nice young woman—pleasant, friendly, made herself right at home. The dogs took to her right away."

"Why was she staying here?" Marti asked.

"The university arranged it. We've taken in so many students over the years, it's become a tradition. Mother was particularly pleased that Larissa was here. They had both traveled extensively and had quite long chats about places they visited."

"Did Larissa talk much about what she was doing at the Smith place?" Vik asked.

"No, but she was very excited. As small as it was, this was

her project. She was on her own. It's refreshing to see someone that young so aware of their responsibility. So conscientious."

Conscientious enough to take copious notes, Marti hoped.

"Did she find anything?" Vik asked.

"Not that she mentioned. I was hoping she would. The Smiths' estate could be such a significant place historically."

"How so?" Marti asked. All she knew was that there had been a Smith among the original settlers in this area and the property had been in the family ever since.

"Well, there's a lot we don't know about Idbash Smith. In fact, nobody really knows anything at all. There has always been speculation as to whether or not he was involved with the Underground Railroad, and questions as to if, and how, he might have helped the Potawatomis who sneaked further north instead of being relocated to Kansas. Nobody in the family has ever commented on any of this. If anything of historical importance were found . . ."

Marti considered that. Not only did the Smiths' property originally belong to the Potawatomi, but runaway slaves could have hidden there as well. African-American history was gaining recognition when she went to school, but back then discussions remained on a national rather than a local level, and centered on current events and civil rights. There was little mention of their history, beyond footnotes on "important" African-Americans, like Frederick Douglas and George Washington Carver. Even when she listened to her children talking about the history of northern Illinois, their focus was on the Potawatomi. When she got a chance, she would have to ask them about the Underground Railroad.

Vik caught her eye and raised his eyebrows. She realized she hadn't been paying attention to what was being said, and asked to see Larissa's room.

Ms. Channon showed them inside. The staircase was near the front door, so Marti only got a glimpse of a room with blue-and-yellow-striped chair covers and the same colors in floral wallpaper. Someone liked flowers. There was a vase of pink peonies on a hall table. The upstairs room Larissa had occupied was large and airy. This time the walls were papered in green-and-white stripes and the curtains and bedspread had a leafy motif.

Marti preferred to search with only officers present, but Ms. Channon sat on the bed, folded her arms and waited. Vik stood by the window. The coroner's inventory of Larissa Linski's personal effects was scant. Other than her clothing there had been fifteen dollars—two fives and five ones—a dollar and half in change, and a medal in her purse. No jewelry, two bobby pins, and a barrette. Larissa had packed light also: jeans, shorts, T-shirts, socks, sweaters.

An army-issue canvas duffel bag was half-filled with various implements. Even without consulting the list of supplies she had brought along, Marti could see that Larissa had been thorough: small shovels, tape measures, brushes of various sizes and widths, safety goggles, gloves, picks, scrapers, a magnifying glass, a magnifier with a stand, a vise, a box of Baggies, and Baggies filled with Q-tips and cotton balls. There was a laptop in the closet along with a briefcase with a thick notebook inside. Marti explained that she needed to take both as well as the duffel bag and promised to return them.

Vik hefted the duffel bag and slung the strap over his shoulder. "I suppose you're going to take this to McIntosh," he complained as they walked to their car.

"With luck he'll be able to help us," Marti said. She had glanced at Linski's notebook and thought she could figure out at least some of the drawings. She would need a glossary of archaeological terminology to figure out what Larissa had written. Even then, she would probably need help interpreting what some of it meant.

"Look, Marti, Gordon was direct and to the point with Dr. Cyprian sitting right there, but don't forget the last time we worked with him. If anyone can find a detail or idea that isn't worth a damn, it's him. Detective Wannabe McIntosh. He's still watching too many *Quincy* reruns."

"I'm hoping he can figure out what's in the notebook and tell us about what's in this bag." Or perhaps what wasn't and should be.

"Right. If he doesn't get bogged down with something stupid like what color the dirt is. Strata—smatta." He waved his hand as if he were shooing an insect. "The only dirt that's important is what fell on her."

Marti shifted the computer to her other hand.

"And that," Vik said. "What if we need a password to get in? What if she used a code?"

"One thing at a time."

"This could all be a waste of time."

"When have we let a little thing like that interfere with an investigation?"

"Investigation," Vik said. "Remember that. That's all this is right now. Your nose twitching?"

"Not yet."

"Neither is mine."

When a bird gave a loud whistle, a few chirrups, and whistled again, Vik said, "A cardinal. Annoying as hell."

By the time they were on Route 120 and five miles from Lincoln Prairie they had agreed that they would not visit the Smith residence until after they knew what was in the notebook and found out if anything useful was on the computer. They remained at odds about letting Gordon McIntosh tag along when they returned to the dig site.

This was only the third time in twelve years that Harry Buckner had been invited to come into the house. He had been interviewed in the kitchen, and the week before last had come into the old man's den to check out a map and figure out where to dig those holes. Now the old man wanted to see him again. He didn't like coming inside. The kitchen wasn't so bad, but here . . . He stood by a bookcase, away from the lamp on the desk that the maid said was over a hundred years old; away from the blue-and-white glass globe that was tilted on its silver axis; away from the chess set made of brown and white marble; away from the table with fancy bottles of liquor and gold-rimmed glasses.

Harry shifted from one foot to the other. He kept his hands in his pockets. Where was the old man? He didn't want to dig any more holes, not after what happened, but he would if he was asked to. This was an easy job. Ride around on a lawn mower, ride around on a plow, vacuum up fallen leaves, billions of leaves, but he didn't have to rake them. And he had a place to stay. He was a long way from Idaho, a long way from Zoe's grave, a long way from the mountain road where she died. He could think of her now the way she had been when she was a little girl or the way she looked when she went to high school dances. There was nothing here to remind him of the way she looked when she was dead. When those thoughts came, depending on what time of year it was, he could look up at the sun coming through the branches of the trees, or walk through the orange and yellow leaves that covered the grass, or just watch the snow fall, and push all the bad memories from his mind.

"Harry."

"Yes!" The old man's voice startled him. "Yes, sir." He turned to see Mr. Smith standing there with another map. This map was a brownish yellow and cracked just like the other one. Harry followed him to the desk and stood as far away from the lamp as he could.

"Will someone else be helping . . . looking for . . ."

"No. We won't need any outside help with these holes." He pointed to a place on the map in a stand of oak trees. "The trees are planted in a circle here and you'll go right to the center."

"I'm not sure I can get the backhoe in there, sir."

"I looked. Go in from this road." He pointed. "You'll have to go this way." His finger traced a path around the trees. "Not much room, but enough. Try to back up without scraping the tree trunks. Just take your time. You can do it."

"Yes, sir," Harry said. He didn't want to do it, didn't know why he was doing it.

The old man pointed again. "What about this site?"

Harry knew exactly where he was pointing. "That's the apple orchard."

"And you can find this exact spot?"

"Sure."

"Good man," Mr. Smith said. He cleared his throat, and then said, "You liked the girl who was working here."

It seemed like an odd question for Mr. Smith to ask, but then this was only the third time since he'd been working here that they had talked about anything.

"She reminded me of my daughter," Harry explained.

"Your daughter? Oh. Yes. That's why you kept an eye on her."

"Yes, sir." He could tell that Mr. Smith didn't know anything about Zoe. "I went out there at least twice a day to make sure she was okay. I just didn't go early enough Saturday."

They had put him to work way up front near the road, thinning out the tulips. It seemed like a strange time of year to do it, but there had been too many last year. Instead of throwing the extra bulbs away, he had planted them near the barn.

"Did she mention anything about finding something?"

"No, sir, but did she? She sure wanted to."

Mr. Smith shook his head. "I know, that's why I asked. It would have meant a lot to her family if she had."

Harry was surprised by that. He didn't think rich people cared about much of anything besides themselves. He wouldn't have expected Mr. Smith to give any more thought to Larissa's family than he had given to him and his Zoe. "Nice of you to feel that way, sir. Too bad she didn't find something."

He didn't know a lot about old Indian stuff, but if he found something, he was going to keep it.

It was hot when Marti and Vik returned to the dig site. Gordon McIntosh had to inspect every tree, bush, flower, and leaf that bordered the clearing. While he did that, Marti took photographs of all three holes and the area surrounding them. Thanks to her computer search, she had a general idea of what she was looking at but she didn't know how to evaluate what she saw. They had requested an expert on cave-ins.

"Hopefully," she said, "by tomorrow we'll confirm that those boulders could have come loose and fallen on her without any outside assistance and be able to close this."

When Gordon wandered over he held out a Baggie with about a dozen cigarette butts inside.

"Collecting evidence?" Vik asked.

"Could be," Gordon answered. He didn't sound the least bit annoyed by the sarcasm in Vik's voice. "I found these in one spot right under that tree." He pointed into the distance.

"Which tree?" Vik asked. "There are a lot of them around here."

When they had established the exact tree, Gordon said. "Someone was standing there watching."

Vik gave him his "duh" look, but said nothing.

"And as for this dig, not that I would call it that, it doesn't make much sense. According to her notes, Linski was told to check out the third hole only. So why did they dig the other two?"

"Maybe it was dependent upon what she found in that one," Vik reasoned. "Got anything else for us?"

Before McIntosh could answer, a voice called from behind them. Marti turned to see a man wearing a business suit coming toward them. As he got closer, she noted the short but wavy gray hair, and his sharp, narrow features came into focus.

"What are you doing here?" he asked, stopping a few feet from the hole where Larissa had died. His deep-set dark eyes probed their faces. He was as tall as Marti and Gordon, but had to look up at Vik. "Did anyone give you permission to be on this property?"

When Marti and Vik identified themselves as police officers, he extended his hand. "Paul Smith. Real bad, what happened here. What's worse, we're getting used to it."

Gordon looked at Marti, but this wasn't the time to fill him in on the previous accidents.

"So, what brings you back, besides curiosity?"

Marti ignored the curiosity comment, but it annoyed her. She let Vik answer.

"A woman died here," he said.

"And it was an accident."

"Presumed to be an accident," Vik amended. "That's for the coroner's jury to decide. We just provide the evidence."

"Does that mean we'll be seeing you again?"

"Possibly."

"Well, let's hope not. We like to get past these things as quickly as possible. Best for everyone that way."

Marti wondered if this family had come to expect fatal accidents the way other families came to expect weddings and funerals and births.

"I'll leave you to it then," Paul Smith said, and walked away.

"They need a golf cart or something," Vik said. "As big as this place is."

"What was that all about?" Gordon asked.

Marti wondered about that, too.

"He must have known we were here," Gordon said. "The guard at the gate let us in."

"Curious, maybe," Vik said. "Or worried."

Gordon looked into the hole. "Maybe after this cave-in expert takes a look, you'll be able to give the Smiths the okay to fill this in."

"Before someone else falls in," Vik said. He glanced at the uniform assigned to keep the area secure. "Manpower could be put to better use someplace else." Then he waited while Gordon walked ahead. When Gordon was out of hearing distance, he said. "Is your nose twitching yet?"

"Sure is," Marti said.

"Mine is beginning to twitch, too."

There wasn't much conversation as Marti drove back to the precinct. She wondered what Gordon was thinking. A different perspective on things never hurt. She could pretty well figure out what was on Vik's mind. The big question right now was why Paul Smith had walked the distance from the house to the river, which was considerable, and if there was something there that they were not supposed to find. Or, if something had been placed there that someone wanted them to find. She wasn't sure why that thought kept intruding.

At exactly seven o'clock, Kat Malloy met with Eileen Smith. The maître d' knew both of them and escorted them to their favorite booth in a far corner, away from the windows. Kat slipped him an extra twenty. It wasn't the busiest night of the week, but she wanted to be sure that there wouldn't be anyone sitting nearby. When the waiter suggested a white wine, she agreed.

"So," Kat said as she leaned against the plush velvet upholstery. It had been a long day and the dining room was soothing. Everything in shades of mauve and maroon, deep-pile carpet, heavy draperies, calmness and quiet. "Long day," she admitted. A long day away from Richard, a long day that she was certain Richard had spent with his legislative assistant. She had known Richard too long and too well to deceive herself about that. She took a sip of wine, watched as Eileen pretended to be as nonchalant as she herself was pretending to be. "So, there's been a little excitement in your corner of the world."

"You could say that," Eileen agreed. "But nothing that Richard and Josiah can't handle."

"Nothing that they can't make go away," Kat said. "Everything will go away once this sale goes through." She signaled to the waiter. "Same as usual?" she asked. When Eileen nodded, she placed their order.

Five courses and another bottle of wine later, Kat was feeling relaxed. Good thing she had taken a cab from her condo. "So, everything looks good from here," she said. "The land developer is ready to close. Richard's kept the publicity about the accident to a minimum. Everything is proceeding as planned."

"And I've locked in the deals with the contractor," Eileen

said. "We're getting ten percent of everything, off the top. Did you bring the contracts?"

Kat watched as Eileen spent the next half hour going over them. Eileen had been Franklin's doormat for so many years that it was still too easy to forget that the lady had a law degree from Northwestern and used her brains much the same way Kat used street smarts and savvy.

"Looks good," Eileen said. They called the maître d' over, signed, then he signed as a witness.

Kat was feeling good as she left. She thought of Richard with his little legislative assistant. She who laughed last . . .

It was after eight when Marti got home, and getting dark outside. Trouble, their German shepherd, was patrolling the perimeter of the chain-link fence that surrounded their property.

"Good girl," she said when Trouble came over to her. "Have some treats." She rubbed the dog between her ears. "Good girl," she said again.

Ben was on duty tonight. She missed him already. As soon as she walked into the kitchen she could hear the boys overhead. The house was a quad level. Other than the kitchen, the dining room and living room on this, the main level, were seldom used. Ben, the boys and Marti liked what was now called the "middle place," right above her head. Momma and the girls—her daughter Joanna, and her best friend's Sharon's daughter, Lisa—usually gravitated to the den in the basement. She missed Lisa and Sharon. They were on vacation and would be gone for a month.

Goblin, their cat, was napping in her basket in the pantry. She looked up at Marti, looked away, stretched slowly, then got up and detoured to the stove and then the table before heading in Marti's direction. She purred as Marti rubbed the fur between her ears. Marti checked the refrigerator to see what Momma had fixed for supper—baked ham and a couple of salads—and went upstairs to join the boys. It was almost their bedtime. She could eat later.

Mike and Theo were sitting at a table with pieces of leather and a tray filled with beads. Bigfoot, a mixed breed the size of a Saint Bernard, was lying near Theo's feet. He looked up at her, wagged his tail, and went back to sleep.

"Damn," Theo muttered.

Marti tried not to smile. Ben had warned her that the boys' language would undergo a few changes when they began playing team sports. He had also advised the boys that it had best not happen when the women of the house were within earshot. Momma was appalled that that was the extent of it, but Marti and Ben agreed that what they couldn't control, they would regulate.

"So what are you two up to tonight?" she asked.

"Ma!" Theo said.

"Ma!" Mike repeated.

Neither boy looked up from what they were doing.

"Beadwork?" Marti asked. "Part of your Potawatomi project?"

"You should see all of the great stuff they've got at the Lake County Discovery Museum," Mike said.

Theo was concentrating on getting thread through the eye of a needle. "The women must have done this back then," he said, "but Momma won't even help us with this."

"And Joanna told us she was not a squaw."

" 'Squaw' is derogatory," Theo added. He was struggling with the needle and thread. Marti didn't offer to help either.

"Did you guys know the Underground Railroad came through here?"

"Everybody knows that," Theo said, then, "Hah! Got it!" He held up the threaded needle.

"I've never heard anything about that," Marti admitted.

"They don't say much about runaway slaves in school," Theo said. "They talk about Harriet Tubman, and say she was a conductor, but they don't say much about the slavery part."

"Mostly they talk a lot about American Indians," Mike added.

Theo had his head bent close to the piece of leather he was

sewing the beads to. "Probably because there aren't any in our class, or even in our school."

"And because the Potawatomi weren't fugitives like slaves were. They were just in the way."

"We studied the Holocaust last year," Theo said. "Teachers like talking about that because it didn't happen here."

"That wasn't like slavery," Mike said, giving the leather another enthusiastic stick with the needle. "Or relocation."

"Sure it was," Theo said. "They tried to destroy the Jewish culture and take away their religion, just like they did with Africans and American Indians."

Marti sat in a beanbag chair and watched the two of them. Theo, in profile—cleft chin, high cheekbones, widow's peak— the image of his father, her first husband, Johnny, who had died in the line of duty. Mike had Ben's softer, rounder features, and his father's smile and easy laugh. The time she was able to spend with her family gave her such a feeling of peace and contentment that she wished moments like this could last forever.

She listened as the boys discussed slavery and Indian relocation and the Holocaust, finding similarities and differences. As they talked, they made bead patterns, and she learned a lot about how good teachers helped children learn to think, something that went far beyond learning how to follow directions or take a test.

Now that the boys were going into sixth grade and would be attending a school with over six hundred sixth, seventh, and eight graders, she and Ben were becoming increasingly concerned about keeping them in public school. Not only had the educational focus shifted from learning to testing, but as Sharon had explained before she went on vacation, teachers were now expected to train children to become employees, and employers expected them to follow directions, not think. Marti and Ben found this trend alarming. They also felt that the middle school was too big.

This year, when Theo, her junior scientist, came home and complained because his science teacher didn't know that the endoplasmic reticulum was part of the cell, she was concerned. When Mike, who would read just about anything, and always went for the easy grade, complained because the stories and vocabulary in his literature book were too easy, she became alarmed. When Marti mentioned this to Joanna, she agreed. "It's not about education, Ma. It's about following directions. Why do you think I get Bs and Cs? I could get a few As, but I'd have to follow the teachers' instructions to the letter. And sometimes I'd rather enjoy what I'm writing about, or find out about things I didn't know, or just be a little different and experiment."

After that conversation, Marti, Ben and the boys had visited several smaller Christian schools. They had narrowed their search to two and were going to meet with the teachers the first week in August and then reach a decision.

5

When Isaiah Ben Mosheh saw the name "Samuel" on the computer screen, he felt a familiar pain in his chest.

"Samuel, property of James Thatcher, fugitive, escaped May 9, 1835."

His heart began beating rapidly and his breath came in gasps. He put a tablet under his tongue and tried to breathe normally until the pain subsided and his heartbeat slowed. Then he thanked God for the NitroQuick and tried not to think about the time when medication wouldn't be enough.

He looked again. His eyes weren't what they used to be, even though his glasses had thick lenses. Was this the Samuel he was looking for? Was he nearing the end of the search he had begun nineteen years ago? He was afraid to hope, but over the years he had come to realize that hope was indifferent to logic. If he had known how difficult this would be, how discouraged he would get, he might never have begun this search at all. At first it had been easy. He found a lot of information about family members in his own generation. Then he ran into the brick wall called segregation when, thanks to Jim Crow, separate records were kept for blacks, and in some instances, such as voting, there were no records because blacks couldn't participate. Now he had reached another brick wall, slavery, a time when blacks were property, not people, not citizens, and nameless. He printed the page on the computer screen. Samuel, slave of Thatcher. Was this Samuel the right one?

As always, when he thought he had taken another step into his family's past, Isaiah remembered his grandmother, Ruby Thatcher Gardner. Family had been everything to Grandma. She had told him and his brother all the stories about members of their family that she could remember. Not long before she died, she said to him, not for the first time, "Sometimes I wonder who you really look like." She spoke just above a whisper. "You have your father's eyes, but everything else about you is your great-grandmother Reba's, and she always said she looked just like her daddy. Folks called him T. G. because his given name was Theodore Gardner." She smiled. "I think you look like our ancestors."

"Which is why you used to call me 'old one' when I was a child."

Grandma sighed and closed her eyes. "I go home to the old ones soon. Home, boy. Home to meet those who came here in chains and those who were in the land where our family began." She sighed again. "I think they sent you to me so that I would know who it was that I came from. So I would . . ." Her voice trailed off and she slept.

Isaiah sat in the overstuffed chair by her bed. He whispered, "I'm right here," and put his hand on hers so she would know, even asleep, that she was not alone. He looked at the pictures on the wall—one of Jesus in profile, another, the *Last Supper,* painted on black velvet—then at the bureau where Grandma kept a small basket her aunt had woven and a braid made from Great-Grandma Reba's hair. The basket was filled with roots. Grandma had hand-dipped the candle that burned there. He did not know whom to pray to, the blue-eyed Jesus who stared into the distance, or the old ones who were Grandma's familiars. He looked at the flame that flickered before the makeshift altar and spoke to his ancestors.

Even as he prayed he wondered if anyone heard him. Grandma would not be here much longer. She was so much a part of who he was that he did not know who he would be without her. He was not her child anymore. She had lived to raise him to manhood. But there were places in his heart where he would always be her child, and those places were rubbed raw by her dying.

Grandma's bedroom was his office now, the place where he searched for their ancestors. The dark green wallpaper with white roses the size of his hand had been covered with mint-green paint. Her bed and chair were in the attic. The massive bureau and dresser had been replaced with a desk, file cabinets, and bookcases. The basket filled with roots, Reba's braid, and Grandma's candle all were on a shelf.

Isaiah palmed his hands on the table, pushed himself up and reached for his cane. Longevity was not part of his family's history. He had inherited the infirmities of his parents. His joints ached and swelled. He took insulin. The cardiologist could do nothing more for his heart. None of his doctors were optimistic about how much time he had to complete this search. He looked at the computer screen again. Had he finally worked his way back to the time of the beginning, as Grandma called it? Was he at or near the beginning of his family's time in this country? Reba Thatcher Gardner, daughter of Edward Thatcher. Was this Samuel, slave of Thatcher, the father of that Edward Thatcher? Soon, perhaps, he would know.

It was after seven o'clock when Floyd came in. Isaiah turned on the kettle and spooned instant coffee into two mugs. Floyd was three years younger than Isaiah's sixty-two, but the arthritis had reached Floyd's spine. Surgery had eased the pain, but, like him, Floyd walked with a cane.

"Got me some real supper," Floyd said. "I bet you been eatin' that beet soup. I don't even like looking at it sittin' in the re-frigerator."

As brothers, they could not have looked less alike. Floyd was taller, and light-skinned with curly, reddish-brown hair. Isaiah was dark with kinky hair that he wore in short dreadlocks. They were both widowers, and with the last of their children out and on their own, their lives had come full circle when Floyd re-

46

turned to Grandma's house, the place where they had been born.

"Beat that Bill Davis seven times," Floyd said.

"Checkers or chess?"

Floyd chuckled. "Both. Couldn't make a bad move today." He took the foil off a plate of collard greens and ham hocks and put the plate into the microwave. "Stopped by my baby girl's to see the new grandkid. Boy cried the whole time I was there. Didn't keep her from cooking, though. Girl cooks almost as good as her mother." He paused and Isaiah knew that he was thinking about his wife, and then he shrugged. "Real food, bro. Real meat, too. Pork."

Isaiah had found it impossible to keep a kosher kitchen with Floyd here. It didn't matter that much. He wasn't orthodox. Still, he had liked keeping kosher. It gave him more to do when he wasn't on his computer.

"So, you been ancestor-hunting today?" Floyd asked. "Be nice if we had an ancestor somewhere who struck it rich in the gold rush of '49 and left us a claim to his stake."

"We've got what we need."

"Got us a pension and disability, Irwin. Enough to survive."

"Isaiah," he reminded him.

"Sorry. Called you by your given name for close to fifty years."

"Changed my name fifteen years ago."

"Oh, yeah, right. Back when you became a Jew." He brought the plate of food to the table and unwrapped some hot-water corn bread. "Something wrong with being Baptist?"

Isaiah poured hot water into their mugs.

"Is this decaf?"

"Yeah."

"Damn."

Isaiah thought about Samuel, considered keeping it to himself until he knew more about him, decided this might not be the right time to say anything. He had stopped trying to involve

Floyd in his research a long time ago. Sometimes, when he was in the right mood, Floyd did seem interested. Most of the time, he was scornful. Once, Floyd had said, "You get to a lynching yet?" And Isaiah had understood. Floyd was a proud man. Even though Isaiah explained that there had been free Black men before emancipation, Floyd would rather not know where he came from than know for certain that he was the descendent of a slave.

After Floyd went upstairs to watch television, Isaiah fixed another cup of coffee and opened his journal. He kept records in a file on the computer, but this book, written in his hand, was for his children. Tomorrow he would go to the bank vault where he kept all of Grandma's papers, everything she had told him about their family history, and copies of everything he had been able to document over the years. He kept another journal there. Everything he wrote here tonight would be copied into that journal tomorrow.

When he had written down everything, he closed the notebook. Then he thought about getting ready for bed. He was tiring so easily now. Sometimes, like tonight, he felt too weary to move. But he would finish this. He would record that final page. This was his gift to his children and their children and their children's children. It was the only lasting gift he could give them.

6

Marti sat beside Vik in the shade of a huge oak and watched as a cave-in expert checked out the dig site.

"Hot," Vik said.

"Still hot," Marti agreed. The temperature hadn't dropped below eighty degrees all week.

The river wasn't far from where they were sitting. Clumps of thistle grew along its banks. Here, the grass had been mowed. There were no wildflowers to intrude on the monotony of green. Once this had been farmland; before that, the hunting grounds of the Potawatomi. Had runaway slaves passed this way, too? She tried to imagine what it must have been like back then.

"Idbash must have been part of a trading company to acquire this much land," she said. That was Theo's opinion, and Mike thought so too. "Too bad the Potawatomi had no concept of debt."

"Payback was a bitch," Vik agreed.

"I wonder what Idbash could have done back then that was illegal?"

"This was the wilderness."

"They must have had a few laws, Vik."

"Yeah, but who enforced them?"

"Federal marshals, maybe," Marti said.

Vik seemed to consider that, and then said, "We should have brought lunch."

He called to the uniform who was leaning against a squad car. "Got something important for you to do," he said. "Find a place around here that sells food." He handed him a twenty-dollar bill.

"Anything special?" the uniform asked.

"Just stop at the first place you come to and hope for sandwiches."

Marti watched the uniform leave, then turned to Vik, who had taken out his notebook.

"So what if the Smiths did not clear this with JULIE," he said. "The accident didn't involve any natural resources or utilities."

"The woman I spoke with at JULIE didn't think that mattered." She had seemed to take it as a personal affront and spoken as if it were Marti's fault.

Caleb, the cave-in technician, waved them over. He was tall and muscular and wore a sleeveless shirt. His neck and shoulders glistened with perspiration. His hair was naturally black and cut short at the sides, but curly and dyed royal blue on top.

Marti shaded her eyes as she looked into the first hole. It was hot in the sun.

"Someone dug here." Caleb pointed out one section of the hole that Marti thought looked just like the rest of it.

"Here," he said. "They took something out and replaced the dirt."

Marti looked at Vik, then at Caleb. "How can you tell? It all looks the same to me."

"No. The dirt's been moved. It's been packed in to look like it was always there, but see—" He pointed.

"No," Marti said. "I don't see."

"Well, you have to know what you're looking for. The layering of the dirt is different from the areas that were not disturbed."

"Oh." She couldn't see that either.

"I'll take some pictures."

"Will somebody else be able to see what I can't?" Marti asked.

"Another expert."

"Does that mean another expert could disagree?"

"No, but they could give a variety of reasons for the changes."

"And your reason?" Vik asked.

"That's your job, not mine."

"Thanks, Caleb," Marti said. "We needed that reminder."

Marti retreated to the shade of the trees, with Vik close behind. She picked up her notebook, found the entries relating to Linski's notes. "She didn't go to that hole, Vik. Or, if she did, she didn't record anything. All of her notes were detailed, right down to the time of day. There's no way she wouldn't have included it."

Vik pulled a blade of grass and chewed on it. "I guess that leaves us with a few questions. Like, what was in there? What was removed, if anything? Or maybe, what was somebody looking for?"

"I like that last one," Marti said.

After they had eaten Italian sub sandwiches and finished off one of two six-packs of Pepsi, Caleb joined them.

"The second excavation was untouched except for the backhoe." He wiped sweat from his forehead with the back of his hand and left a streak of dirt. A bandanna kept the perspiration out of his eyes. "You might want to have someone check it out for artifacts."

"You don't do that?" Vik asked.

"Uh-uh."

Marti offered him a can of pop. He drank it down, crushed the can, and went back to work.

"So," she said. "One apparently untouched site. The one in the middle. Someone will have to take a look at it. Why do I have the feeling that it will be a waste of time?"

Vik's wiry eyebrows almost met as he scowled. "Trouble. This family is nothing but trouble. They can't even give away a piece of their land without somebody dying."

A little more than an hour later, Caleb called to them again.

He was standing at the hole where Larissa Linski had died.

"Boulders," he said, pointing to a wall of large fieldstones about six feet high.

Marti looked. There were two holes where the boulders had been that hit Larissa Linski.

"See how the boulders fit together? See how tightly they are packed into the dirt? I have no explanation as to how two of them could have come loose."

Vik swore under his breath. "Of course you don't," he muttered. "Luck of the Smiths."

"What about the backhoe?" Marti asked.

"They didn't dig this far. The roof should have been a good eight, ten inches thick."

"Then how did she fall into the root cellar?"

"The site isn't intact enough for me to determine that. The ground beneath her was unstable. Not the fieldstone walls, just the ground where the roof or top of the root cellar was, or used to be. Her falling in should not have disturbed those boulders."

"How long has the root cellar been there?"

"Can't say."

"Guess," Vik suggested.

"I would guess the early eighteen hundreds, but only because the surveys I've got, which go back to 1842, don't indicate that anything is here. It wasn't something whoever did the survey could see, and apparently nobody told him about it."

"Surveys," Vik said. "What else do they tell you?"

"Just basic land formations, buildings."

"But not this?"

"No."

"And that means?"

"That the root cellar must have been dug before they began making surveys."

Marti pulled out a Xeroxed copy of a grid Larissa Linski had drawn. "What about this? Linski marked this spot with an X. Can you pinpoint the location?"

"Sure."

Several minutes later Caleb said, "Here."

It was a place above the root cellar.

"How can you be sure?"

"She drew it on a grid."

"And?"

"Here. I'll show you." He held his hands apart. "This is the scale. Based on that, the X-spot is here."

"Does the X mean she found something?"

"Most likely."

"Can you give me any idea of what it was?"

He laughed. "I'm not clairvoyant. Based on the way the soil is disturbed, I'd say something relatively small."

"Define 'relatively,' " Vik said.

"Sorry. Can't. The redistribution of the soil is in a small area. She didn't dig deep, she didn't dig wide."

"She didn't mention anything about it in her notes either," Marti said. "If she found something, it ought to be recorded somewhere."

"I heard they used to graze sheep around here somewhere," Vik said. "Maybe it was petrified sheep dung."

"No matter what it was," Marti persisted, "she was supposed to keep a record of everything."

Vik began walking toward the tree where they had been sitting. "She never should have come here. The place is jinxed."

Marti, bringing up the rear, agreed.

Back at the precinct, Marti pulled out her folder on Linski and found the transcripts of everything Larissa had recorded in her notebook and everything that was on the files on her computer.

"Waste of time," Vik said.

"Maybe," she agreed. "I don't understand why there is no mention of finding anything."

"Maybe she didn't. Maybe some little animal made whatever it was."

"Vik, we've got three holes, all excavated with a backhoe. We've got a young college student who was told which hole to look in, and apparently she found something. And we've got that same student crushed to death by two boulders that should not have fallen on her. You saw what those rocks looked like. It would have taken the backhoe to dislodge them."

"Maybe it did."

"Leaving the boulders around them intact? And what about the other hole that had been disturbed? According to Linski's notes, she never went near it."

Vik snapped a pencil in half. "Coroner's inquest is day after tomorrow. I don't know what's going on out there. But this doesn't look like an accident anymore."

Marti thought for a moment, and then said, "We'd better go back to the Channon place. If Linski did find something in that hole, we could have looked right at it and not known what it was."

Before they could leave, Marti got a call from the State of Illinois Attorney General's office in Springfield. One of the state's legal counsels, Anne Devney, wanted to see her and Vik tomorrow morning.

"Why?" Marti asked.

"The Gonzales case."

"Gonzales?" She had to think for a moment. "Hector Gonzales?" He had killed two rival gang members in a drive-by five years ago, right after she came here.

"Right."

"What about him? He got a commutation. What does he want? A pardon?"

"Could be. He definitely wants out. He's got a lot of enemies now that he's back in the general population."

"What's that got to do with me?"

"I need to review the case with you."

"Tomorrow? I've got to testify at an inquest tomorrow. How about sometime next week?" Marti didn't understand the urgency. She didn't need the distraction right now either.

"Sorry, this one says 'expedite.' "

"Isn't there someone in Chicago we can talk with about this?"

"Sorry. I'm it."

When Marti hung up, she said, "We've got a nine-thirty appointment tomorrow morning. We'll have to be out of here by six to avoid rush-hour traffic."

"What's Gonzales's problem? He'd rather been on death row waiting to be injected into eternity?"

"Apparently he thinks he shouldn't be in jail at all."

Vik finished off a Snicker's bar. "I knew this would happen. First you're going to kill them because they killed somebody. Then you're going to kill them but it won't hurt. Then you're not going to kill them. Then they expect to get back on the street so they can kill again. What's so bad about being locked up with sadists, rapists, and psychopaths for the rest of your life, instead of being buried in a box? Some people don't appreciate anything."

Marti called Janet Petroski, the coroner. Janet agreed to postpone the inquest until Friday.

When they returned to the Channon home, Vik did not object when Marti insisted that Gordon McIntosh come along. Mary Ellen Channon was sitting on the porch when they arrived. She put down a book and rose to greet them. Both Irish Setters were napping. One raised its head to look at them, gave a languid wag of its tail, and went back to sleep.

"They haven't released the body yet," Ms. Channon said. "Is there a problem?"

"Takes time," Vik said.

"Oh. Well . . . I'm glad nothing is . . . wrong." It sounded like a question.

Gordon looked as if he was ready to provide an answer. Marti moved closer before he could say anything. She bumped into him, making sure her elbow dug into his side.

"Oops, sorry."

As they went upstairs, Ms. Channon said, "Mother is so upset about this. My sister took her to our place in Door County for a few days. I just haven't had the heart to pack Larissa's things. I think that would make things a bit easier for her mother . . . but . . . maybe tomorrow . . ." Her voice trailed off as she opened the door to Larissa's room. This time she didn't come in.

"Something relatively small," Vik said. "Whatever that means."

To Marti's surprise, Gordon began a systematic inspection of the room.

While Gordon went through the closet, the bureau drawers and the drawers in a small desk and a nightstand, Marti checked the ledges above the doors and windows, and searched for loose places in the carpet. Vik took the bathroom.

After about half an hour, Gordon said, "Nothing."

Marti finished going through Larissa's clothing for the second time. She checked all of the pockets, turned the cuffs of two pair of twill jeans, and shook out the T-shirts, socks, and underwear that had been tossed in the clothes hamper. That done, she agreed, "Nothing."

"I even squeezed out all of the toothpaste this time," Vik said. He held up the tube.

"Nothing else to do here. We've got that archaeologist coming in tomorrow to check out that middle hole. I think we're ready to talk with the Smiths."

Marti smiled. "You've got it, partner." She was looking forward to it.

Ms. Channon gave them a worried look as they left, but she did not ask any questions.

When Marti arrived at the "Smith place," the guard at the gate gave her a map and directed her to follow a road until she came to a place beyond the main house where she could park. She drove for several miles to a paved area not far from a ten-car garage.

"So," she said to Vik, "this is the Smiths' place."

She wasn't sure of the architectural style but the term "castle" seemed appropriate. The main building consisted of three stories of gray stone complete with turrets. The two-story wings added on at either end were made of a lighter shade of gray stone and gave the house a U-shape. Each section of the house had its own formal garden complete with reflecting pools and fountains. There were balconies on the second floor with doors that opened onto them. Each wing had a group of three statues that looked like chess pieces.

Vik nodded toward one of the statues near the north wing. "The one on the horse with his sword in the air must be Vladimir the Impaler. Hell of a way for anyone to die, let alone a kid."

"How did he manage to land on that? It's not like it's a straight drop."

Vik shrugged. "Maybe it wasn't an accident."

They followed the walkway that led to the front of the house. A uniformed maid admitted them and explained that everyone was waiting for them in the library. Inside, the house was cool. They walked across a large room with a marble floor and five crystal chandeliers. The ballroom, Marti thought, imagining ladies in antebellum evening gowns waltzing to the music provided by a tuxedo-clad orchestra. She had never worked the Gold Coast when she was on the force in Chicago. That was the only place she knew of, other than the Palmer House or the Sheraton, where she might find anything like the Smith place.

The library was a vast, oak-paneled room with thick maroon carpeting and half a dozen groupings of sofas, love seats, and chairs. The paintings on the walls were all of hunting scenes with lights attached to the frames. The maid led them toward the far end of the room, where two couples and an elderly man sat near a fireplace.

"American royalty," Vik whispered. "I think we're supposed to genuflect."

Marti looked at him and winked. They both smirked at the same time.

When they reached the fireplace, the elderly gentleman said,

"Josiah Smith." His wrinkled face, prominent brow, and narrow nose reminded her of an Abraham Lincoln impersonator she had seen a few years ago. He did not stand to greet them or invite them to sit down. He did ask for their names and their identification. When he wrote both on a small pad, Vik suggested he verify the spelling.

"Mind?" Marti asked, indicating the nearest seating available, several straight-backed chairs with no padding. When Josiah Smith did not answer, she decided arched eyebrows were an affirmative response and brought one over, placing it where she could look at the group. Vik did the same. Seated, they took out their notebooks. Marti was immediately glad that she was what Momma called "healthy." These chairs were to be looked at, not sat on. Vik was going to have a sore butt and a backache by the time they left.

"So," Josiah said with another lift of his eyebrows. He waited. When neither Marti nor Vik responded, he added, "This seems like a considerable amount of fuss for a rather mundane accident."

"Someone died," Vik said.

"Unfortunate," Josiah agreed.

Marti looked at the others. This wasn't teatime. They all had drinks, nothing fancy, just wine. She thought of the cigarette butts. There were no ashtrays. She recognized Paul Smith and nodded to him. "And you are?" she asked the woman sitting beside him.

"This is my family," Josiah said. "Here at your request." He didn't introduce them.

"Names," Vik said, in his most courteous tone of voice. Marti knew that meant he was furious.

"I believe we've met," Paul said.

Vik turned to Josiah. "Sir, this is still a police matter. It would speed things up if you would cooperate, but we're not in any hurry."

"This is my wife, Jessica," Paul said. "My brother Franklin, and his wife, Eileen."

Marti looked at each of them in turn. Paul's wife looked taller than he was. She was tanned with those fine lines women get when they spend too much time in the sun. Chestnut-brown hair cascaded to her shoulders and she wore an understated white silk pantsuit. Franklin also seemed taller than Paul. Maybe it was the way Paul was sitting, hunched over and scrunched down. Franklin's hair was dyed a dark brown that made him look older and seem vain. Eileen, Franklin's wife, was ordinary in comparison to Jessica except for her eyes, which seemed gray the first time Marti looked at her but were more blue than gray when she looked again. Eileen didn't fidget, but she leaned forward, sat back, and looked about the room as if she was anxious to leave. Marti got the impression that she was one of those hyper types who always had to be doing something.

"Why don't you get on with this," Josiah suggested. "We do have other things planned for the evening."

Marti consulted her notes. She and Vik had agreed that she would ask the questions. If it came to it, they could play good cop bad cop. She was bad cop today.

"How did you choose the site for the dig?"

Josiah looked from her to Vik, as if waiting for Vik to speak. When Vik said nothing, he answered. "The Lake County Commissioners want that piece of land to complete their Historic Des Plaines River Trail."

Marti considered asking him if the excavation was required in order to pass title or meet some other legal requirement but decided not to. "And that was the only reason?"

He nodded.

"Why did you dig three small holes and not one large one?"

Josiah looked at her for a moment, then looked at Vik again, then turned his attention back to her. His eyes were dark and unclouded by age, although he appeared to be very old. He seemed to be wondering why she was doing the talking. "Are you the senior officer here?"

"Why did you dig those holes in that configuration?"

Josiah looked at Paul, then Franklin. He gestured with one hand, as if to dismiss her, or her importance, and then smiled. "We don't know much about those things, officer. What did you say your name was?"

She repeated it and asked if he would like to see her badge again. He declined.

"So, Mr. Smith, you didn't bring in an expert."

"I rather thought that as long as we made an attempt to see if there was anything important there . . ."

Marti waited.

"The commissioners wanted the land to remain undisturbed. We, on the other hand, felt an obligation to determine if there was anything there of historic significance."

"Are you satisfied now that there is not?"

He nodded and took a sip of his drink.

"Why did you hire a college student to handle it?"

"For the same reason I didn't bring in an expert."

When he didn't elaborate, Marti asked, "And why was that?"

"I just told you." He sounded exasperated. "It was a routine check. It wasn't that important. Anyone with a minimum of expertise could handle it."

"Why did you dig in that particular spot?"

"It was a random selection."

"How long had that root cellar been there?"

"I have no idea. I didn't know it was there. I would imagine it goes quite a ways back, but I couldn't say with any certainty."

Marti noted that Josiah was the only one answering her questions. With this many family members present, usually one of them would interject something.

"Was Larissa looking for anything in particular?"

"The deceased was simply asked to go into the holes and see if she could determine any reason to search beyond that."

Holes. Marti made a mental note of the plural. "She was to check out all three?"

"Of course."

"And did she?"

"I think she was still looking at the first one."

Marti noted that also. "So, the other holes have not been disturbed?"

"I wouldn't think so."

Paul caught her attention. He was clenching his hands together so tightly his knuckles were white. "Did you give her any suggestions as to what she might find?"

Josiah looked away, and then looked at her. Did he think she knew something? If so, what?

He shook his head. "As far as I know, that land has been undisturbed for as long as we've owned it."

"Did you know there was a root cellar directly below that hole?"

"Did you hear what I just said?" he snapped.

"Is that a yes or a no?"

"No!"

"My father has been quite upset about this . . . this . . . incident," Paul said. Apparently, it was not okay to use the "d" word.

"Incident, Mr. Smith?" Marti asked. "This is a death investigation. We are investigating the death of Larissa Linski. She died. She is dead."

Marti turned to Josiah Smith. "Was Larissa to check out all three excavated areas, or just the one she was working in?"

Josiah's eyes narrowed and he considered her for a moment before he spoke.

"You asked that already, but yes, she was hired to investigate all three holes."

"Did she?"

"I have no idea. You probably know the answer to that. Mind telling me?"

Instead of answering, Marti said, "Was Larissa told where to dig?"

"No."

"What to look for?"

"No."

"Not to find anything?"

"No! I find that insulting."

Marti glanced at Paul's hands. They were still clenched. Was he angry because her questions were raising his father's ire? Or was it because he had a reason for not wanting her to ask these questions? They would have to find out if there was anything in the middle hole right away. Caleb, their cave-in expert, would be returning with someone familiar with archaeological digs. At least, with a guard posted since the alleged accident, nobody had been able to access anything.

THURSDAY JUNE 27

Day was breaking and traffic was light as Marti and Vik left for Springfield Thursday morning. By the time they were approaching O'Hare airport on I-295, traffic was getting congested and they had to close the windows and turn on the air-conditioning.

"I wonder who in the hell thought this one up," Vik said. "Hell of a way to waste a hot, humid, muggy day. We could be back at the Smith place sitting in the shade, swatting at flies, squashing ants, and maybe even counting more cigarette butts. Too bad people don't use matches anymore. Finding a bunch of those really would have made McIntosh's day."

She pulled into a crowded truck stop for breakfast. The service was fast and the food plentiful and well-cooked. After they ate, they ordered large cups of hot coffee for the road.

"At least we'll get this over with," Vik commented.

"Maybe," Marti said. "I wonder why they didn't call us in when they were deciding whether or not to commute."

"That was a done deal. Not that I can blame the governor for that. Thirteen wrongful convictions and a couple of guys who were hours from the death chamber was reason enough. Not that we have to worry about the Gonzales conviction. Not only was he the right man, we caught him in the car with the gun and had three witnesses."

"I wish things were that easy with Linski's death."

"We had a case in Lincoln Prairie maybe thirty years ago. Good family. Wealthy. One night there was a bad thunderstorm. Tornado warnings, high winds, torrential rain, the works. All three kids—teenagers—and both parents at home. Call comes in, one of the kids finds the parents dead. Nobody knows anything. The kids didn't see anything, didn't hear anything, nothing. Real simple story and they all stuck to it, without deviation. Everyone is convinced that one of the kids did it, but there's no proof—no evidence—no witnesses. A few theories as to why one of the kids might have done it, but not one of them will talk. Ten years ago, one of the kids confessed. If he hadn't, that case would still be open."

"You think one of the Smiths did this or knows who did."

"It happened on their property. The girl was there because they hired her. She probably found something while she was digging. But there will be no witnesses. None of them is going to volunteer anything. They will alibi for each other. And this case will remain open unless we get some damned substantial evidence and motive to support it."

Marti thought of the Smiths, all together, family, but not close. "We're talking survival, in this case, Vik. Maybe someone's survival needs will change."

"Hah! I wouldn't wait for that to happen."

Neither will I, Marti thought. Neither will I. The thought of anyone getting away with murder made her angry, but she knew that it happened. For whatever the reason, the thought of one of the Smiths getting away with murder was deeply offensive.

Marti decided that the best way to describe Springfield was dismal. She had come here in November a couple of years ago. Gray skies and cold weather hadn't compensated for haphazard urban sprawl and a general lack of anything that made the place distinctive. Today, sunshine and ninety-degree temperatures didn't do much for the town either.

About the only good thing about Springfield was that the

monuments to Lincoln were all within walking distance, and when she brought her kids here they had completed the entire tour in two hours. Everyone had been happy to head home.

"I have not seen one decent place to eat," Vik complained as they drove up and down the one-way streets in the center of town. "Geez, you go two blocks from the capital building in any direction and it's not a lot different from the west side of Chicago. I bet the guy who planned this town was a White Sox fan."

Chicago was a two-baseball-club city—Sox and Cubs. Like Marti, Vik was a die-hard Cubbie.

"I'm not sure anyone did any planning, Jessenovik."

They met with Anne Devney in a small wood-paneled office in the capital building. Devney was a slender woman at least four inches shorter than Marti's five-ten. She was wearing a conservative suit with a knee-length skirt in a job where pantsuits were common. She had that resigned attitude of someone who has done the same job for a long time and knew there could still be some surprises, most of them unwelcome.

"So," she said, leading them into a small room crowded with a long table and half a dozen chairs. "This is it, the Gonzales case." At least twenty-five legal-sized manila folders were stacked in three piles. The folders were worn at the creases, some were torn and had been repaired with Scotch tape. Papers stuck out from the top and the sides.

"We don't have to go through all of that," Vik said.

"I'm afraid so, not that we'll finish today. I can only give this two hours."

Two hours later they had not even made it through all of the evidence. Vik was cussing under his breath in Polish as they walked to the side street where they had parked their car.

"That woman is out of her mind," he said. "All of this because a guilty man wants a pardon?"

"The wheels of justice . . ." Marti said.

"Are grinding much too slowly."

"He's been with the general population for what—six months now?"

"That's the problem, MacAlister. His gang is outnumbered by nine other gangs and he's still alive."

"This could take weeks," Marti said. They had to meet with Anne Devney again on Monday.

"Not if one of those other gang members gets to him before the wheels of justice grind to a halt. Prisons are not a safe place to be. That's why he wants to take his chances on the street."

"Well, he's not getting out on my watch," Marti said.

In the currency of the street, she would rather be "Big Mac" and keep some insignificant gang banger behind bars than gain a reputation for not being able to make a homicide bust stick.

7

Marti came awake all at once. Dirt, she thought, dirt. Then, wide awake, she saw that she was not in the root cellar. Beside her, Ben stirred. Without waking him, she snuggled closer, fitting her body against the contours of his. He murmured her name and stroked her thigh. She pictured the fieldstone walls again, the dirt ceiling overhead, saw the roof collapse, felt her nose and mouth fill with dirt. She opened her eyes. The roof. Was it just made of dirt? Didn't it need beams of some kind? Caleb mentioned dirt, nothing else. Maybe nothing else was needed. The coroner's inquest would begin at 10 A.M. Whether or not they ruled Larissa Linski's death accidental, she would have to find out about the roof.

Marti didn't tell Vik about her dream. She did mention the roof, or the lack of it.

"Look, MacAlister. Do not ask McIntosh about that. The man already thinks he's on the case. The less we have to do with him the better. He's a pathologist now. Leave it at that."

"We don't know enough about any of this archaeological stuff, Vik." She was logging two to three hours a night on the Internet but lacked the expertise to be selective. Last night one search turned up 578 listings. Some were obviously not what she was interested in. Other entries were less specific. "What if we miss something?"

"That's why we have experts."

"They can only give us information. They can't interpret it for us."

Marti had gotten used to autopsies. She didn't think she would ever feel that way about inquests. Family members saw the photographs, heard the evidence, learned details that no loved one should ever have to know, especially when the deceased died violently. It was always worse than testifying at a trial. At least then there was a suspect, perhaps even a reason, however incomprehensible, for the death. At an inquest, there was only how the person died and what had happened. When she testified, Marti could never bring herself to look at the victim's family and friends. When it was a homicide and she didn't have a suspect, she felt as if she had not done her job.

The coroner's jury brought back an undetermined-death/gunshot-wound verdict on the skeletal remains. Their decision on the Linski case was to keep it open. Afterward, Mrs. Linski asked to talk with Marti and Vik. They met in a small office in the coroner's facility. Marti thought of her dream. She remembered Larissa's dirt-streaked face and fluid-filled eyes as she looked at Larissa's mother. Petite and blond, Mrs. Linski was an older version of her daughter.

"They don't think it was an accident," Mrs. Linski said. Her voice was flat, her face haggard. There were dark circles under her eyes, as if she hadn't slept in days.

"We don't know anything for certain, ma'am," Marti said. "Not yet."

Vik pulled a chair out for her, made sure she was seated close to Marti. "Coffee, ma'am?" he asked.

"No. No, thank you." The woman sat with her hands clasped in her lap. She looked at the ceiling, then over Marti's left shoulder, then at the floor. "I . . . I . . . where is she now?"

"At the funeral home."

"Then they . . . she isn't . . . she doesn't look like those pictures anymore, does she?"

"No, ma'am."

"She would have been . . . upset . . . to have me see her that way." She wiped at her eyes. "It didn't. I mean it was . . . quick . . . she didn't . . ."

"No, ma'am." Marti gave her some Kleenex. "No. It happened very quickly."

Mrs. Linski had heard the evidence. She knew that was a lie but she nodded, needing to hear it.

"Will you . . . find him? Will you ever know who it was?" She sounded detached now,

Her loss was new. Marti knew that soon the anger would come.

"Oh, we'll find him," she said.

Mrs. Linski looked at her for a long minute. "Yes," she said. "I believe you. At least I know you'll try. I need to know who it was. I need to know why."

Marti nodded. "So do we."

"Sometimes you know too much," Mrs. Linski said. "Sometimes you see things you can't forget. Her eyes . . . why . . . ?" She shook her head. "I want to see her again, see her the way she was before . . . maybe I'll never . . ." She began crying again.

"Mrs. Linski, you might be able to help us."

"How?"

"What can you tell us about Larissa?"

Mrs. Linski dabbed at her eyes and blew her nose. "Her nails," she said. "They were caked with dirt. Every night she came home and did her nails. Funny, that. She wasn't fussy about anything else."

"Did Larissa call you while she was here?"

"Yes. She called me every night."

"What did she talk about?"

"She was . . . happy . . . excited . . . but . . . she had mixed feelings about coming here. This was the first time she was being paid for working a dig. That bothered her. Made it seem too commercial."

"How much was she being paid?"

"Four thousand dollars a week."

That seemed like a lot of money to Marti, especially for a

student, an amateur, but when you had as much money as the Smiths, maybe it wasn't.

"That seems like a lot of money," she said. "Especially for a student."

"I thought so too. But Larissa spent most of last summer on a dig in Australia. She said that was why they were paying her so much."

"Had she been on many digs?"

"Oh, yes. Every summer since high school. The summer before last she worked at a dig out west where they found most of a dinosaur. She had a lot of experience."

And Marti thought, they told her that they hired Larissa because they didn't need an expert.

"Larissa wanted to do a good job," her mother said. "She wanted everything to be perfect. Wanted . . ." Tears came to her eyes.

Marti handed her more Kleenex.

"Her dad always wanted to be an archaeologist. He became a high school science teacher instead. Family responsibilities. He died a few years ago. Larissa was living his dream. And now . . ." She dabbed at her eyes, then blew her nose.

"Did she mention finding anything?"

"I don't know. I don't think so. She said she had something to show me. She wouldn't say what it was. It could have been anything. Wherever she went, Larissa found something—a stone, a feather, something to keep as a memento. She would label them so she wouldn't forget where they came from."

"And if she found something at the dig site?"

"It would be in her notes."

Her notes, Marti thought. But it wasn't.

"If you think of anything else, anything she told you about being here . . . Anything. Even if it seems unimportant, call us." Marti wrote her cell-phone number on the back of her card. "I saw Ms. Channon and two other ladies sitting with you at the inquest."

"My sister. And my oldest daughter. Larissa is . . . was . . . my youngest. She was much younger than my other two girls." She seemed calm, but Marti thought exhausted might be closer to the truth. "Will they let me take her home now?"

Marti nodded.

As soon as they returned to the precinct, Marti called the evidence tech. "Count the number of pages in the Linski notebook. Let me know if any are missing. And see if you can detect impressions of writing on any of the blank pages. If you do, I want to know what it says."

Next, she called Caleb and asked him if there should have been a roof.

"He says it could have been a dirt roof supported with wooden beams, but that the wood would have deteriorated a long time ago and that might be why the ceiling collapsed."

Vik shook his head. "Let's go over this again."

They reconstructed what had happened at the dig site based on current information and listed what they could not explain.

"Why was the root cellar so far from the house?" Marti wondered. "Or was there a house nearby when they built it?"

"Is it a typical root cellar?" Vik asked. "Is there anything about it that's different?"

"What did they use it for? Damn, Vik." For a moment, what they didn't know seemed overwhelming.

The evidence tech returned her call within an hour.

"The notebook is intact," she told Vik. "No pages missing. If Larissa did find something, why wouldn't she write it down? If there was something there, and that's why she died, then she must have told someone. Josiah hired her but that doesn't mean he's the one she reported to."

"Paul came to the site," Vik said. "And someone watched from beneath a tree while smoking."

"We didn't see anything when we were inside the house to indicate that anyone in the family smoked, Vik."

"Nowadays most smokers have to go outside and light up."

"If Larissa did find something," Marti said, "it was relatively small."

"Relatively."

"What could survive in that soil for at least a hundred and fifty to a hundred and seventy-five years, maybe longer? Shells, beads, pottery . . ."

"Metal, bones . . ." Vik said.

"What about leather?"

"Hell if I know."

"There's still too much we don't know." She had asked the boys to get some books on archaeology from the library.

"We agree that this is a probable homicide. We know how she died. It's safe to assume that whoever did it has got themselves an alibi. But motive. What will you kill for?"

"Damned near anything these days, Jessenovik. The question is, what was in that hole that was worth killing for? According to Caleb, the dirt in the first hole was disturbed. If someone took something out of there it must have been something that was big enough for them to find without outside help. That has to be why they needed Larissa, to find something small. And since there is nothing in her notes or on her computer files, we don't have a clue as to what that might be." Why didn't she put it in her notes? If there was anything.

She picked up the Linski file. "Something small," she said aloud. She put in a call to Dr. Altenberg.

"How small?" Altenberg asked.

"Relatively," Marti answered.

"Oh." Altenberg was silent for a moment. Apparently "relatively" meant something to her. "Before the white man came, the Potawatomi were foragers. They went wherever the food supply was. They made all kinds of bags and pouches to carry things in, and pitchkosans, or bundles, which they filled with medicinals, ceremonial items, or whatever identified which clan they belonged to. They decorated these with marvelous beadwork. Finding something like that that had been buried for a long time would be highly questionable but very profitable. They also made things out of the parts of animals that they couldn't eat: deer hooves, porcupine quills. They made tools from animal bones and used bones for artwork, carving them and drawing on them. Something like that would be an exciting find. After the French and English arrived, they had ornaments made of German silver. Things like that would survive under those conditions. Flint and most metal objects wouldn't have nearly as much historic significance."

"Would they have had gold coins?" Marti asked.

"Possibly. Not that they had much of anything by the time they were made to leave here. The French and the English encouraged a 'Buy now, pay later' economy."

"Is there anything you can think of that would be valuable if found?"

"The value would be based on demand. It could be almost anything if it was something that was scarce."

"Thanks." When Marti hung up, she had more questions. What would have such significant value, if found, that it had to be kept secret? Having people find out that Potawatomi, or even runaway slaves, had been on the Smiths' property wouldn't have any negative impact. If those rumors were proved to be true, Idbash would become a hero.

The phone rang again about an hour later, but when Marti answered, nobody spoke; after a few seconds they hung up. Curious, she looked at the receiver, and then put it down.

Ethan Dana stared at the receiver. He couldn't do it, not yet. He didn't want to know what had happened to Tommy, or what Tommy had done. He never wanted to know what Tommy was up to. Usually he had no choice, Tommy told him. This time Tommy's silence had lasted since last August, the longest Tommy had ever gone without calling or coming back. This silence was scary because it was so unlike him. The picture of Tommy, which he had put in a drawer in his office, was scary too.

Solveig came in from the kitchen. "You called, Ethan? What did they say?"

"Whoever it was didn't answer," he lied.

She came over and sat on the arm of the chair. "I know you do not want to know what has happened. But Tommy is family. And all of us, all of Tommy's family needs to know."

Tommy had left last July. He had not come back. He had not called or written since last August. He would have been back by now, or at least would have called, if he could have. If. The thought made Ethan's stomach churn.

He put his hand on Solveig's stomach, felt the baby move. "Maybe we'll call him Tommy," he said. "Johans, for your father, Tommy Dana."

"And Topash for your grandfather," Solveig said. "Johans Topash Tommy Dana."

"That's a lot of names for one little kid."

"Yes, but he will not be little forever, and with these names, he will always know who he is."

"I love you," he said. Solveig was the one person who knew all of who he was and loved all of him.

The sun was setting when Harry Buckner drove the lawn mower through the open doors of the barn. This was his favorite time of day. He would go outside for a while, sit there until the sun set, then go up to the loft and warm up a can of soup for supper. Life was good here. At least it had been until this afternoon, when he dug that last hole. If he had someplace else to go, maybe he would, but there was no other place, no other job either. He was overweight, had a gimp leg, and he was sixty-four. This was the end of the road, and, until today, not a bad road to end up on.

But now that girl was dead. Young. Pretty. Dead. The only sure thing he knew was that it was not because of him. He had gone back today, looked down at the fieldstone walls. There was no way he could have dislodged two of those stones with the backhoe. He didn't know how those rocks had come loose, but it was not because he was negligent or drunk the way the driver who killed his Zoe had been. If only Zoe were here. If only she had had time to get out of the way of that car.

Before he got off the backhoe, Harry had reached down and picked up what looked like a metal collar. It was heavy, like lead, and rusty. It had hinges and two rings that came together so it could be locked. There was a ring that a rope or a chain could be attached to. It could have been used to tether an animal, a sheep maybe, or a goat. It was too small for a cow or a horse. Whatever this was used for, it had been buried for a long time. Now that he had found something, he wondered it the girl had found something too. Old man Smith had asked him about that.

He put the collar down and wiped his hands on his jeans. Was this why he was told to dig in that place among the trees? Were they looking for things like this, and tools, maybe, things people would have used when they were coming here in covered wagons? There was a shed on that land when the map was drawn.

Harry knew the Smith family well enough to know that everything they did was for a reason, and that most of their reasons had something to do with money. The land he was digging up was to be given away, but the rest of the land would be sold. Did that sale depend on what was on the land that was free? No. He didn't want to know that. He didn't want to know anything about any of this. He just wanted to do his job. If only he hadn't found anything in the first place. He would hide it. Maybe then it would be like it had never been there at all. This was nothing, nothing important. Josiah asking about that girl finding something was making him feel uneasy, that was all.

Marti rested her head on Ben's shoulder and let him lead her through the slow, easy rhythms of the music. The lights were dim, the conversation little more than an intimate hum interspersed with quiet laughter. They were at a small jazz club on the far south side of Chicago listening to music played by a trio that had been discovered and then forgotten before either of them was born. The saxophone player blew riffs on "Soul Eyes" that even Coltrane would have applauded. The bass throbbed like a heartbeat.

"Ummm-humm," Ben murmured, holding her close. "It doesn't get much better than this."

She inhaled the pungent scent of his cologne and agreed. The music was hot, the beer was cold, her man was ready, and it was almost time to go home. "That hot tub and those vanilla candles are going to be calling to me real soon," she said.

"I hear them now," Ben whispered.

They left the next time the musicians took a break and listened to *Coltrane for Lovers* all the way home.

Josiah awakened to the sound of a woman crying. He sat up but did not reach for the light on the table beside his bed. He had never heard nor seen Jessica or Eileen cry, but he was certain this wasn't either of them. This sounded like the weeping of someone who mourned. Josiah swung his feet over the side of the bed and felt along the carpet for his slippers. Then he stood, listening. This woman was far beyond any comfort he could give, although he wasn't inclined to comfort her. Rather, he wanted her to be silent, to go away, and to cry someplace else. Her desperation was obvious, and also annoying. The question returned. Who was she?

His room was dark. The curtains were drawn, the windows closed. There was no light, but his eyes were accustomed to the darkness. He had slept in this room for years now. He could make out the tall peaks of the mirrors attached to his dresser, the cumbersome wardrobe, the thronelike chair in the corner. Heavy, bulky furniture, all of it. Older than he was, dated, but timeless. Josiah listened, but heard no unfamiliar sound other than the woman's sobbing. He took his robe from the foot of the bed. Even though it was warm, the long hall tended to be drafty. He went to the door and eased it open, not because he didn't want to frighten the woman but because he didn't want her to know he was there. The crying did not become louder, nor could he see who it was. He peered out.

She was sitting on the top step of the stairway. He couldn't see her face, only her back and her shoulders, hunched as she wept. He did know who she was, not by name, only because he had often stood by the window at night and watched as she walked past the oak trees toward the apple orchard and disappeared. Tonight as he watched, she began to rise. Alarmed, he closed the door. As he turned both locks, his hand shook. The woman, a harmless a presence outside, seemed less benign now. Why had she come inside after all of these years? Why had she come into the house?

Vik had the contents of several folders spread out on his desk when Marti arrived at work. She sniffed. No coffee. Cowboy and Slim hadn't arrived yet. They didn't always come in early on weekends. Most Saturdays there was enough Friday-night vice action to necessitate a trip to weekend court for bail hearings.

There was a strudel, filled with apples and raisins, on Vik's desk.

"Mildred and Helen baked yesterday," Vik said. "She warmed this one up this morning."

Marti wondered if that meant that Mildred, Vik's wife, had had a good day, or if her spinster sister was the one who had baked. Mildred had MS. Helen had moved in with them a few months ago.

"Is she doing okay?" Marti asked. Vik hadn't seemed as worried lately.

"It's stabilized again."

"That's good. What are you working on?"

"I was talking with Stephen last night about some of this construction stuff."

"I take it Stephen is not a chip off the old block." Vik had come in less than a month ago with a sore thumb because he had hit it with a hammer.

"Stephen takes after my brother, not me. He's good with his hands, worked construction all through college."

"Did he come up with anything?"

"He had some ideas. He said the cellar might have had a roof with a wooden framework and sod on top, or they could have rolled logs close together. He also said the roof would have to be replaced maybe every eight to ten years."

"And that's why it isn't there anymore."

"Yeah, but some things didn't make sense to him."

"What?" Marti sat at her desk and reached for her mug. Then she remembered it was empty. Where the hell were Cowboy and Slim?

"It's too deep. Too hard to access. No ventilation." Vik threw up his hands. "Then he explained a lot of stuff I wasn't much interested in. The gist of it was he didn't think it was a root cellar."

"Oh?"

"Because of the way it was constructed. But he got me thinking. There were no backhoes back then. Why would anyone dig that deep with a pick and shovel? And, according to Steve, at least three of the walls should have been dirt. When you think about it, getting all of those fieldstones down there and in place took a hell of a lot of time or manpower. It was built more like a fortress than a storage place, maybe as some kind of defense against the Indians."

"No," Marti said, "the Indians were used to white men by then and they got along okay."

"There is something else. We're assuming that there were steps leading down and a door at ground level. Caleb didn't find anything like that."

"I never thought about how anyone got down there," Marti admitted. "Maybe they threw something down there? But what? And why?" She thought for a moment. "Something valuable and/or illegal. Guns, maybe," she guessed. "Maybe old Idbash was a gunrunner."

"Hell, I bet half the folks heading west could have been called that. If Linski found some bullets, whoopee."

"We need to know why Larissa Linski died."

"Maybe there is no why, Marti. Maybe this was an accident. The Smiths have had stranger things happen out there."

"An unlucky root cellar? A haunted dig? Come on, Jessenovik, this hasn't looked like an accident since we saw those fieldstone walls."

When the phone rang, Marti looked up from the reports she was going through. She was surprised to see that it was almost three o'clock. Probably someone else was calling about the picture of the facial reconstruction. So far today, there had been seven calls. Six of those callers were not even seeking an American Indian. Three were looking for a missing woman. As they spoke, most hesitantly, a few belligerent, she could hear the bleak and terrible desperation that had made them pick up the phone.

This time it was Mary Ellen Channon. "Someone has been in the house."

"Where are you?"

"Upstairs."

"Leave now," Marti told her. "Go to your car, turn it on and sit there with the doors locked and the windows up. If anyone approaches you, leave. I'll have a uniform there right away."

It took Marti twenty minutes to drive to Grayslake. She would have used the siren or the Mars light, but two local officers had been dispatched right away and their arrival confirmed within minutes.

Ms. Channon was sitting on the porch and seemed calm. "I took Larissa's family to the airport," she said. "Everything seemed fine when I got back, until I went upstairs. Two doors were ajar. I know they were closed when I left. They're always closed."

"How did they gain entry?" Vik asked.

"We never lock the doors during the day."

"That might be a good idea from now on."

"You could be right," Ms. Channon conceded.

"Which doors were ajar?"

"Mother's, hers is the first room on the right, and Larissa's room . . . the guest room . . . right next to it."

As they went upstairs, Vik said, "Note that two closed doors were left ajar. Could this be Christmas in June? What do you want to bet Santa left us a present?"

"A relatively small present," Marti agreed.

They found it in the closet. A corner of the carpet had been pulled up and made to look as if that had hidden it from sight.

"Looks like an animal hoof," Vik said. "But not a relatively small hoof."

He was wearing latex gloves and put it into a plastic bag which he held up. "And"—he shook the bag—"It rattles. A toy. It was Santa."

"He could have left us a new toy. This one has dirt on it."

"Bet I know where the dirt came from. No telling where they found the toy."

"We'd better get it to the lab, Vik, so they can hurry up and tell us what we already know."

On the drive back they decided to keep their distance from the Smith family.

"Somebody knows Larissa found something," Marti said. "Realized that our expert could have figured that out too. What didn't occur to them is that we could guesstimate the size of the find. Let's just sit on this. See who comes to us."

Isaiah had come to love the Jewish rituals. He loved the prayers, the traditions. He kept the Sabbath. "So God blessed the seventh day and hallowed it, because on it God rested from all the work that He had done in creation." Every Friday evening Isaiah walked to the synagogue for Shabbat. He went back on Saturday morning for Shacharit—morning prayer, then Torah, and Musaf. Afterward he usually stayed for Kiddush, sharing a glass of wine with the other members of the congregation. Even though he was the only Black, he felt welcome there, at home in a way that he had never felt in any other religion. Sometimes he tried to explain why he had become a Jew, or, as he believed, returned to the religion of his ancestors when they were in Ethiopia. Although he could not prove that his ancestors came from there, he wanted that to be true. Solomon, after all, had a son, Menelik I, by the Queen of Sheba, a black woman. His children humored his wishful thinking, but they respected his commitment.

He kept the Jewish Bible, the Tanakh, on a small table in the living room. On Shabbat he lit two candles and placed them on either side of the book. Two Sabbath candles burned in his den also, the room that had once been Grandma's. He had placed a small doily that Juanita, his wife, had crocheted, under Grandma's basket of herbs and the braid made from Great-Grandmother Reba's hair. He was not just remembering them, but the Creator who had made them. He was celebrating all the times they had been happy together. He was honoring his ancestors and giving thanks to the God who gave them life.

Over the years, Grandma's house had changed, not all at once, but gradually—a chair here, a sofa, a table, a lamp. The living room had become the place where Isaiah remembered. Grandma's china cabinet with all of her special plates and serving dishes was here, and her sideboard, still filled with real silver tableware and monogrammed linens. He had refused to scrape off or paint over the red-flocked wallpaper on the upper half of the walls or replace the dark oak paneling on the lower half. Two sepia-tinted photos in oval frames hung above the sideboard. Grandma was wearing her favorite Sunday hat, the one that made Isaiah think of what she must look like in heaven. The center of the hat was a little white cap with a large rhinestone brooch pinned to the front. Layers and layers of white organza ruffles trimmed with silver ribbon fanned out like angels' wings. The other photo was of his parents, who he could not remember: his mother seated in a fragile, ornate chair, and his father standing behind her with one hand on her shoulder. Pictures of Juanita, their children and grandchildren were on the other walls, and, since Floyd had come home, photographs of his family as well.

For Isaiah, the Sabbath was a time to remember. His wife had passed less than a year after Grandma and if his life changed when Grandma died, it almost stopped when Juanita passed away. He wasn't sure what would have become of him if he hadn't had children to raise. On the Sabbath he talked to Juanita, not out loud, but in his mind. He recalled things their four kids had done, the times they had celebrated—the graduations and birthdays and weddings, the births of their three grandchildren. He had felt Juanita's presence during those times, just as he did now. He believed she was always near, in a dimension just beyond his line of vision.

Today, he talked with Grandma, too. He told her about Samuel, runaway slave of Thatcher. He asked for her help. He had looked up more slave owners named Thatcher, but had not been able to find another one with a slave identified as Samuel. Finding the name of any slave was difficult to impossible. Slaves were not citizens. There were no birth records, marriage licenses, land deeds, or anything else to tie them to a place or a time. They were counted in census records, but not named. Recently, he had heard that some owners had insured their slaves, and that those records had names, but were not yet available.

He had found a marriage license for Edward Thatcher and Mellie Bishop. Eventually he found birth certificates for Edward and Mellie. Edward had been born in 1868. Samuel Thatcher was his father, and Cynthia, no last name, his mother. Edward had a daughter named Reba. She was Isaiah's great-grandmother. He had found a few of Reba's relatives, and a marriage license indicating Reba had married Theodore Gardner in 1910, but when he tried to go back in time and identify someone related to Edward Thatcher, it was as if they didn't exist. That was where he was now. Lost. The only clue that he was on the right path was Grandma's name, Ruby Thatcher Gardner. The only thing he knew of that might help him determine if this was the right Samuel was to get a copy of Edward's marriage application. That document would have required the most information about

Edward's family history. Getting a copy meant a trip to Chicago, and although Chicago wasn't that far from Battle Creek, it was a longer trip than he could manage. They were having a guest speaker at his genealogy club meeting tonight. Someone who specialized in searches that preceded 1870. Perhaps this speaker would speak on something that would help him, or maybe he would ask him a few questions. He could almost hear Grandma's voice. "In due time," she said. "In due time."

9

Marti didn't wake up Sunday morning until the alarm went off. Something about that made her feel uneasy. Waiting for the other shoe to drop, Momma would call it. Ben was alone in the kitchen. She gave him a long, slow kiss, then poured a cup of his "fireman's brew," the only coffee she had ever tasted that was better than Cowboy's.

"Where's Momma?" she asked.

"Having breakfast in bed."

"Ben, are you serious? Momma has never done that." Her uneasiness returned. "She isn't sick, is she?"

Ben laughed. "Actually, she is sitting in the chair by her window having her morning coffee and reading the Sunday *Tribune*."

Marti could not ever remember her mother doing that. "You have worked a miracle," she said, pleased.

Joanna was the first one downstairs.

"Ummm," Joanna answered when Ben said good morning; then, "Are you using canola oil?"

"Water's hot if you're ready for tea," Ben told her. "And these don't taste right without real butter on them."

"Guess so," Joanna agreed, still half asleep.

Ben caught Marti's eye and winked. He flipped a pancake big enough to cover a plate.

"Bacon?" Joanna said when she came to the table. "Again?" She rubbed her eyes and yawned. "You just cooked bacon on Thursday. I thought we agreed once a week."

"I'm going to your make-up game this afternoon," Marti said, hoping to distract her. It was softball season. She enjoyed watching Joanna play softball even if it seemed to take forever for something interesting to happen. Maybe that was why. The action was slow enough for her to keep up. And, unlike volleyball, she understood the scoring system.

"Church this morning and my game this afternoon," Joanna said. "Christmas in June?"

"Something like that." Marti thought about what they had found in Ms. Channon's closet yesterday afternoon. Maybe they would know more about it by tomorrow. They were out of leads now and that worried her. The Linski case was getting colder. She and Vik had agreed to take the day off in the hope that getting their mind off the case would help them come up with a few leads or ideas by Monday.

Marti was working on her second pancake when the boys came in.

"You don't have all the syrup out," Mike said.

Theo opened the cabinet. "I want butterscotch!"

"And chocolate," Mike added.

"What is this, pancakes or ice cream sundaes?" Joanna grouched. She had omitted the butter and poured honey on hers. Marti thought honey and most food and drink were mutually exclusive, but it was Joanna's sweetener of choice.

When Momma came downstairs she was still in her bathrobe and slippers.

"Are you okay?" Marti asked.

"Never better. And hungry, too. I don't think I'll ever reach the point where I can sleep in, or have breakfast in bed, but I could get used to coffee and the morning paper before I come downstairs."

Momma sat next to Joanna and Marti looked at them, so alike in profile with Momma's auburn braid pinned to her head like a crown and Joanna's auburn braid almost reaching her waist. They had the same full, generous features and hazel eyes.

Marti looked up, caught Ben smiling at them. Her hair was cut short, but otherwise all three of them looked alike.

Harry drove the backhoe between the oak trees until he reached the place where they were planted in circles. The leaves were turned the way they did when it was going to rain. It was hot, muggy. Harry felt the sweat trickling down his chest and soaking into his T-shirt. He shifted gears and maneuvered around the trees, scraping some, until he reached the center. Mr. Smith was waiting for him. Mr. Smith never came to the places where he worked, at least not while he was there. Harry thought of the collar he had found. Did the old man know? Would he be fired for keeping it? For a moment, he wanted to jump down and run. Instead he remained on the backhoe and looked away as the old man came closer.

"You know where I want you to dig."

"Yes, sir." Harry didn't look at him.

"If you find something you will tell me."

"Yes, sir."

"You will be . . . compensated . . . rewarded . . . if you do."

Harry swallowed hard. Compensated? The old man must know about the collar, but how? "I don't understand, sir."

"I want to give you something. You've worked for us for a number of years. What do you think would be fair?"

Harry gripped the steering wheel. He just wanted to stay here, have a job, a safe place. No, what he really wanted was to go home, go back where Zoe was, where he could visit her grave every day. It had been so long since he had been there.

"I would like to go home, sir."

But where would he live? How would he survive? Compensation. A reward. The old man was talking about money. He had just asked him how much money he wanted and he didn't even know what he had found.

"Sir." His throat felt dry. "Sir." His voice sounded raspy. "A . . . a . . . trailer, maybe. Just a small one, secondhand." But how would he live? He didn't have much of anything paid into

Social Security. "And some jobs give you a pension. I wouldn't need nothing much. Just enough to get by on if I couldn't find work." Maybe he was asking for too much. "Of course, if you couldn't, sir." Maybe working here for twelve years wasn't long enough. "I . . . I . . . I would . . ." He cleared his throat. "I'm getting old. I would like to be home with my Zoe."

"Why, of course," Mr. Smith said.

Harry looked at him. This was the first time he had seen Mr. Smith smile. From the looks of it, he didn't do that very often.

"You had better get to digging. Get the job done. Rain is forecast for later today. You just get this job done, and I'll see to it that you go home."

"Why . . . thank you, sir. Thank you."

He expected Mr. Smith to ask for what he had found, or even ask what it was, but he just turned and walked away. Maybe he was just guessing and didn't know for sure that he had found anything. Harry watched the old man's back until he couldn't see him anymore. Home. He was going to go back to Idaho, back to the forests this place reminded him of, back to the mountains he missed, back to Zoe. There was a trailer park not much more than a mile from the cemetery. Her grave was on the hill that overlooked the river. He had planted a spruce tree there because she loved Christmas when she was a little girl, and every December she picked out a Douglas spruce. He was humming as he lowered the backhoe.

Just as Isaiah spent Shabbat honoring God and his ancestors, he spent Sunday afternoon in the company of his children, alternating his visits among the three of them. Today had been a special day. His grandson, Omari, who always asked about his research, had asked if he could help with it. One day this week, Isaiah would begin teaching him. Even better, Omari was eighteen now and old enough to visit those places he could not travel to and collect more information.

Floyd came into the kitchen as Isaiah was measuring some Arabian coffee his daughter-in-law had given them. Floyd visited his children and grandchildren too. Every Sunday by late afternoon they were home, Isaiah feeling content, Floyd ornery and disgruntled.

"All that searching you're doing," Floyd said. "Be something if you found someone who had some money back then instead of being some poor, barefoot sharecropper." He began putting together a sandwich with a thick slice of smoked ham.

"Poor folk maybe, most of them," Isaiah agreed. "But none that I've found have ever caused a scandal."

Even though Floyd knew that in every generation Isaiah had uncovered, he had found military records for someone in the family who had served with honor and even distinction during wartime, even though he had not discovered any criminals or dishonorable men, Floyd still feared that there was a lynching out there somewhere in their past.

"Them living righteous but poor might be enough for you, but neither of us is gonna be here forever. I'd like to do a little living before I die. Be nice to take a real vacation, go someplace other than Forrest City, Arkansas, every two years for a family reunion." He cut a slice of cheddar cheese. "Be nice to go to Vegas, maybe, or get a nice little sports car. A red one. Convertible. Never have had a brand-new car, neither of us. Even your boy got himself a new car, Irwin."

"Isaiah."

"Right. I keep forgetting. Want some cheese? Can't have no pork now, can you? My Cindy fixes it just like Grandma used to."

"We don't need no car no more, Floyd," Isaiah said, ignoring the jab about pork. "It's getting hard for both of us to get in and out of one with these knees."

"We could be like white folks, get us a stretch limo and a chauffeur."

"How many white folks you know got that?"

Floyd had built a very carefully constructed house of sticks where the white man was concerned. Even though he played checkers and chess with Bill Davis almost every day, Floyd did not like most white men, but all that he had—job, pension, even his name—came from them, and all that he wanted, the white man already possessed. So Floyd pretended a respect that stopped short of deference, and tried to sidestep anything that might destroy that pretense of mutual respect and equality.

"No need carrying all that anger in your heart, Floyd. Life is what it is."

"You want to be like them Jews wandering in the desert all them years, like Job sitting on a pile of shit. That's fine for you, not me. You can spend the rest of your life trying to figure out where you come from. Me, I'd rather look where I'm going. And that ain't never been nowhere. Ain't never been nowhere at all."

Isaiah didn't have an answer for that. They were poor men, both of them, came from poor folk, would die poor, but not as poor as a lot of people who had much less.

"We ain't got nothing to complain about, Floyd."

"So you say. Your Martin will be moving into that new house he's building before the summer's over. I don't care what nobody says, it ain't right that a child outdoes his father, not even when that's what we want for them." He considered some mustard, then shook his head. "Nah, just spoil the taste of the ham."

"We got—"

"And don't bother saying we got food and a roof over our head. We didn't even buy this house, neither of us. House belonged to Grandma. She worked all her life for a white family to get what little she had. Brought their cast-offs home like she had gone to the store and picked them out herself. She gave it to you all bought and paid for."

"Only because you and Sylvie had a place and me and Juanita and the kids were already living here and taking care of her. Place is yours much as mine."

"Well, you just keep lookin' for them ancestors, bro. See if you can find us a rich one." He laughed, but there was no humor in it. "Fat chance of that. Got to give it to you, though. You've stuck with being a Jew and kept looking for some slave relative for years longer than I expected you would."

"I might be on to something." As reluctant as he was to say anything to Floyd, last night's speaker had asked him a lot of questions and given him some good suggestions.

"What else is new? You been on to something for years now."

"I might have found Samuel."

"We talking about a field slave, or a house nigger?" Floyd asked.

"Runaway if he's the right one."

Floyd gave him an unexpected grin. "Now that wouldn't be so bad, bro. Better to have one in the family who at least tried to get away." Floyd thought for a moment, then said, "No, that wouldn't be so bad at all. A fighter. So, how'd you happen upon old Samuel?"

"I think he might have been a Thatcher."

"You mean you think his owner's name might have been Thatcher. Samuel didn't have no last name. Didn't have nothin' that couldn't be taken away from him."

"Right."

"What was so hard about finding him? Great-Grandma Reba was a Thatcher. If you didn't spend so much time going over every little detail and finding every cousin twice removed, you would have found out about old Samuel ten, fifteen years ago. Whatcha gonna do now, spend the next three years making sure he's the right one?"

"I just might."

"Never did understand you bookish folk. Always going to night school, getting a diploma. Taking them college courses. History. Philosophy. Hah! Never done you much good, has it?" Floyd bit into his sandwich. "Ummm-umm. Sure you won't have some? Nothing beats a good piece of smoked pork." A few bites later he said, "You know, bro, I used to worry that you'd be on your deathbed like Grandma and still wondering who you were. Now I think it's what's keeping you alive. So don't pay no mind to me. You just take all the time you need. The kids will appreciate it, even if I don't. Your kids and mine."

Isaiah realized that Floyd meant that and was surprised. He wondered about Floyd's kids appreciating anything. Floyd's two boys had inherited their father's disdain for most things that were non-material and a craving for things that implied status. The difference was that both of Floyd's kids got enough education to have the things Floyd would never be able to afford. Now if they would just stop being so selfish and share some of it with their father, like his kids shared with him.

"So what about slave owner Thatcher?" Floyd asked.

"The one I'm looking at owned property near Jefferson City, Missouri. Four men who were trusted slaves, and given an identification tag to allow them safe passage within the city limits, were listed on a runaway notice. One was named Samuel."

He had spent almost four years getting here and still could not be certain that he had arrived at the right place.

"Don't tell me that nobody in the family has traveled further than Forrest City and Battle Creek since we was in chains."

"We got cousins in Chattanooga."

"Well, that's one hell of a long way from here now, ain't it?"

Isaiah hadn't found anything yet to indicate that this Samuel had been caught. That was one possibility that Floyd hadn't thought of yet. Isaiah decided not to mention it. He was going to have Omari help him find out if this was even the right Samuel before he looked into that.

Marti reached the ballpark just in time for Joanna's softball game. Rain was forecast for early evening. The sun that had been shining when they left church was hidden behind the clouds. Joanna's team was in transition, according to a quote by her coach in the *News-Times*. According to Joanna, that translated into "We suck." Two key members from last year had graduated from high school and were too old to play, a third had got a concussion in a car accident, and a fourth had gone to Oregon for the summer.

As Marti watched, Theo and Mike took a cooler filled with Gatorade to the dugout. They had volunteered to be bat boys and gofers. Ben waved at her. He was filming the game.

"Remember," Joanna had told him that morning, "get the shortstop and the girl playing first base. If they can see what they're doing wrong and work on it, they'll be straight."

Marti knew most of the parents. She avoided those who yelled the loudest and complained the most about the umpire's calls. That left a couple on the far end of the top bleacher. She had talked with them before. They seemed friendly enough, but based on the questions they asked, it was obvious that neither of them knew much about the game.

Marti returned the woman's wave as she climbed to the top of the bleachers and sat on the wooden bench.

"We're at bat, right?" the woman asked.

"Not yet," Marti explained. "We've got the field."

The woman looked confused. The man nodded and said, "That's why our team is practicing throwing the ball and catching it."

"The away team bats first, so that the home team gets to bat last," Marti reminded her.

"Thanks." The woman still looked confused, but the man gave Marti a thumbs-up.

One hour and three innings later, Joanna's team was taking the field again. So far, the shortstop had not stopped anyone, and every line drive down first base was a base hit. They were behind six to nothing. There was an automatic seven-run advantage rule and the game was called half an hour later, with the score nine to two.

"That wasn't bad," Joanna said as they pulled out of the parking lot.

"It looked pretty bad to me," Theo said.

"I know, but we did some things right this time. They were just a better team."

"You planning on winning any this year?" Theo asked.

This was their sixth loss in six games.

The clouds that had been hovering in the distance began moving in. Watching them, Marti thought of the holes that had been dug on the Smiths' property, the hole where Larissa Linski had died. It was a good thing they had gleaned what little information there was. The rain would obliterate everything. Tomorrow they could give the order to fill the holes. Too bad the rain wouldn't stop them from wondering if there was anything they had missed.

Drops of rain began falling as Harry Buckner drove from the shelter of the trees. Dark clouds had gathered to the north and were moving in. He liked thunderstorms, but he was in a hurry to get back to the barn before this one broke. He had lived in Kansas and Tennessee, places where storms like this spawned tornadoes, but that wasn't as likely to happen here. He would watch the lightning strikes from the window in the loft for a while, then warm up something for supper and listen to the rain bombarding the roof. Later, when the storm had passed, and the night was clear, and the moon came out, and the air smelled clean, he'd think about how Zoe used to wish on a star and believe that her wish would come true.

Thunder rumbled and big drops of rain began hitting his face as he reached the barn. He left the backhoe outside and ran for the door. It was dark inside but he didn't need a light. He made his way to the stairs that led to the loft just as he had for the past twelve years. Tick, the old barn cat who had lived here longer than he had, greeted him with a yowl and ran along beside him, meowing. The mice stayed outside during the summer and were harder to catch. Harry took half a tuna-fish sandwich out of his lunch bag. That would hold Tick for now. Then he checked the shelf where he had put the lead collar. Gone. Nothing. That was why the old man hadn't asked him what he had found. He already knew. For a moment Harry wondered why the old man had even bothered asking him about it. To pay him off. To find out his price. Old metal. Why was it even worth anything? No matter. It was worth something to them. Worth enough to get him back home, where he could be with his Zoe. He thought of the girl again. Larissa. He wondered what she had found, then reminded himself that her accident couldn't have been his fault.

Harry went to the window, opened it, watched as lightning flashed across the dark sky and jumped down to the ground like the bony fingers of a giant hand. He took a step back as the rain blew in, then heard something behind him. Before he could turn, he was pushed forward. As he fell, he thought, "That bastard." He didn't think of Zoe at all.

It began raining when Marti and Vik were about eighty miles from Springfield. By the time they reached the turnoff to the city, light rain had become a downpour, wind gusts were battering the car and the sky was so dark that Marti wondered if it might spawn a tornado. Several traffic lights were out and by the time they reached the capital building they were fifteen minutes late for their nine-o'clock appointment with Anne Devney.

As they walked from the parking lot the wind turned their umbrellas inside out.

They were soaked by the time they made it to Devney's office. A secretary greeted them.

"She's been called to a meeting. It shouldn't take long."

When Marti's cell phone rang at ten forty-five, Devney still hadn't shown up. It was Lupe Torres, their backup. Another accident had been reported at the Smith place.

When she hung up, Vik asked, "Who is it this time?"

"Harry Buckner, the guy on the backhoe who dug the holes." For some reason she thought, Zoe's father.

"Dead?"

"How'd you guess?"

"Another accident, right?"

"You've got it. But coincidence can only take them so far."

"Then let's hope this is the end of the road."

Lupe called back as soon as she reached the scene. "Looks like he fell out of the window in the upper level of the barn."

"Take pictures," Marti told her. "Lots of them. Interior, exterior, close-ups, distance. Everything you can think of. And go over everything the evidence techs do. Make sure they don't miss anything. You know how Vik and I want the scene processed."

Anne Devney came in while she was talking. "Accident," she said when she hung up.

They went to the small conference room. The file folders were in four stacks now. "There might be a few interruptions," Marti advised her.

"You really should turn that cell phone off," Devney said.

"Sorry. Can't do that."

Lupe didn't call again. She had worked with them on a number of cases. She knew what she was doing.

Devney found it necessary to go over points in the case that they had covered on Friday. By the time they got to the pre-trial files, it was noon. By the time they left, it was after one o'clock. The rain had stopped, but the sky was still dark. Marti could see lightning strikes as she drove. They didn't stop to eat. She made the three-and-a-half-hour trip back to Lincoln Prairie in just over two hours.

Lupe Torres was waiting for them. "I've got the photos." She had had them enlarged.

"That was fast," Vik said.

Lupe always seemed pleased when Vik complimented her.

Marti picked up a photograph that showed the garden in relationship to the barn. Harry Buckner had landed in a vegetable garden, behind the barn. His body was facedown in the mud. The tilled earth, which must have been kept moist with repeated watering, had absorbed the rain, and the runoff had collected in the furrows between the rows of plants. Some bushes were heavy with still-green tomatoes, others with long, pointed chili peppers. There was a row of sunflowers that were about four feet high. The area had full sunlight.

"Where is this barn?" Marti asked. This was the first time she had seen it.

"Far northwest corner of the property," Vik answered. She didn't ask him how he knew that. His sense of direction was unerring. She thought it must have something to do with growing up in a small town with streets that weren't all laid out in straight east-west, north-south patterns.

Lupe had used a wide-angle lens for the next shot. Although the area immediately surrounding the barn had been cleared, it was isolated by trees and dense bushes. Behind the barn, where the vegetable garden was and the body had been found, there was also a narrow road where machinery had made ruts. Closer to the trees, grass grew about a foot high. Thistle and other weeds grew higher. Marti was surprised by how much of the Smiths' property was undisturbed. That must be why everyone involved with land restoration and conservation wanted some of it.

"Old barn. Timber-framed," Vik said. "Gambrel roof."

"What's that?" Marti asked. She didn't think it was important. She just wanted to see if Vik knew, or if he was just guessing.

"A gambrel roof?" he asked.

"Yes."

"City girl," he scoffed. "See how it has two slopes on each side? An old barn," he repeated. "I wonder if anyone is trying to save it, now that they're getting rid of the land."

"It's not like it's the family castle," Marti said. Like Vik, she thought it was a more interesting building, but who else would? "It's so far away from anything but that back road; I bet nobody even knows it's there."

Vik pointed. "Buckner must have come out of that door, fell forward."

"Door," Marti said. "It looks like a window to me."

"It's a barn," Vik said. "They would store stuff in the loft, haul it up there with a rope, lower it down, or just toss it into a wagon or a truck. Doors," he repeated.

"How long ago were you a farmer?" Marti asked.

Instead of answering, Vik said, "Who found him?"

"One of the guards," Lupe told him. "Chet Simms. He said Buckner was supposed to be mowing the south lawn this morning. When he didn't show, the guard was sent out to the barn to wake him."

Marti made a note of the name. "Did any of the Smiths show up?"

"Not while I was there."

Why didn't that surprise her? Marti looked at the shots of Buckner. She could not see his face at all. His arms were spread wide, as if he had attempted to fly. The door consisted of two long wooden panels that would meet at the center when closed. Why would Buckner have opened it during a storm? Why would he have stood close enough to the opening to fall? How could he have lost his balance?

"Here's the backhoe," Vik said, picking up another photo. "Out front. He must have been digging again."

"I made sure the evidence techs checked the grooves in the tires," Lupe said. "Dirt, but no mud. They didn't think anyone had moved it during or after the storm. They also searched as far back as the fence and for three hundred feet along both sides of the fence for tire tracks or footprints. They didn't find anything."

Marti stopped at Wendy's for burgers and fries on their way to the Smith place. She thought about eating bacon twice in one week and picked up a salad, too. When they reached the Smith place, Lupe directed her to the barn and put a call in to have the guard who found the body meet them there. While Vik admired the roof, Marti went inside. It was cool and dark. A riding mower and a plow were parked to one side. One stall was filled with rakes, other gardening implements, and shovels. The other stalls were empty, with cribs for hay. Leather harnesses hung on the walls. They were old and worn and stiff from lack of use. Narrow stairs went up to the loft. There was no railing. Marti tested one step, then another. They seemed sturdy.

"Get in here, Jessenovik!" she called as she reached the top. Before he could, a black cat jumped down from a shelf and picked its way down the stairs.

The loft was a place where a man with few possessions lived alone. The cot was unmade; a cabinet held cans of chili, soup, and ravioli. A bowl and a spoon were in the sink, a clean pan was on a hot plate. The coffee maker held half a pot of cold coffee.

"No Sunday go-to-meeting clothes," Marti said. Just work clothes, thick-soled shoes and three pairs of boots. When she opened the top bureau drawer she found a photo album filled with pictures. A little girl with dark hair and dark eyes who must have been Zoe, with a much younger Harry and a smiling woman who Marti assumed was Buckner's wife. As she turned the pages, the little girl went to school and the woman went away. Then Harry went away, probably because he was holding the camera. The little girl visited Santa Claus and the Easter Bunny and a couple of cartoon characters. She grew up and went to school dances, toasted marshmallows over campfires, and posed on skis against a backdrop of snow. After a dozen more pages of a smiling young woman, Zoe went away. The final picture was of a grave surrounded by floral arrangements. One had a pink ribbon that said "Daddy's Girl" in gold letters.

"No mail, no nothing," Marti said. There weren't even any bills.

Vik was checking the storage shelves that had been placed at intervals along one wall.

"Something was here," he said.

It wasn't the shelf the cat had jumped from. The dust had been disturbed. There were a partial palm print and a few finger prints.

"Looks like somebody put something here," Lupe said. "I'll call and make sure the techs caught it."

Marti checked the shelf where the cat had been. There was

almost no dust at all. Someone had put an old flannel shirt there and the cat was using it for a bed.

When they went back outside, a uniformed security guard was waiting for them at the front of the barn. The dirt was so hard-packed here that last night's rain had done little more than dampen it.

"Chet Simms?" Vik said.

The man nodded.

"You found him."

"Yes, sir." The man took a drag on his cigarette and shifted from one foot to the other.

"Why were you looking for him?"

"I wasn't."

Vik waited.

"I . . . umm . . . it's Monday. He mows the west lawn on Monday. He didn't show."

"Has that ever happened before?"

"I . . . um . . . I don't know. Maybe. Maybe not. Happened today."

"You were in the guardhouse at the entrance to the property on the east side?" Vik asked.

The guard looked at him, then nodded.

"Then how did you know he wasn't on the west side?"

"I . . . um . . . um . . . I . . . no lawn mower."

"Did you try to make voice contact with him?"

"Uh . . . no . . . there's no . . . he doesn't. He just takes care of the grounds. There's no reason to talk to him."

"Did he have a schedule?" Vik was beginning to sound frustrated.

"I guess, kind of."

"Why were you expecting to hear the lawn mower?"

The guard didn't answer.

"Thanks," Vik said, dismissing him.

The guard inhaled twice, then threw the cigarette butt on the ground.

100

As he walked away, Vik called, "Be careful. Don't have any accidents."

Marti waited until the man got into his Jeep and drove off, then put on a latex glove, opened a small plastic bag and retrieved the cigarette butt.

They went to the guardhouse at the rear of the property, the one closest to the barn. Inside, it was like a large living room except for a bank of screens fed by cameras. Marti checked them. Ten screens. She couldn't pinpoint the locations but could see that all of the cameras were placed along the perimeter. There were no interior locations, no camera that would record someone approaching or entering the barn.

"We need to ask you some questions," Vik told the guard.

"Sure," the man said. "Nobody's told us not to talk to you."

"How many shifts do you have?"

"Three," the man said. "Six guards on each. One of us is always here and at the main guardhouse. The others patrol."

"On car or by foot?"

"SUV."

"Do they each have a specific area?" Vik asked.

The guard pointed to one of the maps that were framed and hung on the walls. "This is the Smith property." Instead of a square or rectangular shape, the property lines were irregular. Some joined at angles. Others outlined small blocks joined at one corner to the whole. At the top of the map, the land curved along the river.

"Now." The guard hung an overlay on the frame. Dark lines created six sections. "Each guard works one of these areas. They always patrol the same place. Otherwise it gets confusing."

"How often do they patrol?"

"Each section is close to sixty acres. They just drive around and come to one of the guardhouses for breaks."

"We've never seen them," Vik said.

"That's because you're here during the day, when Buckner,

or whoever replaces him now, is working. The guys working those areas try to stay out of the way."

"What about the fence? Has it ever been breached?"

"A few times. Local kids. Parts of it are electrified now. Low voltage. I can show you on another overlay."

The electrified sections looked to be random.

"Can you tell them from the other sections?"

"No. That's the idea."

Vik had him point out where the barn was in relation to the fence. The nearest fence was wired.

"Do you keep reports?" Vik asked.

"Not unless there's something to report."

"And last night?"

"No. Poured rain, lightning, thunder, the whole nine yards. That's about it."

It was time for another visit to the Smith family. Lupe stayed outside. This time the Smiths were assembled in what the maid referred to as the parlor. It was after eleven in the morning, an odd time for everyone to be at home. Marti wondered if any of them worked.

The room was about half the size of the library and the furniture was all curves and curlicues and looked like a traveling exhibit Marti had seen at a museum when she was in college. French, she thought, or maybe Italian. Marti didn't wait to be invited to sit down. The chairs were comfortable this time. Vik decided to remain standing. He was bad cop today.

"Do you want to see our identification again?" Marti asked.

Josiah Smith gave her a haughty look, but said nothing.

"How long was Mr. Buckner in your employ?

Paul Smith answered. "Twelve years."

"And you hired him?"

"Actually, the cook did. We have very little to do with the hired help. Our security people checked him out."

Marti was surprised that Paul spoke and not Josiah, who was

102

looking away from her now and toward a window. He hadn't wanted to speak to her the last time she was here and had apparently decided to follow through on that.

"What should Buckner have been doing this morning?"

Paul hesitated. "I have no idea."

"Did anyone know what his schedule was?"

"The security people, maybe. I guess they keep some kind of records, make some kind of patrols, I don't know what exactly. Something sufficient so that nobody is on the property at any time who shouldn't be."

A muscle in Josiah's jaw twitched, and Marti got the impression that he would like to speak but had opted not to, at least not yet. She preferred talking with Paul anyway. He had more to say.

"What was Mr. Buckner's normal routine on Sunday?"

"I have no idea, but he would not have been working."

Marti made a mental note of that.

"When is the last time you saw him?"

Paul thought for a moment. "Actually, I have no idea. To tell you the truth, I rarely saw him at all."

She made another mental note when he said to "tell you the truth."

"Did he work on Saturday?"

"Yes. No. Well, I'm not sure."

Marti waited.

"We played tennis on Friday. Someone might have asked him to clean up, retrieve the balls, pick up the trash, glasses, whatever."

"Someone," Marti said.

"Yes."

"Who?"

"The guard, maybe."

"Does that mean you did talk with the guards?"

"Oh, yes. No, not personally. No. I would assume that someone said something to one of the guards, or that the guards noticed something needed to be done and told him to do it. If not, then to tell you the truth, Harry didn't do any work Saturday or Sunday that I know of."

Again, Marti noted what Paul said.

"How many guards do you have?"

"We contract with an agency. I think there are maybe four to six here at any given time."

"Do they patrol the property?"

Paul hesitated, "Well, I . . . I suppose . . . they do whatever guards do. You'd have to ask—"

"Do you have any more questions?" Josiah spoke abruptly.

Sharp old man, Marti decided. He knew Paul was talking too much. She debated asking if Buckner had done any more digging, but didn't want the old man to know that was even on her mind—not yet, anyway.

"There was only—" Paul began.

"No!" Josiah interrupted.

Marti wondered what Paul had been about to say.

"Does anyone in that family work?" Marti asked Vik as they walked to their car.

"I don't know which one does what, but one son has some cushy obscure government job, the other is a bank president. One of the wives is in real estate. Big real estate—office buildings, industrial property. The other wife does something at the Mercantile Mart or the Stock Exchange."

"With a place like this to maintain, that doesn't sound like much more than pocket change," Marti said.

"The old man is loaded. I'm surprised he's selling. They're only getting about fifteen million. I'll bet they're worth ten times that much."

Marti thought of the expression "house-poor" and remembered driving up to a huge Tudor and going into a house that was empty. The owners slept on a mattress on the floor. Sometimes appearances were everything. "Where do you get your information?" she asked.

"Read the newspapers. Ask a few questions. If they were in financial difficulty, these accidents would make a lot more sense."

It took the state's attorney three hours to get a judge to sign a warrant authorizing them to search the grounds of the Smith estate for additional excavations. At 7 P.M., they were back with a dozen sheriffs and six uniformed officers. That was not nearly enough people to do an adequate search, but Vik had a map of the property based on the zones the guard had shown them. Each section would be gone over twice, each time by a different team. It was already close to sunset, but Marti didn't think they would find anything without the element of surprise. She didn't want to give the Smiths another day to cover their tracks.

"You really think we'll find something?" Vik asked.

"No," Marti admitted. "But Buckner did something with that backhoe."

"What good will it do us to find another excavation site if we don't find anything in it?"

He was asking the same questions the state's attorney had asked. She repeated her answers: "Well, that they have a reason to dig. That they are either looking for something or trying to make it look as if they found something. That two people could be dead because they found something they weren't supposed to. That they are now knowingly in violation of the law according to JULIE."

"And?"

"If we find another site, at least we know something's going on here. We raise a little suspicion."

"Marti, we work homicide, not grand theft."

"Vik, two people are dead. What do we do? Go home? If Linski or Buckner found something they were not supposed to and there is another dig site, maybe finding it will help turn up a few clues."

"Okay," Vik agreed. "You could be right this time. I just hope that doing this is a better idea than doing nothing for a while and letting them come to us."

"What do you think the odds are on that happening? These people are rich, isolated, and respected."

It was after midnight when the first new dig site was found in a grove of oak trees, and two in the morning when a second site was discovered in the apple orchard. Marti made sure a guard was posted at each site and ordered one more complete search. It was after four when she and Vik walked to the Smith mansion. The place was not lit up but the lights in a room at the back of the house were on. Paul admitted them. Inside, the hallway and the first room they walked through were dark. Paul did not turn on any lights but led them to the kitchen. His wife, Jessica, was spooning instant coffee into a cup.

"And I don't care who else wants some," she said. "The water is hot. Make your own." She was wearing a loose-fitting top over spandex capris. Her thick chestnut hair hung to her shoulders. The tallest of the Smiths, she looked as if she worked out every day.

Franklin was sitting on a stool at a counter, playing solitaire. He didn't look up when Marti and Vik came in. His wife wasn't in the room. Marti looked around, wondering where Josiah was.

"We found two more dig sites," Marti explained. "We thought maybe you could tell us when Mr. Buckner dug them up."

Nobody spoke for at least a minute. Then Paul cleared his throat. "I . . . I really don't know about this . . . I really can't tell you . . . the truth is . . ."

"We will say nothing." Josiah spoke, from behind.

Marti turned toward him. Josiah looked exhausted. And old. There were dark circles under his eyes, as if he had not slept in days.

"You may speak with our attorney," he said.

"Certainly, Mr. Smith." She smiled.

"No, we can . . . that's . . . not necessary," Paul said.

"It most certainly is," Josiah insisted. He looked at Paul and raised his eyebrows. Paul did not protest further.

Franklin's wife came in just as Marti and Vik were leaving. Eileen was shorter than she seemed to be when sitting down, but like her sister-in-law, looked as if she spent some time at the gym. Or here in the gym, Marti thought. As big as this place was, why not?

"We'll have to get Caleb back out here in the morning," Marti told Vik as they left. "See if he can tell us anything."

"Anyone but McIntosh."

Marti ignored that. They might need Gordon again. He had been helpful so far. "We'll have to make sure the evidence techs take more soil samples," she added. "Check them against the ones we have." She might not gain more information from these two new dig sites but one thing she was sure of—there was something about this land that was damned important to the Smith family. If two people had died because of it, the family wanted whatever it was to remain a secret.

11

TUESDAY, JULY 2

When Marti went down to the kitchen in the morning, there was a stack of library books on the table. She had almost forgotten that she had asked Theo and Mike to pick some up for her. It was early. The house was quiet. Ben was on duty. Everyone else was still asleep. She checked the titles—archaeology, Potawatomi, slavery, even a book on the Underground Railroad in Illinois. She was getting used to using the Internet, but there was nothing quite like a book. She weighed one in her hand. A book. Something solid. Printed words that wouldn't disappear if she clicked on a mouse. This wasn't a new book, but one that had been opened and read and read again. She held it to her nose and sniffed. The aroma of ink on the printed page took her back years to when she was a child in Chicago going to the public library with Momma. She would roam the stacks and come home with a bag filled with promises.

Deciding which book to take with her to work was a difficult choice. Finding time to read it would be even harder, but the anticipation of the surprises she knew she would find would beckon to her until she did.

She had only gotten a few hours' sleep. The Buckner autopsy was scheduled for 8 A.M. They were supposed to be in Springfield at 9 A.M. There was no way they could be there on time. And she felt too tired to try. Anne Devney was making such slow progress with her review of the case that they would be working on it until Christmas. One day wouldn't make much difference. She left a message on Devney's voice mail.

After the autopsy, Marti and Vik went to the Sunrise restaurant for breakfast. While Vik slathered butter and syrup on a stack of French toast, Marti cut into a Western omelet with her fork and pushed the pieces around on her plate.

"What's with you?" Vik asked. "At least this time we know up-front that it wasn't an accident. There were bruises the size of a palm on Buckner's back."

"He was a big man. Two hundred and sixty-seven pounds. It's not that easy to push someone that big out of that door."

"Depends," Vik said, using the French toast to sop up the raspberry syrup.

"Why don't you just use a spoon?" she suggested.

"Enough momentum, a running start," Vik went on, ignoring her comment. "And almost anyone could have tipped him out the window."

"And Larissa Linski? The fieldstones?" she asked.

"Leverage. At least that's what Stephen says."

"So, you think anyone could have killed Linski or Buckner and size is not an issue."

"No, I didn't say that."

"Well, say something, Jessenovik."

"We don't have enough information or evidence to reach any conclusions."

"We've got two people dead in a week!"

Vik poured more syrup. "You're saying whoever killed them would have to be someone who was strong. And I say maybe."

"That is a thought," Marti agreed. She speared a chunk of omelet, then let it drop to her plate. "The Smith family," she said.

"Frustrating," Vik agreed. "Look at that homicide case back east a couple years ago. The man's family was half as rich as Midas. He evaded the law for years."

"Until someone told on him," Marti said. "It took a hell of a long time for guilt by association to kick in. I hope that's not what happens this time."

Vik scowled. "This isn't just like any other case, is it? They do have privileges. We can't bring any of them in for questioning without some solid evidence." He poured more syrup on the French toast.

"You might as well just drink that," Marti said.

Vik licked some off his finger. "We're not ready to question any of them yet, but every time I talk with them, I hate the way they close ranks."

"And just sit there looking down their noses at us and saying nothing," Marti added. "They haven't figured out yet that we are just as tenacious as they are. We'll build a case this time, same as always."

"Ummm." Vik chewed and swallowed, then said, "We have to talk with that guard again after we meet with Caleb. And we need to check out Buckner's job application, get his social security number. So far they haven't been able to identify any next of kin."

Marti signaled to the waitress for more coffee.

"We're not dealing with professionals, Vik. We're going to treat them with deference and respect, let them think they're home free. They'll make a mistake."

"They've already made a few small ones," Vik agreed. "They didn't expect us to figure out that there was something taken from where Linski was digging. And they tried to cover their ass with that deer-hoof rattle. I'm sure they didn't give any thought to the possibility of bruises on Buckner's body, or bruises that we could identify as not being caused by the fall. Of course they have had a lot of experience with accidents."

"They probably think if that's what they make it look like, that's what everyone will assume."

Isaiah sat back and looked across the kitchen table at his grandson, Omari. He couldn't keep himself from grinning. "You're really interested in this," Isaiah said. "I thought maybe your father put you up to it because he's worried that I'm doing too much."

110

"Actually, Grandpa, he did. But man, this is awesome. I can't believe what you've been doing. And you started before I was born!"

Omari had just completed a year at a local junior college. Isaiah liked to think that Omari looked like him, and he did somewhat. They both took after Grandma's side of the family, with darker skin and kinky hair. But Omari was taller and had his mother's deep-set brown eyes and her smile. Omari was always good-natured and smiled a lot.

Omari had spent most of the week reading Isaiah's journal and going through the files he kept on each family member he had identified, along with copies of any documents he had found.

"There is still a lot of work to do here," Isaiah cautioned. "And you see how organized you have to be. I've made it back to Edward Thatcher. He was born in 1874. His father was Samuel Thatcher. But unless Samuel was a freeman—and I've not been able to find anything indicating that—he was a slave, and Thatcher would have been his owner's name. I'm not sure I've got the right Thatcher."

Omari leaned forward. "So, what do we do now?"

We. Isaiah liked the way that sounded. He wasn't going to have to work alone anymore.

"You're going to have to do a lot more reading. You've got to know our real history, all that they didn't teach you in school, before you can understand what we're trying to find out and how hard it is, and why it's so hard. Then you'll do a little traveling, take a few trips. There are places that have records that I can't get hold of because I have to go to them and I can't do that anymore." His health being what it was, his trip to the family reunion next year would probably be too much. Besides, he didn't like being that far away from a hospital he knew and a doctor he trusted.

"Travel? For real? I've only been to Washington, D.C., on our eighth-grade graduation trip, that and the black college tour I went on in the South. Family reunions don't count."

"Worry about catching up on your reading first. Instead of trying to find Samuel, we've got to stay with Edward and try to find out if he has any brothers, sisters, cousins, whatever. I hit a stone wall when I tried, and it's kept me from getting to Samuel, so we have to try again. Now, you always start with the death certificate and work back from that. Edward died in St. Louis, Missouri, in 1921."

"Is that where we're going to start looking? How do we find out?"

"That's what I'm going to explain next. Now you've got to remember, this takes time. Don't try to rush it. Black folks don't have records going way back the way white folks do. Sometimes, when someone was born it was months, even years, before it was recorded. Sometimes the only record you have is a census count and no birth records at all. Sometimes, the birth record will say 'baby boy' or 'baby girl' and not even give their Christian name."

"And you haven't found Edward's birth certificate yet?"

"No, just his marriage license, but it gives his father's name as Samuel Thatcher and his mother as Cynthia, no maiden name, which makes me think she was a slave and didn't use her owner's name."

Isaiah was still concerned that Omari would not understand how difficult the research would be. "I tried jumping from that marriage license back a generation to Samuel, but I couldn't do it."

"And you found this Samuel slave of Thatcher because you were looking at Missouri, Tennessee and Arkansas. Was that the only Thatcher you found in those three states?"

Isaiah was pleased. The boy was smart and catching on fast. "There were a few others, the name's not that common, but this was the only one who listed a runaway slave named Samuel."

"So," Omari said, "you're thinking that if this Samuel is the right one, and he was a runaway, the odds were good he'd get to the Missouri River to throw off the dogs, and follow that to Alton, Illinois and continue along the Illinois River to the Des

Plaines River. Illinois was the nearest free state."

"Good thinking, but don't get ahead of yourself. We want to find the right Samuel, not any Samuel. So we have to stay here for a while, find out as much as we can about Edward and everyone we can identify who was connected with him. That might lead us right to Samuel without any guesswork." Kids today seemed to want everything right now. "You sure you can handle this? It takes patience."

"You've been doing it for almost twenty years."

"Suppose it takes you that long to find Samuel?"

Omari thought for a moment, then said, "I think I have to find him, Grandpa. I think I have to." He thought again, and then said, "Knowing this much, I have to know the rest. It'll drive me nuts if I don't at least try. And not being sure it was the right Samuel would be worse than not being able to find him at all. I see why you've taken so long." He tapped the folders with his finger. "We know these people really are family."

"Good," Isaiah said. "That's good. Now you're thinking. We've got a general area to look at instead of the whole country. But don't get ahead of yourself. Death certificate says he was forty-seven years old. Died young. Heart attack. That's how I know he was born in 1874, but I can't find no record of that. I got on the computer and went from Saint Louis to Little Rock looking for records, then from Saint Louis to Chicago. That's how I found out he was married in Cook County.

"Now the marriage license doesn't tell you much. But in order to get a license, you have to fill out an application. That's where the information is. I've called the Cook County Recorders office four times asking for a copy of the application. Best answer I got was that if it still exists it is archived somewhere. I tried to work around that by going back another generation to Samuel, but it won't work. So, I need you to go to Chicago. There's an African-American Genealogical Club there that meets at Woodson Regional Library. I called and there's a brother who will put you up and help you make your way through the recorder's office."

"Awesome, Grandpa. This is awesome." Omari got up, came over and hugged him. "You are awesome."

Isaiah hugged him back. It felt so good to be sharing this with someone, so good not to be searching alone. "I've got to get started cooking for today and tomorrow. And I need you to go to the cleaner's for me sometime this afternoon so I'll have something to wear to temple this evening."

"Can I come?"

"Are you sure you want to, boy? I'm real glad you're helping with this, but religion is a personal thing and you been raised Baptist."

"So were you. Is all this stuff what got you going to a temple?"

Isaiah thought about that. "Not really; I was reading about black folks living in villages in the Holy Land, black people who have always lived there and have known no other land, no other country. Then I read the parts of the Bible that tell about Ethiopia and Sudan and Cyrene, African places. Finally, I went to Shabbat, the Sabbath service. Most of the prayers and songs were in Hebrew, which I couldn't understand then. But my soul heard the words, my heart felt what was sung. So, I stayed. Are you ready for some lunch? Getting toward noon and I haven't even had breakfast yet."

Isaiah layered bell peppers, sliced tomatoes, and onions in a casserole dish. He scrambled eggs and poured them over the vegetables, then put cheddar cheese on top. He made toast and poured boiling water over instant coffee. While he was cooking, Omari turned to the news channel, then added milk and sugar to the coffee. The books Isaiah had given him on African-American history were stacked on the table. For a moment Isaiah felt sad. Those books were filled with much more truth and pain than the history lessons and civil rights stories that Omari had been taught in school.

When Marti and Vik reached their office, Slim and Cowboy, the two vice cops they shared space with, were on a search-and-destroy mission. It was earwig season. Marti suspected that Slim was afraid of bugs. Since he was carrying a Glock nine-millimeter, she didn't do anything to find out.

"Think we got them all, partner; for now, anyway," Cowboy drawled. He pushed back his five-gallon hat, releasing a shock of blond hair bleached almost white by the sun.

Marti watched as he ambled over to the coffeemaker. "You should have done that first," she complained.

Slim—tall, lean and caramel-tan, sauntered over just as Marti opened her briefcase. She took out a sheaf of computer print-outs.

"Well, well," Slim said, giving her a dimpled cupid's-bow smile. The odor of Obsession for Men didn't seem as strong as usual. "Looks like Mrs. Officer Mac has entered the computer age. What you got there?" He picked up the top printout. " 'History of Lake County.' What's got you off on this, that accident at the Smith place? Someone in their family has been here since before God created the Indians. You find their name anywhere?"

"They're here." She had found lists of names of the first settlers in Lake County. Idbash Smith and his sister, Rachel, were among them.

"I think their property is the only land left around here that hasn't been turned into condo land, rich folk's palaces, or shopping malls," Slim observed.

Cowboy ambled over too. "Damned shame that they're finally selling. They might have the only virgin forest left in this part of the state. Were you looking for anything in particular?"

"What they could have done that was illegal."

"The hell you are," Cowboy said. "A hundred and seventy-five or eighty years ago? Or now?"

"Both, maybe."

"The Smith family?" Slim said. "Rich folk? Is nothing sacred anymore?"

Vik picked up his mug. "Damn. Still empty." He turned it upside down. "What's taking so long? Do you have to grind the coffee beans?"

Cowboy dismissed that with a shrug. "What the little lady's got here looks a lot more interesting than making coffee."

"Then I'll make it myself," Vik threatened, without making any attempt to get up.

"It's coming. It's coming. Needs to brew for a few more minutes. Now"—Cowboy turned to her—"what have you got? They have any lawmen here back then?"

"I don't think they had much of anything here before the Indians were relocated. The Potawatomi had the use of the land until 1836. The earliest land survey we were able to find for the Smith property was 1840. I think they might have waited until the Indians were gone before they started doing land surveys."

"Probably so nobody would know how much land they got that they shouldn't have," Slim said.

"You cynic," Cowboy responded. "The early settlers were heroes, not thieves."

"Whatever," Marti said. "The survey our cave-in expert found doesn't show any root cellar."

"You're still stuck on that?" Slim said. "Nobody could see it. It was belowground. What are you thinking, Big Mac, that there was something down there that shouldn't have been?"

"Something relatively small," Vik said.

"How do you know that?"

"We don't," Vik admitted. "But we do think that something was probably found there and removed."

"Hummmm," Cowboy said. "Friend of mine's father found a musket ball embedded in a tree he cut down a few years ago."

"That's small," Slim said. "Could there have been a gunrunner in the Smith family?"

"Crooked politicians, I could believe," Cowboy drawled. "Even fraudulent land-grabbers, but gunrunners?"

"No way," Slim said. "Back then everyone had a gun. What are the odds someone would get killed now over something like that?"

116

Cowboy adjusted his five-gallon hat. "Murder." He rubbed his hands together. "That's where we're going with this."

That was where they were going, Marti thought. They just didn't have a case yet. There was something important about that root cellar, though, or Larissa would not have died there.

"Think there might be a hooker in this somewhere?" Slim asked. "Maybe the Smiths had the first house of ill repute in Lake County but used someone else's name on the deed."

Marti wondered about using someone else's name. She assumed that since the Smiths were selling the property, it had to be in their name, but according to what she had found out on the Internet, Idbash could have worked out land deals with people who were not Potawatomi. She didn't understand the legality of any of that. She had made a note to find out if she could look up land deeds going that far back. If there were none, she could forget about it. Right now it wasn't important enough to prioritize.

"Interesting family," she said after Cowboy and Slim left. "There's not much about Idbash except rumor, but his sister Rachel was very well-known. She kept her own name. She was a suffragist, an abolitionist, gave speeches. I even found some newspaper articles she wrote. Quite a lady."

"I'm sure the Wagners have been capitalizing on that ever since."

"The senator seems to have fallen a long way from the tree."

"I heard he's pretty good."

"As a lady's man," Marti agreed. "He has quite a reputation. And as a legislator if you lean to the far right. Ultraconservative—anti abortion, pro death penalty, nothing like his great-grandmother Rachel at all."

"Sounds like you were on the Internet half the night, MacAlister."

"No way," Marti said. She didn't want to admit how much time she had spent researching the Smith family. Finding so many listings that included them had amazed her.

*   *   *

While they waited for Caleb in the shade of one of the oak trees, Marti downed her fourth cup of coffee and ate another doughnut. She needed the caffeine and sugar jump-start. She and Vik were both so tired that she had requested a driver.

Caleb was fifteen minutes late. His formerly royal-blue hair was now a brilliant crimson.

"I'm not an archaeologist," Caleb told them as he stood at the edge of one of the holes. "I don't see how I can help you with this."

"It'll be sometime tomorrow before we can get anyone else," Vik said. "We need to get on this now so we can keep a guard out here. Just tell us anything you can."

"I'm not sure I should disturb anything."

"Was it dug up before or after it rained?"

"Before."

Marti turned to Vik. "More soil samples."

"What else can you tell us by looking at it?" Vik asked.

"The soil is evenly distributed for about two feet."

"Yeah," Vik said. "Good soil."

"Loam. Good for growing things. And no stones or rocks. This dirt was put here on purpose. It wasn't deposited by a retreating glacier. See the dirt beneath it? See the difference? That's from the glacier."

"So there might have been a farm here," Vik suggested.

"I don't see any evidence of that."

Vik didn't speak for a few seconds, then he said, "That's it? Nothing else?"

"Nothing that I can think of. I am going to take some pictures."

Marti and Vik retreated to the shade of a tree.

"I need about fifteen hours of sleep," Marti said.

"I didn't even bother going to bed."

"Geez, Vik, even a couple hours is better than nothing."

When Caleb came over he sat with his back against the tree and stretched out his legs. "Well, there are backhoe tracks, and

118

footprints in the holes and places were the dirt is disturbed. There are also four places where the grass is tamped down, like something heavy was there for a while. This happened very recently. Nothing is there now."

"It couldn't have been the backhoe?"

"No way."

When Caleb advised them that the apple orchard site had not been disturbed, they decided to leave it alone and call in an archaeologist. After he left, Marti said, "How many ways out of here are there? Whatever those four things were, they could have gotten rid of them."

"There are only two ways out, the main gate and a place out back for deliveries. Everything else is fenced in. High fences, twelve feet."

"Electrified in places," Marti added.

"It might not be too hard to get two more uniforms out here."

"We can ask."

Lieutenant Dirkowitz met with them as soon as they returned to the precinct. He offered them a diet pop. Marti didn't like diet anything but this did have caffeine. She accepted.

"You two need more than this. You need some sleep. Long night?"

"We found more holes at the Smith place," Vik told him.

"So," the lieutenant said, "what do you think that means?" He picked up the defused hand grenade.

"We're not sure, sir," Marti said. "But there was another accident out there Sunday night and their groundskeeper is dead."

"So I hear."

"Have there been more phone calls, sir?" Vik asked.

"A few."

Marti didn't say anything. Neither did Vik.

"Anne Devney called from Springfield. She was a little upset that you couldn't drive down there today. I suggested that it might not be the smartest thing to do on three hours' sleep. Went right by her." He finished off his can of pop. "Oh, and then there are the Smiths. They are concerned that you are not spending enough time on the Linski case. Think it should be closed by now. They suggested that we might find someone who has the time to conduct a proper investigation." He thought for a moment. " 'Proper.' That was the word that was used." He shook his head. "Makes you wonder what a proper homicide is. Bring me up to speed on what was presented at the Linski and the Buckner inquests and what's happening now."

After they had done so, he said, "None of the Smiths has mentioned this 'toy' you found, or the possibility that it exists?"

"No, sir," Vik said.

"But we see them under controlled circumstances," Marti added. "Always as a group. Always with Josiah Smith present. I think the oldest son, Paul, might be quite talkative if we spoke with him alone."

"Keep that in mind," Dirkowitz said. "But don't bring anyone in without clearing it with me first. And have a damned good reason."

"Sir," Marti said, "I thought we might take a look at some of the other accidents that happened there."

"Sounds reasonable," the lieutenant agreed.

Vik gave her a look that suggested she might have mentioned that to him first. She turned one hand palm-up. She had just thought of it.

"Any theories?" Dirkowitz asked.

"Nothing that justifies killing anyone," Vik said. "It must have something to do with the fact that they're selling the land. But what?"

"We have uniformed men posted at the two entrances to the property," Marti said. "We want to keep them there."

"You think someone will try to move something?"

Dirkowitz opened another can of diet pop and offered them one. This time they both shook their heads. Marti could still taste the last one.

"If there was something in any of the holes, it might be the smart thing to do," Marti said.

"We can't keep them from leaving the premises or search their vehicles when they do. They could put whatever it is in a car trunk or SUV. We'd be none the wiser."

"I know, sir," Marti agreed. "And I know this might not be the most effective use of manpower. But we don't have enough to get a search warrant for the house. We were lucky to get one for the property."

"The earliest we can get an archaeologist to look at the new sites is tomorrow afternoon. Maybe not until Friday," Vik said.

"Who did we ask?"

"The Archaeology Department at Northwestern."

The lieutenant picked up the phone and put in a call to Northwestern University. When he hung up he said, "She'll be out this afternoon."

Vik frowned. "Don't men do this kind of work anymore? I hope she doesn't talk as much as Dr. Altenberg."

"We'll keep those two officers guarding the areas until the archaeologist clears the sites. And since the Smiths have questioned our ability to be effective, we'll keep the men at the entrances, ineffective as that might be." The lieutenant paused long enough to finish his can of diet pop. "Now, a couple of things. I don't want you to have any contact with the media. The Smiths have a lot of control there. And technically, the Smiths get no special treatment from us. The specifics on how we handle them may differ, but we will follow procedure. Don't do anything other than talking with them without letting me know first. And . . ." He checked his watch. "You two are going to go home and get about four hours sleep. Dr. Gabi Kirkemo will be on site at three o'clock."

Dr. Kirkemo arrived with one assistant and four students. She checked out both sites where holes had been dug and decided to work on the one that was undisturbed despite Vik's protests.

"Whatever was here is probably gone," she said. "There has not been any excavation at the other site. I begin there."

Dr. Kirkemo assigned her assistant and two of the students

to the disturbed site among the apple trees. Vik stayed with them. Marti tagged along to the second site, located among the oak trees. As far as she could tell, they did nothing for two hours but draw lines, confer, and take measurements. She wanted to ask what that had to do with anything and urge them to dig but did not. If that's what the other team was doing, it had to be driving Vik crazy. Or worse, he was driving them crazy.

By the time they set up their equipment, which consisted of different-sized screens which they called sieves, got out spades and trowels and began removing small amounts of dirt in a pattern based on the grids, Marti was almost asleep. Dr. Kirkemo and her teams worked until it was beginning to get dark.

"Find anything?" Marti asked the doctor, although she knew they hadn't.

"I don't think we are deep enough yet."

Marti had expected them to dig, find something, or not, and return to Evanston.

"How long will this take?"

"It is hard to say. Hopefully, not more than a week."

"That long?"

"It depends. There is one thing that might be interesting. The trees where the earth is disturbed are quite a few years younger than the trees that surround it."

"Which means?"

"That a circular area here was cleared, then replanted. This hole is close to the center of that clearing. The circular pattern of planting is not typical. The trees surrounding these are planted in rows."

"How long ago are we talking about?" Marti asked.

"Oh, a rough guess, based on the size of the younger tree trunks, maybe a hundred and fifty to a hundred and seventy-five years. We will have to take cuttings from each to know for certain."

Marti went to the tree nearest the hole, then walked away from it in one direction until she could see what Dr. Kirkemo meant. She reached a stand of trees that had trunks nearly twice the circumference of the trees where the dig was.

When she returned, Dr. Kirkemo said, "There is another thing. The trees in the area surrounding this circle of oaks are much more diverse. Maple, elm, cedar, birch."

"What do you think that means?" Marti asked.

"Potawatomi. Syrup and sugar from the maple trees, saplings and birch bark for tepees, cedar to scatter on the floor to control odors, elm and hickory bark for storage containers. However, I must advise you that the presence of this variety of trees and their possible uses does not mean that we will find artifacts."

"But we could," Marti said.

"Yes."

"Then don't rush it. I wouldn't want you to miss anything."

When Marti told Vik how long it could take, he shrugged.

"So? A few days? A week? What's the big deal about that?"

That was the crux of it. What was the big deal? Whether Potawatomi had lived here or escaped slaves had hidden in the root cellar, they still didn't know what was important enough to kill for.

"Do we know what's supposed to happen to this land?" Marti asked. Vik had consulted the maps.

"All of this will be sold." He waved his arms in the direction of the trees. "The orchard, too. The trees, especially the oak, will bring damned good money. Shame to cut them down, though."

"Finding artifacts of any kind will bring everything to a halt."

"I'm not sure about that," Vik said. "They can't build here until everything is recovered, but they still might be able to sell."

"There is so damned much that we don't know."

"Because we're cops," Vik said. "We solve murders. We don't go on digs. We don't sell real estate. And we're damned sure not rich." He shook his head. "I was wondering if maybe the old man doesn't really want to sell and is trying to hold things up. Maybe it's the sons who want the money."

Marti felt a headache coming on. "We need a decent night's sleep," she said. "I can't even think straight right now. We've got to talk to the guard again. The one who found Buckner."

"That can keep until tomorrow," Vik said. "They've got him rehearsed by now anyway."

Ben was there when Marti got home. Everyone else had gone to Joanna's night game. He gave her a quizzical look. "Headache?"

She nodded. "What are you doing here?"

"I dropped off Momma Lydia and the kids, told them what time I'd pick them up. I was sort of hoping a very tired lady cop would show up while they were gone." He took her in his arms. "The hot tub awaits you, and then one of my famous omelets and a total body massage."

As tired as she was, she managed to stay awake for it all.

When Vik got home, Helen and Krista were waiting for him. He went to Krista. "Is your mother all right?"

"She's sleeping."

"Bad day?"

"She fell but she didn't hurt herself. She was just upset, that's all."

"You're sure she's all right? Did you call the doctor?"

"We took her to the emergency room. They said she might be a little sore and have a few bruises. But nothing is broken. She'll be okay."

He went into the room that had once been his den but had been converted into a bedroom because it was too difficult for Mildred to go upstairs. He sat beside her. Her breathing was slow and even but her face looked flushed against the pale blue pillowcase. He touched her forehead. She didn't feel warm. She was okay. Today she was okay. It had just been a fall. But she became upset when the muscles in her arms or legs became weak, and he hadn't been here to comfort her.

He had planned to take a long, hot shower. Instead he put

on his pajamas and slipped into bed beside her.

"Matthew," she said, her voice heavy with sleep.

"I'm here now," he said in Polish. He gathered her into his arms. "Moje serce." My heart.

He felt the warmth of her tears on his shoulder and held her close and cried, too.

Josiah stood by the window. Where was she? He had not seen her since the other night when she came into the house. Why had she come inside? Why was she crying? Until then, she had always walked toward the apple orchard. A guard was stationed there now. Did that upset her? Was that why she didn't come now? Or was she in the house somewhere, waiting? That thought made him nervous, but he told himself that he was too old to be frightened by anything.

Idbash had spoken of her a number of times. "The woman comes in the night. I watch her from my window as she wanders among the trees. Who does she seek?" Idbash did not fear her either, nor did he know why she came. Still, seeing her sitting on the steps had been unnerving. Since then, Josiah had not been able to sleep at night. He lay awake until dawn, waiting, listening for the sound of her weeping. And he had another lock put on his bedroom door. Now he closed the draperies and turned away.

There were a number of Idbash's documents that he needed to look at again. He picked up the agreement signed by Idbash as a superintendent of government agents in 1822. "The tracts of land here stipulated to be granted to Idbash Smith shall never be leased or conveyed by the grantees, or their heirs, to any persons whatever, without the permission of the President of the United States."

These tracts were Smith land now. At least he thought so. Or did this agreement still apply? So much time had passed, and so many treaties had been signed. He could not risk drawing attention to this by making any inquiries that might help him find out. The grantees were the Potawatomi. Could this land still belong to them? There always seemed to be some dispute in some state over who owned land that had once belonged to Indian tribes.

He did not understand the last paragraph at all. "The United States, at the request of the Indians aforesaid, further agrees to pay to the persons named in the schedule annexed to this agreement the sum of seven thousand, two hundred and five dollars, which sum is in full satisfaction of the claims brought by said persons against said Indians, and by them acknowledged to be justly due."

There was no attached schedule. Josiah had tried to work his way through this sentence by sentence, but the meaning was still unclear. He thought it meant that Idbash had received the money as the government's agent because legally Idbash could not have owned the property in his own right until the Indians left in 1836.

He pulled out a Xeroxed copy of the government act establishing trading houses with the Indians in 1806; he reread the portions of the articles that he had highlighted.

"Every agent . . . will not directly or indirectly be concerned in any trade, commerce or barter . . . interested in carrying out the business of trade or commerce, on their own, or any other than the public account, or take or apply to their own use any emolument or gain for transacting any business or trade . . ."

Josiah didn't know if that applied to land. He didn't know how long this act had been in effect. He wasn't sure if, legally, Idbash had actually come into possession of the land or if indeed the family did now own it. He knew that the documents he had now were sufficient to establish ownership and enable him to sell, but if anyone was to look beyond that . . . if anything was found that raised any questions about what had happened here when Idbash took possession of this land . . . even if they did prove ownership, the process could take years.

He opened the journal again, although he didn't need to. He went to one of Idbash's last entries. "I will leave much to my children. Enough for their children as well. All I have done, I did for myself and my own comfort, but I considered them at all times. My father came to this country impoverished and died soon after, leaving me nothing more than his good name. I lived like an Indian until I came here, with little shelter and eating from the land. I stayed in this place because here I could exceed my father's ambitions. I have lived so long and seen and done so much that I wake from nightmares when I sleep, but my children and their children shall sleep undisturbed by my dreams."

Josiah closed the book and turned off the light. He returned to the window and pulled the curtain aside just enough to peek outside. Had Idbash's nightmares included the woman? She was there, in his dreams now, when he slept.

12

When Marti sat down at her desk, the light on her telephone was blinking. She pushed the button and an androgynous voice advised her that she had five new messages. Each was from Anne Devney. Each demanded an immediate response. It was only 7:45 A.M. She returned the call right away, expecting voice mail and a recorded message. Instead, Devney picked up the phone.

"An autopsy!" Devney said when Marti explained why she couldn't come to Springfield yesterday. "This certainly has priority over something like that."

"We each have our own priorities," Marti replied.

"This needs to be yours."

"In your opinion."

"You will have to come down tomorrow. This has top priority in our office."

Marti started to ask how Hector Gonzales, petty thief, dope addict, gang banger, and killer had become so important. Instead she said, "He's been convicted, commuted, and is incarcerated. I've got to track down someone who is still out there."

When Anne Devney persisted, Marti agreed to meet with her tomorrow.

"What was that all about?" Vik asked when she hung up.

"We're meeting with Devney at four tomorrow afternoon."

"Damn. Tomorrow is the Fourth of July." He had been late for roll call and snapped at anyone who came near him. Now he cursed in Polish.

"How's Mildred?"

"She fell yesterday."

"Is she okay?"

"Fine, physically. Just depressed."

Marti knew that despite the slow progression of the MS, Mildred was seldom depressed.

"Know what?" she said. "Nothing is moving here. Nothing. We're at a standstill. Let's go talk to the guard again, then I think you should take the afternoon off."

"We have to see Dr.—"

"I will check on Dr. Kirkemo this afternoon. If she finds anything in the meantime, she'll call."

"Marti . . ."

"Take the afternoon off, take Mildred for a nice drive to the country or the beach or somewhere, stop for dinner and have a quiet evening at home. In fact, I think you should spend tomorrow together too. It's the Fourth of July. You know—barbecues, fireworks, John Philip Sousa, flags, parades. I was only planning to come in for a few hours."

"Was," Vik said. "Now there's another trip to Springfield."

"I can handle that. We'll just go over everything we've already looked at and spend half an hour looking at something else. For something with such a high priority, she sure is slow as hell."

"As soon as I leave, MacAlister, something will break."

"If it does, I'll call you."

"We don't have the forensics on the cigarette butts and the prints and the dirt."

"If we don't have them by the end of the day, we won't get them until Friday. If they come in, I promise to call."

Vik looked at her for a long minute.

"Vik, you're not going to mind missing something here as much as you'll miss spending time with Mildred." She didn't add that, given his mood, he wasn't worth much here anyway.

After another minute, Vik nodded. "She was doing okay, taking it easy but feeling pretty good, not so fatigued. She was beginning to use her cane more than her walker. Now this. Maybe some time together away from the house will do us both some good."

To Marti's surprise he booked a room at a bed-and-breakfast in Lake Geneva, and gave her a number where he could be reached. "I'll be here first thing Friday morning. Now let's go talk to the guard."

When Marti and Vik went back to the Smith place, the guard who had found Buckner's body wasn't on duty. When they asked to speak to Josiah or Paul, they had to wait half an hour. Once again, the family was assembled in the parlor. This time Franklin's wife wasn't there.

Josiah was standing by the window. He turned as they entered the room. "You asked to meet with us because the guard who was on duty yesterday is not on duty today? Do you actually expect me to know about something as trivial as that?"

"All we wanted was the name of the security agency," Marti said.

"Then you should have called. This is quite unnecessary."

Marti took her time, looking at each of them in turn. "Yes, it is," she agreed.

The security agency that provided guards for the Smith place was located in a professional building on Bellview Road. Marti checked the directory for the suite number, and she and Vik walked up a flight of stairs. The suite reminded Marti of the place where she took her car for tune-ups and minor repairs. One room, no window, two desks, a chair, three posters tacked to the wall, a three-legged table with a stack of old magazines and lots of dust. A young woman sat at one of the desks. She was talking into a headset attached to a cell phone and kept tugging at the skimpy knit top that covered her breasts.

Vik leaned against the wall and waited, arms folded. Marti walked to the desk.

"Yeah, you know, I mean . . ." The young woman popped her

gum, then laughed and said, "Well, gotta go. Yeah. Customers. I'll call you back in a couple of minutes."

She looked up at them and said, "Yeah?"

They showed her their badges.

"Yeah. So? We get you guys in here every so often. What do you want this time?"

"We want to speak with the guard who was on duty at the Smith estate on Monday."

"Yeah. Chet Simms. The guy who found the body. He's taking the day off. Wanted a long weekend." She popped her gum as she opened a file drawer. "Here." She wrote on a slip of paper and handed it to Marti. "His address."

"How long has he been working here?" Vik asked.

"A lot longer than me. Three, four years at least." She checked the file. "I take that back. Six years. Wow. I wasn't even in high school yet. Boss won't let them work anyplace important until they've been on the job at least a year. And the Smith estate is real important."

Chet Simms lived in a tan brick bungalow on the southwest side of town. It was a quiet, tree-lined street with similar but not identical houses. A camper was hitched to an SUV parked in the driveway. As they approached, a black-and-tan dog ran to the chain-link fence. He began to bark when Marti rang the bell. The guard recognized them as soon as he opened the door.

"Come on in," he said.

They entered a small, well-kept living room. The patio door was open, and the dog was standing outside wagging his tail. It was a mixed breed, and as it panted, it drooled.

"It's okay, boy. Everything's okay. They're friends," the guard said. He spoke as if the dog had its teeth bared and was ready to lunge at them. "I remember you two. Come in. Have a seat. It's lucky you caught me. The wife and I are heading out as soon as she gets back from the store. I told you all I know about finding that guy."

Marti wondered if he was this relaxed because he was in his

own home or anticipating the trip, or if it was because he had been briefed by one of the Smiths and had had time to rehearse what he was supposed to say. There was also the possibility that the first time they spoke with him he had been unnerved by finding a body.

"Anything like that ever happen to you before?" she asked.

He shook his head. "No. Man. I don't even like seeing 'em in coffins. God." He shook his head again. "I didn't even know the guy, but damn . . ."

"Why did you go looking for him?"

"He wasn't mowing the lawn. We got a call from the house. They wanted the lawn mowed."

So it wasn't because the guards hadn't heard the lawn mower.

"Are they usually like that?"

"The cook is a real pain. Knows everything and makes a big deal about it. She runs the place if you ask me."

Marti recalled that it was the cook who had hired Buckner. They would have to talk to her. She looked at Chet, decided that her second guess was probably correct and he had just been upset the last time she questioned him.

Outside, she said, "I'm inclined to think he's telling the truth and was just reacting to finding the body yesterday."

"Me, too," Vik agreed. "Interesting what he had to say about the cook, though. I think that justifies having a talk with her."

"She hired Buckner," Marti reminded him.

This time, Paul Smith was allowed to greet them with only his wife, Jessica, present. He led them to the kitchen, sat on a stool at the counter, and unfolded a newspaper. Marti had not expected to have an unsupervised visit with Cook.

Jessica went into a room-sized pantry lined with shelves and freezers. "Cook! They're here."

Cook. That was the only thing anyone in the family had called her. Marti debated asking the woman her given name. She decided to wait and see how the conversation went.

Cook was white-haired and plump and almost as tall as Paul's wife. Poor Paul, Marti thought. So far, everyone in the house was taller than he was.

"He was supposed to mow the west lawn every Monday morning," Cook said.

Marti detected a hint of what she thought was a brogue.

"He was not there, so I sent someone to get him."

"Did that happen very often?" Marti asked.

"No. Harry was always reliable. Always. But his weight. I have to admit I thought maybe he wasn't where he should be because he had a heart attack or something."

"How did you know he wasn't there?"

"I couldn't hear the mower."

"So he didn't check in with you or anything?"

"He had a schedule of his responsibilities. In winter, he plowed as necessary."

"Did you talk with him often?"

"Occasionally. Mid-July he would begin bringing tomatoes from his garden. He grew tomatoes that were as big as grape-fruit."

"Do you know of any family?"

"Only his daughter, Zoe. Poor man. Sometimes you love the memory more than the person. I think that for him it was both, and also the future that never happened for her."

"Did he fill out a job application?"

"Just papers for taxes and insurance. The accountant would have all of that."

Marti turned to Paul. "We cannot find any next of kin. You'll have to either give us the name of the accountant or get Buck-ner's paperwork. We'll have to have his social security number. If he gave any references or names of family or friends, we'll need that, too."

Paul hesitated, looked at his wife, then nodded.

"Today," Marti said. She turned to Cook. "Do you know when his daughter died? Or where?"

"Not the year, but it was in the winter. The road was icy that night and the driver was drunk. I think he lived in Idaho then, but it could have been Iowa. Something that began with an I. Or was it Utah? I'm not sure. One of those places."

Marti expected Josiah to show up, but he hadn't put in an appearance by the time they left. But then, Paul seemed as intimidated by his wife as he was by his father.

"Interesting family," she said as they walked to their car. "Cook seems nice enough."

"Sounds like Buckner kept to himself. From what I can tell there are the guards, the maid who lets us in, and Cook. Someone has to keep the place clean, though. I can't imagine either of the wives making a bed."

"They probably have a service come in. As big as that place is, there aren't enough people to make much of a mess."

Marti returned to the office alone. She caught a whiff of Obsession for Men, but Slim and Cowboy were gone. She checked the coffeepot. Empty. No doughnuts either. She had been so anxious for Vik to go home, she hadn't suggested stopping for lunch. She thought about going down to the garbage machines, compared what she would find there to real food, and decided she didn't feel much like eating anyway. Before she could decide what to do next, the phone rang.

"Detective MacAlister," she said.

"Are you the one who's looking for Tommy Strongwind?"

"Who?"

"Tommy Strongwind. They have a copy of his picture at the Indian Affairs office."

She had almost forgotten about the computerized facial reconstruction.

"Where are you calling from?"

"Madison, University of Wisconsin."

"What makes you think it's Tommy Strongwind?" she asked, jotting down the name.

"It's him."

"Who is he?"

"My cousin."

Marti sighed. Either they talked too much or they said too little. At least this sounded like she might be speaking with a relative.

"Tell me about him."

"He took off again last summer."

"Where did he say he was going?"

"He didn't."

"Then what made you think he had taken off?"

"Tommy did that a lot but he always came back."

Unlike the others who had called, this young man did not sound confused or desperate.

"What's your name?"

"Ethan Dana."

"And you're sure this is your cousin, Tommy Strongwind?"

"Yes."

"Can you tell me anything about his family?"

"He's Indian. Potawatomi. We still have a few relatives up north on the reservation."

"When's the last time you talked with them?"

"Couple of years, maybe."

Before Strongwind disappeared.

"I need you to find out if anyone's spoken with him or seen him since you did. Show them the picture. If they agree that it's him, ask them to call me."

"Okay."

"Can you take care of that right away?"

"Is it important?"

"Yes."

"Then I'll drive up as soon as I can."

After she hung up, Marti picked up the copy of the *News-Times* that was folded on Vik's desk. The headline she was looking for was in the lower left-hand corner of the second page. "Worker dies in accident." In a three-sentence paragraph, it gave Harry Buckner's name, mentioned the storm, and listed an address without identifying it as the Smiths' place. There was no mention of the accident involving Larissa Linski the week before. Marti wondered whom Josiah knew at the *News-Times*. The lieutenant was right about the Smiths controlling the media.

While Krista packed a small suitcase for her mother and Helen packed a lunch, Vik put folding chairs in the trunk and a sweater and blanket in the backseat. Sometimes, even though it was summer, Mildred got cold. He got her settled on the front seat with a few small pillows to keep her comfortable, then leaned over and patted her knee.

"It's been a while since we've gone anywhere."

"And on a workday, Matthew."

"Marti will call if she needs me."

They spent most of the drive to Wisconsin talking about Steven, their daughter Krista and their grandson. By the time they reached Lake Geneva, they were recalling things that had happened years ago when they were newlyweds and he was a young cop. They never ran out of things to talk about. Vik worried that it might be because they didn't spend enough time together.

"Are you tired?" he asked.

"No. I'm enjoying the ride."

"Good. It's nice country here. We'll drive a little while longer, then go to that place with a view of the lake for an early supper."

By the time they reached the bed-and-breakfast, Mildred was tired. He helped her take a shower, then sat in the bed beside her and read a book after she went to sleep. It had been a good day for both of them.

Marti waited until Dr. Kirkemo and her assistants packed up their equipment for the night. It was dusk and mosquito season, but thanks to the bats, bugs were not a problem.

"Nothing," Marti said.

"Something," Dr. Kirkemo said. "But not what you're hoping for, not yet."

"What's the something?"

"Strata."

Gordon McIntosh had mentioned that. Maybe now she would find out why it was important.

"We have gone through the first layer of dirt. It's loam, a very fertile soil. Before the trees in this circular area I pointed out yesterday were planted, this land was cleared, leveled and covered with a rich, organic soil that would facilitate growth."

"Which could mean . . ." Marti began.

"Any number of things. What happened here is that the trees grew quickly, which also means that they looked like mature trees within a short period of time and blended in with the other trees that were already here."

"What if you don't find anything?" Marti asked.

"We will either extend the dig site or begin another one within this perimeter."

"Then you think something is down there."

"I could be wrong about that, but it's worth making sure. I am an architectural archaeologist. If I find something, I will know what kind of dwelling it came from and be able to determine the configuration of the village. Then we will not dig randomly but in specific places looking for specific artifacts or indications that the Potawatomi did establish a village here."

When Marti got home, everyone was out back on the deck having supper. Ben had barbecued spareribs, Momma had cooked greens, Joanna had contributed two salads. Although she didn't think much of Joanna's vegetable casseroles, most of Joanna's salads were great. The six-bean salad she had prepared for tonight was one of Marti's favorites. She fixed a plate and sat in a comfortably padded chair. The sun was just setting, citron candles kept the mosquitoes at bay and there was just enough of a breeze to make it seem cooler than it was.

Later, while Joanna and the boys cleaned up, Marti and Ben went up to the middle place. She wanted to look at the books the boys had brought home from the library. She hadn't even had time to open the book she had taken to work.

"What are you researching?" Ben asked.

"Research? I'm not sure what I'm doing. Spinning my wheels, most likely."

"This case is different, isn't it?"

"It's a lot like a case here that goes back about thirty years." She repeated the story Vik had told her about the storm and the three teenagers and dead parents.

Ben considered that. "You don't have any circumstantial evidence?"

"Not enough. Not yet. And nothing so far that will stick to anyone in the family."

"Tough case."

"You said it."

"Is it because of who they are?"

"Yes and no, but that's more a matter of perception. If they were not who they are, circumstantial evidence could weigh more heavily against them. Because of who they are, we have to have an airtight case."

She went over to the computer and turned it on.

"You've been on the Internet a lot lately."

"You would not believe the things about this case that I don't know."

Ben looked at the stack of library books. "Potawatomi," he said. "The Underground Railroad. Archaeology."

The Underground Railroad. What if the root cellar had been a hideout for runaway slaves? Suppose it was that far below ground to keep the dogs from getting their scent? There was a bounty on slaves. They had to hide because they weren't safe here. Their owners and bounty hunters could catch them and bring them back. Maybe there hadn't been a roof. Maybe something else had covered that cellar. They could have used a ladder to climb in and out. But if that was the case, then why did Larissa Linski die there? She no longer believed that was an accident, and she certainly didn't believe in the accident ghost, or witch, or bad fairy.

They went to see Marti's godchild on the Fourth of July. Thanks to Anne Devney, she would miss the fireworks tonight. Staben House, where Sissy and little Gracie were living, always had a big cookout. With Sissy there, the whole family had become involved. Today, Ben and his partner Allan were the chefs. Momma was reading to the preschoolers. Theo and Mike played horseshoes and volleyball with the older children. Joanna organized a treasure hunt.

Marti played with Gracie for a while. At three and a half, Gracie was a trusting, affectionate child who greeted her with a smile and a hug and laughed a lot.

Then Marti and Gracie's mom, Sissy, sat inside where it was quiet, and talked. Sissy, always underweight, had gained a few pounds. She didn't look at the door every two minutes anymore, as if she was expecting someone to break it down, and she didn't jump anymore when the phone rang.

"How's it going?" Marti asked.

"You were right. They're pretty tough on me here. But they care. And for once in my life it's good to have people around me who think I can take care of myself, and Gracie."

"How's the job?"

"I hate it. Sitting there waiting for the phone to ring, taking messages and making appointments is driving me nuts. I need more to do. But I don't know how to do anything else."

Marti waited.

"I want to go back to school so I can get a real job, but I don't know what I want to do, and there's Gracie. I'd have to find day care. Good day care. Someone to love her."

"That's the scary part, isn't it?" Marti said. "Finding someone you can trust."

Tears came to Sissy's eyes as she nodded. "I know what could happen to her. And if anything did happen, they would take her away from me."

"I'm her godmother," Marti said. "I think this is something I should help you with. Why don't you get enrolled for fall semester and let me look into day care for Gracie?"

"I am so afraid for her," Sissy whispered. "One of the mothers here watches her for me now. But that's just because she's not looking for work yet. Her baby is only three weeks old. Even though Gracie's here, I still worry. I still call two or three times a day. I can't help it."

Marti wondered if Sissie, after being on her own or in foster care most of her life, would ever get over worrying about her daughter. Some people could guess at what was out there. Sissie knew.

Downtown Springfield was crowded, perhaps because of the holiday. Marti wasted fifteen minutes trying to find a parking place before she gave up and went to an indoor parking garage connected to a hotel. There were no vacant spaces until she reached the fourth level.

Instead of going to the capital, she met Devney at the library. Old, but recently renovated, it was a beautiful building. The center was open from the ground level to the ceiling three floors up. Anne Devney led the way to a small meeting room with two windows. The room was tucked in a corner, had comfortable chairs and bookcases. Five folders were on a coffee table. "I think this is where we left of," Devney said as she chose one.

Three and half hours later Marti returned to the garage. The sun had set and the streets were all but deserted. Two women were half a block ahead. She turned. Nobody was behind her. As she walked, she arranged her keys between her fingers. Her gun weighed heavy in her purse. Holstering her weapon had seemed unnecessary when she left home. She was wearing her service shoes with the steel heel shanks. A sudden burst of music came from a pub as the two women went inside. Marti kept to the center of the sidewalk, away from the doorways, away from the cars parked at the curb.

She paused as she reached the garage and looked about. A man was waiting for the elevator. He was wearing faded jeans and a cap with the visor pulled down. He didn't look at her. She let him step ahead of her and enter first, then stood with her back to the wall. She gripped the keys. The elevator was warm. The man got off on the third level.

When Marti exited, most of the parking spaces were filled. Hotel guests, maybe. It was quiet. No voices. No music. No car doors slamming. Had the man one level below left this quickly? She kept to the center of the driveway as she approached her unmarked vehicle. It did not have a remote door opener.

Marti put the key in the lock. Smelled paint thinner. Heard breathing. Someone grabbed her from behind. She raked her heel down his shin. Came down hard on his instep.

"Goddammit!" a man howled. His grip loosened.

She thrust both elbows back. He grunted.

Another man vaulted over the railing. Cap. Crowbar. She raised her arm. Pain went from her wrist to her shoulder.

"Police!" she yelled.

The man behind her got her in a choke hold. She buckled her knees. She dropped. He lost his balance. She pitched him forward.

She butted the man wearing the cap with her head. He screamed. Blood spurted from his nose. She kneed him. He yelled. Doubled over, he clutched at his crotch.

The man behind her grabbed her hair. Turning, she hit him with the heel of her hand. She hit him again as he backed away. Marti grabbed his wrist, twisted his arm behind his back, forced him to lean over the trunk of her car.

"Do not ever touch my hair again." She punctuated each word by pulling his arm higher. "Next time I'll break it."

She cuffed him. The other man was gone. His cap was on the floor.

It was almost ten o'clock by the time she left the local police station. Her arm hurt like hell but she could drive. If she had to spend half the night at the hospital, she preferred the hospital closest to home. Ben would meet her there.

13

FRIDAY, JULY 5

When Vik came in Friday morning, Marti realized it was the first time in weeks that he didn't have dark circles under his eyes. He wasn't frowning either, although the expression on his face was still far from cheerful.

"What happened to you?" he asked. "Fall off the deck while the fireworks were going off?"

She had a cast from her left wrist to just below the elbow.

"Cracked radius," she said.

"How did that happen?"

"A couple of guys picked me as a mark."

"While you were in Springfield?" Vik asked.

She nodded.

"Just two? What did you do to them?"

"One broken nose, two black eyes, fractured ribs, broken toes, a fractured tibia, and swollen testicles."

"Geez. They really pissed you off." He smiled. "I always knew you could take care of yourself, MacAlister."

That had been Ben's reaction too. They knew she could take care of herself. That pleased her. Her kids didn't know about this yet, but she was hoping they would react the same way.

"I'm also on painkillers, Jessenovik. You're duty driver today."

Vik fixed them both a cup of coffee. Slim and Cowboy had come and gone.

"You look rested," she said, and thought, or maybe just less worried, or less guilty for spending so much time away from home. She was familiar with both.

"Sorry I'm late. We decided to stay another night and drove back this morning."

"Is Mildred feeling better?"

"I think she felt better as soon as we pulled out of the driveway. She hasn't gotten out much lately, except for Mass. And she didn't have much of an episode. It was just upsetting because she had been doing so well. Anything from the lab yet on the soil samples and cigarette butts or the prints?"

"Nothing." She dropped a stack of Xeroxed copies on his desk. "Files from the drowning accident and the impaling at the Smiths' place."

They made notes independently, then compared them.

"Franklin's son drowned," Vik began. "Only child. He was fifteen, drunk, and had amphetamines in his system. There was bruising—chest, back, arms, legs. Medical examiner thought it was more consistent with a fall than a fight. According to the guard, the kid was alone in the house. The rest of the family was at their summer place in Michigan. They all alibied each other. Presumably he fell down the stairs, made it to the wading pool, and then hit his head when he fell in. At least that was acceptable to the coroner's jury. They ruled it accidental."

Marti read from her notes. "The impaling has a lot of similarities. A cousin, seventeen. Wagner side of the family. Alone. Drugs and alcohol. Everybody has an alibi. The coroner's jury ruled it accidental but it sounds like the medical examiner thought it could have been a suicide. Being nice to the family maybe. Or to the senator. It looks probable that this kid jumped. Vladimir the Impaler was far enough away from that balcony to make accidentally landing on his sword almost impossible."

"Hell of a way to go," Vik said. "Unless the kid was on something and thought he could fly." He checked his notes. "No bruising like Buckner has. Maybe he did jump."

"And maybe the fifteen-year-old did fall down and drown. According to the school records, these kids were nothing but trouble. The parents ended up taking them out and having them tutored at home. Let's pull the autopsy photos."

Two hours later they still had nothing conclusive.

"That kid who drowned had a lot of bruises," Vik said. "Looks more like a fight to me than a fall down the stairs."

"We need to take a look at the prior accidents," Marti said. "See if there's a pattern."

"Then we'd better check with the coroner's office. If we ask the *News-Times* to go through their archives, the Smiths will find out before we get the photocopies."

The prior records went so far back they were in storage. "Monday at the earliest," she told Vik.

When Isaiah woke up, he knew without opening his eyes that he was in the hospital again. Floyd had called an ambulance for him when his arm began hurting. Before they could get there the pain had begun moving up to his shoulder, then to his chest. Sharp, constant pain, different from the other heart attacks. He was conscious when they began giving him oxygen and felt them starting an IV, but he didn't know what happened after that. Someone had remembered that he didn't like lying flat, because his head was elevated. And nothing hurt now, but his chest was sore. He opened his eyes, looked toward the window, saw the sunshine, and gave thanks to God for another day. Then he looked around, saw the monitors, the IV pole, the window that looked out on the nurses' station. Intensive care. This had been a bad one. Tired, he closed his eyes. Sleep. He needed sleep.

The next time Isaiah woke up, Omari was there. They looked enough alike so that it was almost like looking at himself when he was a young man. He could almost hear Grandma's voice as she said, "Old one." He closed his eyes. "It is time, Omari, time to go to Chicago. You . . ."

"Don't try to talk, Grandpa. I already called the Woodson

library and they put me in touch with a member of their genealogical group. Do you want me to wait a few days before I go?"

Isaiah shook his head. "No. Go now. Find Samuel."

"I'll find him," Omari promised.

Isaiah smiled.

Marti and Vik drove to the site where Dr. Kirkemo was working. A lot more dirt had been removed and sifted.

"It looks like things are moving along here," Vik said. "Find anything?"

Dr. Kirkemo smiled. "Porcupine quills, bear claws."

"Whoopee," Vik muttered.

"And mussel shells."

"Zebra mussels?" he asked.

"No. Ocean mussels."

"But we're not anywhere near the ocean."

"Exactly." Dr. Kirkemo smiled again. "Someone brought them here—used them for trade maybe, or gave them as gifts."

"I give," Vik said.

"Potawatomi," she told him. "I'm guessing that there was a tepee where we're looking and that these belonged to a family member. The other team hasn't found anything but they have established that something was removed from their site. I'm going to bring them over here tomorrow. I am going to stop digging here, though; for now, at least, and try to identify a few places where they might have buried their dead."

"Why?"

"Artifacts are not enough to stop development. Human remains are. If there are any, the Potawatomi have the right to rebury their dead according to their customs."

"Have any of the Smiths been here?" Marti asked.

"I haven't seen anyone."

"Good. I would appreciate it if you didn't mention any of this to them."

"I'm working for you, not the family."

Marti went to a table and looked at what was scattered there. Quills and claws and shells. Such simple reminders of a way of life that was gone. How long had they stayed here? Long enough to hunt for a season? Or had this been a more permanent home? Marti closed her eyes and listened to the calls of the birds. Pheasants and Canadian geese would have nested here. If they lived here during the summer, the women would have planted squash and beans and corn.

They would have built fires at night. They would have danced and drummed, according to Theo and Mike. When it was quiet, they would have heard crickets and owls. Bats would have flown overhead. There would have been deer, even buffalo, grazing nearby. What did they think of the stars? Did they have a mythology for the constellations?

She opened her eyes. Sunlight filtered through the leaves and dappled the ground. Did the Potawatomi plant these trees, or were they already there? She imagined flowers, pink and lavender and yellow, dancing in the wind. The relocation of the Potawatomi wasn't just the benign removal of a people who had become trespassers on their own land. This had been their home. Who would want to leave a place like this for the flat, monotonous plains of Kansas?

"Marti?"

Startled, she looked at Vik. His relatives had known oppression in Poland. Her people had been brought here in chains. Conquering, subjugating, enslaving, removing, killing, war. Concepts as old as time, but why? She had spent most of her adult life seeking out those who killed others. But there had been so many centuries of killing. The little she did now was not even a deterrent. At least with Linski and Buckner, she thought there might be a reason for their deaths, no matter how illogical that reason might seem to her. Sometimes the only reason was that the other person happened to be there.

When Marti and Vik got back to the precinct, the forensic reports were there. Vik scanned his copies, then said, "Damn."

"Right," she agreed. There were a few surprises.

The surface dirt on the deer-hoof rattle matched that of the dirt in the hole where Larissa Linski had died, but the dirt in the grooves of the hoof did not match that at the Linski site or the two new sites.

Marti tasted her coffee. It was cold. She gave it to the spider plant. "The deer hoof could have come from anywhere. They just want us to think Linski found it in that hole."

"Too bad we don't have any witnesses who saw who went into the Channon place and hid it."

The cigarette butts were not the same brand. PCR tests, which gave faster but less complex DNA results, indicated that the security guard was a non-secretor, but that whoever smoked the other cigarettes did secrete. The palm- and fingerprints did not match Harry Buckner's and they were not on file.

"So," Marti said. "We need DNA samples and prints from all of the Smiths. I'll clear it with the lieutenant."

Vik tossed his copies of the reports into his in-basket. "At least we've eliminated a few possibilities and limited a few others," he said; then: "Why in the hell couldn't they have just sold the land and been done with it?"

When Marti called the lieutenant, he said he would arrange to have an evidence tech go to the Smith place and take samples for DNA testing as well as palm- and fingerprints.

"Does he mean today?" Vik asked. "Does he have to get permission from some politician first?"

Marti shrugged. "He'll see that it gets done. It'll be more interesting to see if they've got enough clout to delay the process, and if they can, for how long."

Marti was finishing off a slice of pizza when the phone rang. Vik took the call and motioned to her to pick up.

"Detective MacAlister?"

The voice sounded familiar, but she couldn't place it.

"It's Ethan Dana."

She thought for a moment—the facial reconstruction. "You're calling about your cousin." Maybe it was Tommy Strongwind.

Nobody had called since Dana's last call and he was the first person to call twice.

"I'm going to the reservation this weekend. Can you tell me why you're looking for him?"

Marti took the folder out of her file drawer and extracted the computerized picture. For a moment, she hoped this wasn't Dana's cousin. "We aren't looking for him," she said. "Whoever this is, we've found him."

There was silence.

"What you have is a computerized reconstruction of what we think the person we found might have looked like."

"Then he's . . . Tommy . . . damn . . ."

"We don't know that for certain yet."

"What happened?"

"We don't know that either." She didn't mention the bullet that had nicked his rib. "This might not be your cousin."

"It is unless he has a twin, and I think I'd know if he did."

She was surprised that a computer had created that much of a likeness.

"Can I tell the family and tribe members what's happened? They'll want to bring him home."

"We'd appreciate any help we can get. What we really need is anything that would give us a positive identification. Bone fractures, X rays, dental records. Any medical records. And anyone else we can contact."

"Sure," Dana agreed. "I'll do whatever I can."

"Do you have any idea why he would come here?"

"No. No. Nothing. Why would anyone go to Lincoln Prairie on purpose?"

Marti thought he had said that much too quickly.

After she hung up, she said, "This caller seems pretty certain that our skeletal remains are his cousin."

Vik was looking at the DNA and forensic reports, grunted. "Strange case, isn't it?'

"The skeleton?"

"That, too, but I was thinking of the Smiths. All that land. All that money. And none of them seem happy. Hell, they aren't even friendly, not even with each other, unless they wait until nobody else is around. A man works for them for twelve years and they don't even know what he does, who he is, if he has family." He drummed his fingers on his desk. "Hell of a way to live. Strange."

"It does make you rethink the trickle-down theory."

Vik looked at her, then said, "You're right. The odds on that bunch sharing the wealth with anyone else are slim to none. Starting with Idbash, all that family has done is take. I'm wondering why they agreed to donate some of the land. Not that they're giving away much of it."

Josiah paced about his study, unable to sit down. He had been appalled when the police arrived, and having to submit to being fingerprinted had been beyond the pale. There was no way he would have complied if his attorney had not insisted. Conveniently, Richard had not been available when he called to protest.

And now this. He checked his watch. Seven-ten. Paul was late, as always. He could not remember a time, not even at his birth, when Paul wasn't late, if only a few minutes. It was as if Paul was born with the intention of displeasing him. And Paul had done so all of his life.

Josiah tried to sit down and pretend a calm he did not feel. He tightened his grip on the arms of his chair, trying to resist the need to get up and walk about. He would not let Paul see how agitated he was. He tried completing the morning's *New York Times* crossword puzzle but couldn't concentrate. Instead, he went over to the liquor cabinet and poured himself a Scotch. He brought the decanter to his desk. It was another ten minutes before there was a knock on the door.

When Paul came in, he said, "Well, Father, we've had our mouths swabbed and hand- and fingerprints taken. What's next, a trip to the police station for questioning?"

149

"Do not come in here twenty-three minutes late and speak to me that way. Sit down."

Paul sat across from him. "This house has become a substation for the Lincoln Prairie Police Department." Paul spoke in that soft, even tone that always sounded mocking. "It seems like they're everywhere these days."

Josiah picked up a pencil, realized he did not intend to use it and put it down. Why was it that a man's sons were such a continual vexation? He had given Paul everything that his father had given him. Money, leisure, education, travel. He had appreciated those necessities. Why couldn't his sons? Franklin was courteous, at least, but from Paul he got nothing but this sardonic disrespect.

"Why are the police here at all, Father? Doesn't anyone on the Wagner side of the family know someone who can see to it that they go away? We have benefited considerably from our Wagner connections. Why can't they do something now?"

"It is damned inconvenient," Josiah agreed. He had spoken with Richard again, and even called that concubine of Richard's, Kat Malloy. To his surprise, Kat had agreed with Richard—leave well enough alone. Since she had been with Richard for over ten years and had considerable influence in her own right, and because she was often more astute than Richard, Josiah had not persisted. Maybe this investigation should run its course. Richard had seen to it that Franklin's son's death was ruled accidental—after a police investigation had indicated it was not.

"That was an accident," Josiah said. He realized he had spoken aloud, counted to three, then said, "We do have far too many accidents here, but that's what they are—accidents."

Paul leaned back and stroked his chin. "I think not, Father. Not this time, and certainly not when Franklin Junior died. No." He shook his head. "Those two detectives don't think so either. Too bad we couldn't have kept these most recent accidents in the family. The authorities would probably be much more sympathetic." He stood up. "I don't think we'll get much sympathy this time. And please, Father, whatever is going on, don't tell me."

"That's right, Paul," Josiah said. "Don't get involved. Don't offer to help. Don't ask any questions. Stay as far away from this as you can. Give nothing. Just continue to take. Look down at me. Look down at my father, your great-grandfather, Shemuel, and Idbash, my great-grandfather. And, all the while, continue to take. After all, this is your birthright, isn't it?"

"Why did you send for me?"

"Because I want you to stop talking so much. I have instructed you repeatedly as to how to answer the police officers' questions, preferable in monosyllables that they can understand. You don't have to speak in complete sentences, or answer in more than one sentence. They aren't here to socialize. They are here to get information. Don't give them any."

"I don't find it as easy as you do to lie and tell half-truths."

"It's called keeping your mouth shut. Try it."

"What else do you want me to do?"

"Just what you've been doing—nothing."

"We were treated like felons today. And you put us in this position. This is your fault. Why don't you just sell this damned land and be done with it? I would prefer to have my own money, my own land, and my own home." He walked to the door, then turned. "Control. That's what it is, isn't it? As long as we're here and the trust is doled out to us for the rest of our lives, you have control." He yanked open the door and walked out, slamming it behind him.

Josiah crumpled a piece of paper as he stared at the closed door. Idbash had wanted this land to remain in the family in perpetuity. Now his great-great-grandson, Paul, wanted his share, his own. What made any of this their own? What gave them the right to it? Idbash's legacy? Poor Idbash. His father had left him nothing. He had had to forage for everything— food, shelter, the clothes on his back. Was that what compelled him to amass this land, this fortune? Had Idbash somehow transmitted that feral response to poverty and need to his descendants?

Even now, Josiah was as fearful as Idbash must have been when he thought of not having enough. But what was enough? He had accepted his inheritance as his by right. And now his sons were ready to do that also. But he knew what had happened during Idbash's lifetime to give them all of this wealth. And at what cost to others. At what cost. For most of his life all that happened in that distant past had not been his concern. Now that he was forced to sell this land, it was. And he no longer believed that the profit could ever outweigh that cost. He had been as arrogant as Paul. He too had considered all of this nothing more than his due. Now, he was no longer certain. Josiah felt his fingernails digging into his hand and released the wad of paper.

Josiah still could not sleep. He had considered having his doctor call in a prescription, but he had resisted taking medication all of his life. He was not going to allow that one aberration in the woman's behavior cause him to do so now. If only he knew for certain that she had gone outside. If he could just see her a safe distance from the house, walking among the trees. But, he feared she was still inside. And, he thought he knew why.

He had turned off the lamp by his bed but left the draperies open to let in the moonlight, creating shadows on the walls and panels of darkness and light. The maid had fluffed his pillows, turned back the covers, and adjusted the air-conditioning to a level that he considered comfortable. He listened for night sounds that the house didn't make, wished that the stairs creaked or there were trees close enough to brush against the windows, or even a draft to move the curtains. The house had been built too well. There was nothing to relieve the silence, not even the ticking of a clock.

It was after midnight, and he was still wide awake when he heard the doorknob turn. She was here. His heart began thudding in his chest. His breath came faster and was shallow, even though he tried to breathe deeply. The knob turned again. There were three locks on his door now, he reminded himself, and no way she could get in. He lay still, not moving, as if not making a sound would cause her to go away even though she must know he was here. The knob rattled, as if she was twisting it one way and then the other. He told himself it was okay to wipe the sweat from his forehead but he did not move.

The silence was so abrupt that he kept listening for her. He waited, straining to hear another sound, any sound. His heartbeat slowed. His pajama top was damp with perspiration. It might have been four or five minutes before he moved. It seemed longer. He eased out of bed, tiptoed to the door and listened. Nothing. Not a sound. At least she wasn't crying tonight.

He waited for what seemed like at least another five minutes before he unlocked the door, then another minute or two before he opened it just wide enough to peer into the hall. When he didn't see her, he opened the door wide enough to stick out his head. Then he stepped out of his room. She was not on the stairs and not in the hall. He was alone. He closed the door, locked it and leaned against it. She was gone. Turning, he saw her standing at his bedroom window.

14

Marti went to Joanna's game Saturday morning. The stands were filled with parents. Most of them were in the section reserved for the home team. Joanna's was the visiting team. They still had a losing record, but they had won their last game and lost the one before that by one run. Joanna had become as much coach as player. Ben was near the dugout again, camera ready. The team would be over tomorrow to watch the films, then they would go to the field for a few hours and Joanna would guide them through a practice session intended to help them improve.

What impressed Marti the most was that after being on winning teams for years, Joanna had refused several offers to play on other teams with better records. And it wasn't just that Joanna didn't get discouraged. She seemed to see this as a challenge. As Marti watched, the first baseman tagged a runner out. Joanna led the cheers.

Marti caught Ben's eye and waved. He laughed and swung the camera at her. She waved again and yelled, "Yay Cougars!"

A few minutes later Theo and Mike left their bat-boy duties long enough to run up to her with a cold bottle of Gatorade.

"We're ahead by one run," Mike said. "We're going to win."

"It's only the first inning," Theo reminded him.

"I know, but it's the first time we've scored first all season."

Her optimist and her pessimist. As Marti laughed and hugged them, she wished she could stay for the whole game.

*   *   *

When Marti and Vik returned to the dig site they brought lunch for everyone. Momma had packed sandwiches, Mildred and Helen had baked cookies. Marti had stopped on the way and picked up two cases of cold pop and a couple of bags of potato chips and Fritos. It was hot in the sun, ninety-four degrees, according to the weather report. But as Marti walked among the trees it felt much cooler. By the time she had spread out a blanket, arranged the food and Dr. Kirkemo and both teams had joined them, Marti wasn't bothered by the heat at all.

"Right now we are digging at these two sites," Dr. Kirkemo advised them. "And we know that we have that top layer of soil before we will reach anything, which will make things go faster. I have laid out a village based on the location of the trees and where the artifacts were found. If I am correct, the burial grounds will be in one of two places." She selected a turkey-and-Swiss-cheese sandwich. "If we had time, I would go about it at a much slower pace, but I do have other responsibilities that I must attend to soon. Others can take care of the complete excavation."

"We appreciate what you're doing," Marti said.

"It was what you might call a command performance, but a nice respite from what I would ordinarily be busy with at this time of year when I'm not teaching." She made a face, then said, "Cataloging."

The others laughed.

It was almost four in the afternoon when there was a shout from one of the dig sites.

"A femur! I found a femur!!"

Everyone gathered around Dr. Kirkemo's associate professor.

They spent five minutes consulting the map and then were assigned an area to dig that was in relationship to the find. In another hour they had more bones. It was after six when a skull was unearthed. Dr. Kirkemo held it in her hand. It was small.

"A child," she told Marti. "But look." She pointed to an indentation on the left side.

"Was the one blow enough to cause death?" Vik asked.

Dr. Kirkemo nodded.

"Were they attacked by another tribe?"

"Not unless this happened in the 1650's, when the New York Iroquois began expanding south of the Great Lakes. Other artifacts will help us with the dating."

By dusk they had unearthed more bones and one other small skull with a similar indentation.

"They didn't have human sacrifice," Marti said.

"No," Dr. Kirkemo agreed. "Nor did they brutalize their children. We have no way of knowing what happened here. But there is nothing in Potawatomi culture to allow for the killing of children. Were it one child, it could have been some kind of accident, a fall, perhaps, but two children with the same injury is not accidental."

"What do you think happened?" Marti asked.

"Based on historical data, it was most probably done by either the Iroquois or by the white men who came later. Once the Potawatomi reached this area, they were stronger than the tribes already here and they were, for the most part, a peaceful, friendly, nonviolent people."

"Can we date these bones?"

"We'll refer this also to Dr. Bass in Tennessee. And we will search for more artifacts once all the bones are exhumed."

"Will this stop the sale of the land?" Vik asked.

"That I don't know. But I don't think so. It will delay development within the parameters of the village. The Potawatomi had no need to live in close proximity. This might be the only village on the Smith property. I don't know if there are any surveys that would tell us for certain."

When Marti and Vik left, the sun had set and the two teams had set up lights so they could continue to work.

Josiah sat in his bed, propped up by pillows. He must have passed out when he saw the woman, but aside from sore ribs on his left side as well as an aching shoulder and arm, he thought he was okay. He had sent for Cook this morning. She wanted him to call the doctor but more as a precaution than a concern that he was more seriously hurt. Cook had cosseted him all day, bringing warm tea and small meals, doling out Tylenol and feeling his forehead. She opened the draperies and he had lain watching the sun make long patterns on the carpet that shortened as the day grew longer and waned to twilight. It was dark now, except for the moonlight.

Would the woman who once walked in the woods return to his room tonight? He did not believe he was the one whom she sought. If he was, he would be dead by now. She knew that the bones of her dead were here. She just wanted a final resting place for whoever it was she had loved.

Love. Had he ever loved anyone as much as this woman must love? His wife had been chosen for him by his father. He had bedded her, respected her, been pleased when she gave him two sons, and then left her bed for this one. His responsibility to his father and Idbash having been met, he no longer had need for that part of his life. She died alone one night. The maid found her in the morning. The doctor suspected she had taken too many sleeping pills and acerbated the effect with too much brandy but entered natural causes on the death certificate. And that was true; she had died from the natural causes of living in this house with him.

Love. Josiah had felt some affection for his sons when they were young, but had little need for their company as they grew older and more sullen and opinionated. The time he had spent with his own father had always been a formal event. Meals, guests, a trip to the opera or a play or the symphony. That was pretty much the way it was with him and his sons. He had not chosen his sons' wives, but perhaps he should have or at least given them some disincentive.

Eileen had remained with Franklin after the death of their son, but Josiah wasn't sure why. He didn't know if they blamed themselves for the boy's death, or if they blamed each other, but he had not seen one gesture of affection pass between them since then, not even at the boy's cremation.

Paul and Jessica had grandchildren, whom he only saw at Christmas. They were not close to their children either, and lived like a couple who only had each other, which didn't seem so bad to Josiah. They did have each other. They didn't seem to take a great deal of pleasure in each other's company, at least he didn't think so, but there was a bond between them, something that made them inseparable much of the time.

As for him, he didn't mind being alone. His most frequent guest was this woman who now invaded his room. And, if he was close to anyone in this house, it was Cook. He thought about dying. He was eighty-five now and in good health, but nobody lived forever. Idbash and his father and grandfather had gotten up one morning and had massive coronaries. No fuss, no lingering, and little inconvenience. He had lived his life, even enjoyed it, especially when he was younger and had traveled abroad. He saw little reason for being here now, other than managing Idbash's and his father's many assets. Despite the woman's many nightly visits he could not envision any afterlife, which was a relief. One was more than enough. He had known neither ignorance nor want. And now as he approached the end, he neither needed nor wanted anything at all. He would not regret his passing, nor would anyone else. In this family, there was no viewing the remains, no church service, no funeral; just cremation and a twelve-line Psalm of committal at the family vault. Did he want more for his sons? Perhaps, but like him they did not seem to have the inner capacity for more. Like him, this life would be enough.

He wanted to get up, go to the window, get a reassuring glimpse of the woman—outside once again where she should be. But he lacked the energy to move or enough interest in her comings and goings right now to endure the aches and pains movement would cause. He closed his eyes—for a moment, it seemed. The sound of the doorknob rattling awakened him. He stiffened, then relaxed. Only Cook had the keys. Then he looked toward the window where she had stood. No, she had not come into his room tonight. He was still alone.

Marti was tired when she got home. It was caused more by the weight of the two small skulls than the length of her day even though she had awakened a little before five-thirty that morning. Momma had declared a no-cooking day. Sub rolls, a variety of lunch meats and cheeses from the deli, lettuce, and sliced tomatoes, pickles, onion, and bell peppers were available. Marti decided on Italian cold cuts and piled on tomatoes and bell peppers.

The boys burst into the kitchen.

"We won again!" Mike announced.

"But we almost lost," Theo explained. "The shortstop made a really good catch and saved the game."

"And Dad took the whole team out for pizza!" Mike grinned.

After she had eaten, Marti got on the computer. Ben and the boys followed her but went to work on the Potawatomi project. Tonight that involved working with birch bark. Instead of asking what they were trying to make, Marti realized that she had learned a lot about the Potawatomi and that Dr. Kirkemo seemed to know everything about them. She keyed in Underground Railroad, and got more listings than she could process in one night. She tried slavery in Illinois instead. Again, too many entries. She thought she might have asked the boys about that, but if she did, she couldn't remember what they had answered, so she asked them again.

"The salt mines," Mike said. "I asked Mrs. Zaragoza while we were at the library."

"Mrs. Zaragoza said the Illinois constitution of 1818 let them have slaves there," Theo added.

"Could they have made an exception in northern Illinois also?" Marti asked.

"It was only legal in the salt mines," Mike repeated.

"But they could rent slaves, or borrow them from people in

other states," Theo said. "I asked Mrs. Zaragoza about that too. She thought it was neat that you were working on a case with Indians and slaves."

Marti thought of two small battered skulls. "What about children?" she asked.

"Mrs. Zaragoza said they could be indentured servants too," Theo said.

"She said that means they were kind of on loan and you didn't really own them," Mike explained.

"But only if their parents said so," Theo added.

"Which was darned mean," Mike said. "I'm glad they can't do that anymore."

Marti looked at the computer screen again. She couldn't stop thinking about those two children. She needed to help Ben and the boys.

"Is there something I can do?" she asked as she joined them. They couldn't think of anything, but all three of them liked having her attention, so she watched.

The canoes they were working on were a foot long. The birch bark was soaking in water. When she touched it, it felt much different from the way it looked, tough and strong and not paper-thin or easily cracked. The wood for the ribs of the boat was soaking also. When she asked if the canoes would float, Ben said yes.

"We should use pitch," Theo explained. "Like the Potawatomi did. But we're going to use waterproof glue instead." Otherwise, there wasn't much conversation until Ben said, "Lead mining."

"What?" Marti asked.

"Lead mining," he repeated, concentrating on wood strips the width of toothpicks that he was taking out of a bowl of water and bending and nesting one inside the other. "But maybe Galena is too far west."

"They mine lead in Galena?" She had never heard about that.

"Not anymore," Ben said without looking up. "But they used

too. I'm not sure when but they would have done it in the eighteen hundreds."

Marti returned to the computer, found lead mining, printed off several pages, added Galena and printed several more. She read for a while and made a few notes. Then she went on the Internet again and found a listing of mining-stock owners in Illinois. She printed the section that listed owners in the early-to-mid eighteen hundreds. Idbash Smith was among them.

Isaiah felt exhausted even though he had not been out of bed since they admitted him to the hospital. He couldn't walk to the bathroom and had not even been allowed to get into a wheelchair and go to the hospital chapel for Shabbat. The rabbi and several members of the congregation had come to see him. And Omari had called from Chicago that morning, not long after the doctor had come in. Isaiah told the rabbi but not Omari what the doctor had said, that everything depended on how much heart muscle he had left.

He had gotten used to being in hospitals. He hardly noticed the noise anymore. The only thing that still bothered him was always having a light on in Intensive Care. They dimmed the lights but they were always on. He was wishing he could put them out when Floyd came in and sat in the chair by the bed.

Isaiah opened his eyes but keeping them open took too much effort.

"Hi," he whispered. "I'm doing okay."

Isaiah was almost asleep when Floyd spoke.

"Omari made it to Chicago. He's staying with those people you said would help him."

"He called."

"Good. He says first thing Monday morning he's going to check out those records on Edward and find out what you need to know."

Isaiah nodded. "Ummm."

"You need to rest, bro. Just rest. This will pass."

"Ummm."

"Irwin . . . no . . . Isaiah. If that's the name you want to be called by, then that's what I'll call you from now on."

"That's okay," Isaiah said, but he knew what it took for Floyd to say that. He knew that calling him Isaiah now instead of Irwin would make Floyd feel better when he was gone. "We . . . brothers . . . always been . . . always . . . will be . . . that . . . don't have nothing to do . . . with . . . agreeing about things . . . has to do with . . . sticking together."

"And we always done that," Floyd said. "No matter what."

Isaiah nodded.

Floyd patted his hand. "You rest now . . . Isaiah . . . Doctor says you got to get a lot of rest."

Floyd had just called him Isaiah not once, but twice. Lord, you can dismiss thy servant in peace, Isaiah thought. Then he thought again. But not yet, Lord, not until Omari finds Samuel.

Josiah listened as the lock turned. Cook was here. He had turned on the lamp beside his bed and was listening to classical music on the radio. Occasionally a man spoke but Josiah didn't pay attention to what he said. For one of the few times he could remember he just wanted to hear the sound of another voice.

"Mr. Josiah," Cook said. "I've brung you some soup. You haven't touched hardly anything today. That's not like you." She put the bowl on the nightstand and went to get a lap tray. "The boys think you're in a snit about your discussion with Paul last night. I didn't see any reason to tell them otherwise."

She arranged the soup, a spoon and a napkin on the tray and went to an alcove where there was a small refrigerator.

"Now, here's some crackers and your water and some cranberry juice. I'll be back in half an hour to collect your tray."

As she turned to go, he said, "Don't forget to lock the door, Cook."

"No, sir. I won't."

"And should I fall asleep, be sure to wake me. There's something I need you to do."

Cook was back in thirty minutes. After the tray was moved to the hall and his glass of juice had been replenished, Josiah gave her two keys. "My den," he said. "The desk, middle drawer, and the sideboard, top drawer."

Cook returned with the metal lockbox that contained Idbash's journal, went back and came back with the chest filled with maps and other documents.

"Keep these," he said. "Put them someplace safe. Under no circumstances are you ever to give them to any member of this family. Understood?"

"Yes, sir." Her voice trembled. "I never would, sir." She spoke just above a whisper. "Not now that you've told me not to."

"I know you won't, Cook. That's why I'm giving this to you."

After she left, he tried to remember her name. He thought it was Brigitte, or maybe Colleen. Something Irish. He had called her Cook since the day she arrived.

15

Vik awakened early Sunday morning. Still tired, he made sure Mildred was sleeping and tried to get back to sleep himself. Mildred had been doing much better since their two-day trip. She was smiling more, and using her cane again instead of her walker. She had even helped Helen cook yesterday. He was going to take her to nine-o'clock Mass this morning, then, before he went to work, to a restaurant for breakfast and then a drive to the lake. Beside him, she stirred, then snuggled closer.

"Matthew, you're still here." She stroked his thigh. "Guess what," she said. "I'm not sleepy." She rose up on one elbow and kissed his mouth.

Marti looked up when Vik came in, pleased that there still were no circles under his eyes. There was a quickness in his step and a slight upturn of his mouth that wasn't quite a smile but said that everything with Mildred was okay.

"Blueberry muffins," he said, putting a bag on her desk. "Helen baked them while Mildred and I were at Mass. Slim and Cowboy come in yet?"

"You missed them by about twenty minutes."

He poured a cup of coffee. "Nothing like having a case that's going nowhere fast."

"We are making slow progress," she corrected.

"Too slow."

164

Marti told him what she thought the root cellar might have been used for. To hide slaves, then said, "And I might have found something on the Internet last night. I don't know what it could have to do with any of this, though."

Vik came over to her desk. "What?"

"Lead mines."

"In Galena?"

"Right." Was she the only one who didn't know that? "Guess who owned stock certificates in a lead mine?"

"Idbash Smith?"

She nodded. "And during the 1820's, a lot of the galena and smelted lead were smuggled out of the state to avoid federal regulations and federal taxes."

"The family is loaded and that's probably part of the reason why."

"I know. I don't think it means anything important," Marti admitted.

"What the hell is galena? Besides the name of a city."

"It is sulfate of lead, and don't even go there."

"The early 1820's? I thought Idbash settled here in 1829."

"That's what it said in the other research I did on settlers in Little Fort and Lake County, but if we go by the dates on these stock certificates, he was here by 1822."

"Couldn't he have bought the stock while he was back east or wherever he came from?"

"I don't know that much about buying stock at all, let alone in 1822, and I have no intentions of trying to find out. I did find out that Idbash owned one of the mines that significantly underreported its production for at least eight years."

"I bet Idbash wasn't just involved in that smuggling. I bet it was his idea. He's beginning to sound like that kind of guy."

Marti opened the bag of muffins. The aroma of warm blueberries wafted out. "Delicious," she said after she bit into one. "Point is that in the early 1820's, mining was backbreaking work. Everything was done by hand, with chisel and sledgehammer. And they had to use explosives, which was dangerous."

"Not to mention lead poisoning, which was fatal. Those Indians who were slaughtered could have been involved too."

"Those Indians were mining lead before the French and English came here. And if slaves were kept hidden in that root cellar, what if it was dug that deep so they couldn't escape? They could have been used as another source of cheap labor."

Vik drummed his fingers on his desk. "But what would make that important enough to kill for now? Proving that Idbash killed some Potawatomi might make them decide against naming a park or a school for him, but it wouldn't impact the sale of his property or reduce its value. Hell, who knows, the way things are today, it might make that land worth more."

That, Marti agreed, was still the question they could not answer. And unless they did, she didn't see how they would have a case. "Harry Buckner dug at the Potawatomi site. And we've found something there. Maybe he found something, too. It might be easier to make that connection."

Vik leaned back and put his hands behind his head. "Killing children," he said. "That won't make much of an impact. Happens all the time. But Buckner, maybe you've got something. He was old, alone, friendless. Who knows. With the way we still treat Indians and other minorities, not enough people will care about that."

Marti looked into her coffee cup. Empty, just like this case. Relevance was definitely lacking. "How likely is it that one of the Smiths would actually kill someone?"

"Maybe that's our answer," Vik said. "If they hired someone . . ."

"It wouldn't be anyone local, too risky. It would have to be a professional hit. Let me call a few contacts in Chicago."

She thought about the two small skulls again and shuddered. Had Idbash been capable of that kind of violence against children?

* * *

Omari sat down at the dining room table and looked out the window. This part of Chicago, the south side, they called it, was an interesting place. He had expected a ghetto, with ramshackle housing, or, worse, projects; the homeless, drunks sleeping in hallways, gangs and drive-by shootings. Instead this was a quiet neighborhood with small brick bungalows lined up behind chain-link fences, with trees and grass and flowers. The street was quiet except for an occasional siren nearby. There were birds in the trees. It wasn't much different from being at home.

Mrs. Jackson lived here with her son, Carlton, who had stayed up with Omari half the night going through all of the papers Grandpa had sent. Carlton had sorted them into neat piles that covered the table, then read through each stack. He didn't say much but he seemed impressed, excited, even.

"Well, Omari, you're up early." Carlton spoke from the doorway. He was about fifty, and light-skinned, with hair the color of sand. "I've always been an early riser myself."

"Yes, sir."

"Mom sleeps in a bit these days. She's slowing down. We both are. I'm going to make breakfast."

"Let me help."

"Sure. Do you know how to scramble eggs?"

They had to clear a space on the table for their plates. After they ate, Omari loaded the dishwasher while Carlton cooked oatmeal and scrambled more eggs and took both upstairs to his mother. When he returned he brought some manila folders.

"Now we can get down to business. Let me see that list of things your grandfather told you to do." He scanned it, then checked the labels on his folders, said, "Forgot something," and went back upstairs. When he returned, Mrs. Jackson was with him.

Omari watched as Carlton pulled back a chair for his mother, then brought her some coffee. Mrs. Jackson was eighty-two. As Grandpa would say, she was "sassy." Shiny gray hair framed her face. Her smooth light skin was almost unlined. She sat very straight, her back just touching the chair, and looked at them through wire-rimmed glasses.

"Good morning, Omari. I would so like to meet your grandfather." She looked at him and smiled as she made a sweeping gesture over the table. Her fingernails were polished a deep red. "He must be quite a man to have worked at this for so long with so little help. And you are quite a fine young man to be helping him."

Omari liked the way she talked. Her voice made him think of a Sarah Vaughn album his Uncle Floyd played a lot. She was elegant, a real lady. He had never met anyone quite like her. She began going through Grandpa's papers. After a while, she looked at Carlton and said, "Our friend, Mr. Smith."

"I think so," Carlton answered.

Omari wanted to know what they were talking about, but they were so intent on studying Grandpa's research that he didn't want to interrupt. Without saying anything, Carlton and Mrs. Jackson passed papers back and forth. After what seemed like a long time, Carlton looked up at him.

"The name 'Thatcher' is what got our attention," he explained. "That, and the fact that this plantation was in Missouri when it was still part of the Louisiana Territory. Missouri didn't have many big plantations like they had in the south. Thatcher, though, he had about a hundred and fifty slaves at any given time. He raised cotton and tobacco."

"His place wasn't too far from the Missouri River and almost across from Alton, Illinois," Mrs. Jackson said. "Alton was a river town where some people were sympathetic to slaves, and Illinois was supposed to be a free state."

"With some exceptions," Carlton added.

"A lot of those who came along the river did not want to risk crossing Lake Michigan, so they would take the Illinois River up to the Des Plaines River and go on to Wisconsin."

Omari nodded. He had already figured that out.

"We began researching our family years ago," Carlton explained. "A few years ago we began branching out."

"Whenever we saw a trend," Mrs. Jackson continued, "we tried to investigate, find out what it might be about."

"We noticed this Thatcher because it seemed like we were always finding a handbill offering a reward for one of his runaway slaves. So we tried to find out what happened to some of those slaves. That's when this Smith name came up."

"Some of Thatcher's slaves who we tracked to Wisconsin were helped by an Idbash Smith," Mrs. Jackson said. "We found this in records kept by some of the people who helped them escape. Then we noticed that there were also entries that indicated that some of the slaves the conductors were expecting never arrived. When we went back, we found records of slaves making it to Illinois, some as far as Chicago, some further north, then disappearing."

"What makes you suspect this Idbash Smith?" Omari asked.

"Coincidence," Mrs. Jackson admitted. "And lack of information rather than additional information. We just can't find any other records of a significant number of slaves being expected in Wisconsin and never showing up who were on their way to any conductor other than him."

"So how does knowing that help Grandpa find Samuel?"

"We don't know. Maybe it doesn't," Mrs. Jackson said. "We'll have a better idea after the three of us go through the county records tomorrow. We are going to get there as soon as they open, and we'll probably be there all day. We have a few friends there who don't mind helping us with our research, and we've already called to let them know what we need."

"Now," Carlton said, "this is what we need to do today."

Omari smiled. Wait until Grandpa heard about this. When Uncle Floyd called last night, he said Grandpa was really feeling good about him being here, that it was going to help Grandpa get well. When he called again later today, Grandpa would really be glad he was here.

16

Marti was getting tired of the Springfield commute. The cast on the lower half of her arm didn't impede her driving, but the trips she was making there seemed a waste of time. Vik wasn't complaining, but he had lost all patience with Anne Devney. When he told her today that she was going to have to speed things up, Devney accused him of being uncooperative. As they slogged through the transcripts of the pre-trial motions, neither was speaking to the other. By the time they walked from Devney's office to where she had parked the car, Marti was damp with sweat and irritable.

"I'm glad we're going to see Gonzales this week," Vik said.

Marti hated the thought of going into a prison unarmed. It didn't seem to bother Vik as much.

"How often have you done this?" she asked.

"Couple times."

"Menard?" she asked, "Statesville?'

He named a couple of minimum-security facilities.

"Watch your back," she warned him.

The first thing Marti noticed when they got back to the precinct was that her in-basket was overflowing. "Looks like the memo fairy has been here," she complained. When she sorted everything, junk mail outnumbered reports by three to one. Next she checked her voice mail.

"Ethan Dane called twice," she told Vik. "No message." She tried returning his call and got no answer.

Someone did answer when she called the accounting firm that handled the Smith account. It only took three transfers to get to the right accountant.

"Buckner," the woman said. "Yes. I can give you his social security number, his date of birth . . ."

Marti wrote that down. "Next of kin?" she asked.

"No one on record."

"Friend? Reference?"

"One reference." She gave the name of a company Marti had never heard of in a town in Idaho that she wasn't familiar with either.

"Current wages?"

"$18,720 a year, and of that he donated $5,200 to MADD. A hundred dollars a week."

"Life insurance?" Marti asked.

"Not that I know of. We only paid for health insurance."

"Did you deduct for that?"

"No."

As soon as she hung up, Marti got out a calculator. "Well," she said, "so much for the Smith largesse."

"Oh?"

"They might have paid Larissa Linski four thousand dollars a week, but Harry Buckner only got three hundred and sixty."

"That's all?"

She pushed a few more buttons. "Nine dollars an hour for a forty-hour week, health insurance, and a place to sleep. I forgot to ask if they supplied his work clothes."

"Age discrimination," Vik said. "I wonder if he started working for less and got an annual raise."

"I wonder if he cared," Marti said. "Daughter dead, no family. He didn't list one friend as a reference. Speaking of which . . ." She picked up the phone. The company Buckner had worked for had been bought out, but the executive secretary remembered her predecessor's name. When Marti thanked her, she said, "This is just a small town, ma'am. Everybody knows everybody else. Lila will be glad to talk with you."

Lila sounded very old. "Harry Buckner?" she asked in a voice loud enough to make Marti suspect she was hard of hearing.

"Yes." Marti checked Harry's dates of employment and raised her voice as she repeated them.

"Yes, yes, that was Harry. Worked right here until his daughter died. Poor man, Zoe was all he had, she was. Wife ran off with a forest ranger. Big scandal back then. Everyone felt sorry for him—Harry, I mean. None of us ever thought he should have married her in the first place."

"Can you put me in touch with his family?"

"Got no family. At least none that I know of. No brothers or sisters. He was of an age when he married, thirty at least. His folks passed long before then, which was a blessing, considering who he married."

"Do you know what happened to her?"

"His wife?"

"Yes."

"She wasn't from around here. Just passing through when he met her. Stopped long enough to waitress for a few weeks, winked at him few times, smiled once or twice and snagged him. Harry wasn't no Rudolph Valentino. She might have been his first real girlfriend. Cute she was, but foolish."

"Did Harry have a best friend?"

"Well now, seems to me he was kind of friendly with one or two of the boys."

Marti confirmed that the boys were still alive and jotted down their names. The first man didn't remember Harry. The second seemed interested at least.

"Harry died, huh? Damned shame about his daughter. He raised Zoe by himself from the time she was little. Just took everything out of him when she died. I don't think he cared about anything after that. Didn't even keep his job, just drifted away. Illinois, huh, not that far from here. I would have thought

Virginia or thereabouts, or maybe even Maine. Someplace where there were mountains and lots of trees. Harry loved the mountains, the forest; camped there a lot, buried Zoe there."

Marti asked him the same questions she had asked the secretary and got the same answers. Then she put in a call to the Social Security Administration to see what would show up on Buckner's Social Security number. Getting that information would only take thirty to sixty days.

"It doesn't look like there's anyone to bury him," she told Vik. "Unless we can shame the Smiths into it."

"Paul," Vik said. "Maybe. If we could talk with him alone."

Marti reached for the incoming reports. Most were the archive reports she had requested on accidents at the Smith place. After several hours the only conclusion she had reached was that none of the people involved seemed to have had much common sense.

"Who in their right mind would walk through a pasture at night where a bull was loose?" she asked.

"Or run under a tree in a thunderstorm," Vik countered.

"Or try to fly a paper airplane at night?"

"They were a little sturdier than that, Marti."

"Oh? Have you flown in one?"

"Nothing smaller that a Piper six-seater, and that only once."

"A Piper is made of metal, Jessenovik. I don't know what airplanes were made of in 1935. Wood, burlap, and spit, probably." At least that was one thing she had no reason to look up on the Internet.

Oh," Vik said, "here's another barn accident. Very similar. Went right out the door. Same barn, too."

Marti found her copy. "In 1953. Too bad we don't have a clue as to the family dynamics when these accidents happened. True, nobody seems to like anybody else very much today, but none of them are dying right now."

The records went back to 1920. There were eight accidents in all. They reread everything, looking for similarities, divergences, any kind of pattern.

"All males," Vik said. "Four Smiths, four Wagners."

"All of the accidents happened at night. And outside."

"All but the two most recent ones happened away from the house."

"And they don't average out at one about every ten years, Vik. They happen at nine-to-eleven-year intervals, and based on that, we're about due for another."

"Hummm. I wonder if we should warn them about that. Two people dead, neither one a relative, and one of them a female. Maybe the criteria has changed, and the quota."

"Think it's the ghost?" Marti teased.

"Right, the mother of one of those children."

That reminder took all of the humor out of it for Marti. "We haven't heard anything else from Dr. Kirkemo," she said. "I hope that's good."

"Hey," Vik said. "Look what I found. DNA on Mr. Paul Smith indicates that he is our smoker who does not secrete. That gives us a good reason to talk with him without the rest of the family present."

Marti found that report and went through it. "All of the other Smiths are secretors—that's interesting—and we've got their DNA on record, just in case. We'll have to find out if a specific reason was given for taking the swabs. Hopefully not. When we figure this one out I want everything to be open and shut."

Vik snapped a pencil in half. " 'Shut' would work for me."

They called before going to the Smith place. Paul agreed to see them alone. When they arrived he took them through the kitchen where a young girl was preparing a salad, and into a room about the size of a large pantry. There were a table with chairs, a few small appliances on the counter—toaster, coffee-pot, microwave—as well as a cushioned rocker with a basket of knitting beside the footstool. Sunlight filtered through dotted swiss curtains. Marti thought of Cook.

"So," Paul said, sitting down. He looked at Marti as if waiting for her to speak.

Instead, Vik said, "We found some cigarette butts under a tree not far from the Linski dig site."

"And you've figured out that they are mine." Paul kept his hands under the table.

"Yes. Mind telling us what you were doing there?"

"Watching," he said.

"Why?"

"I just . . . Father didn't tell me what was going on there. I wanted to know."

Marti found that interesting, but said nothing.

"Did you find out?"

Paul's face got flushed. "Not until I asked Cook."

"Was Miss Linski the only one digging there?"

"Yes."

"Which hole was she working?"

"The one she was found in."

"What day was this?"

The date he gave was the Thursday before she died, June twenty-first.

"How many times did you go there?"

"I went there again the next day—Friday the twenty-second."

"Why didn't you go on Saturday the twenty-third?"

"I got a call, had to go into Chicago." He hesitated, then said, "I can prove it if I have to. It was a special board meeting at the bank. Five other people were there also."

"On a Saturday?"

"Yes. Something to do with a stock issue being made by a major client."

"What about Franklin? Where was he?"

"I . . . um . . . to tell the truth . . . oh . . . he was with his wife. I don't know where they went . . . business, I think . . ."

"Was anyone else watching Larissa while she worked?"

Paul cleared his throat. Marti wished she could see his hands.

"I . . . um . . . no . . . no. Why would anyone watch her?"

"Why would you?" Vik asked.

Paul looked away and didn't answer.

Vik took Paul through the same questions again. The only time Paul contradicted himself was when he answered that Larissa had been working the first hole the Thursday before she died. He caught himself and said it was the third hole, the one she was in when she died.

"Was she working the same hole both days that you observed her?" Vik asked.

"Yes . . . no . . ." He checked the diagram. "No. On Friday she was working the hole at the other end . . . I think . . . I . . . I . . . to tell you the truth, I'm not sure."

"How well did you know Harry Buckner?" Marti asked.

"What?" Paul looked at her as if he didn't understand the question, then said, "I didn't. He was just . . ."

"Did you know that he has no relatives, no friends, and no life insurance?"

"Of course not. Why would I?"

"The city will have to bury him."

He shrugged. "And?"

"Burials like that get a lot of attention around here."

As Marti watched, his eyes widened a bit and one hand came out from under the table.

"No, no. We can't have that. Umm . . . well. Where's he from?"

"Idaho. His daughter is buried there."

"Ummm."

"Sad, isn't it," Vik said. "Losing a child, especially an only child. Even if they aren't everything you want them to be, they're still yours."

Paul looked down at his hands, flexed his fingers.

"I'll talk to Cook," he said.

As soon as they were in the car, Marti pulled out her notebook. "That man is a terrible liar. I'd say that Franklin wasn't with his wife the day Linski died, that someone else in addition to Paul was watching Larissa, and that he did see her working the hole she died in but not the other one. Got anything you want to add?"

"That about covers it. Cook does a lot more than make sure they eat, doesn't she?"

"She seems to be involved with anything that has to do with the employees, and, I'd guess, running the house," Marti agreed. She wondered why.

"Damned shame you had to mention publicity to get Paul's attention."

"And that you had to refer to Franklin's son's death to get him to do something."

Marti and Vik agreed that they should talk with Dr. Kirkemo before they returned to the precinct. As reluctant as they were to see any more small skulls with one side caved in, they did want to know how things were coming along. The thermometer had remained stuck between eighty-seven and ninety-two degrees for three days. The walk through the woods did nothing to relieve the humidity.

When they reached the site, there were four teams of four working, each in a different area. They watched for a few minutes. Tedious work, Marti decided. The workers squatted and stooped and knelt to put spadefuls of dirt on sieves and let it sift through. Nobody yelled Eureka, so Marti assumed they weren't finding anything. Dr. Kirkemo looked up, saw them standing there and waved them over. Marti didn't ask her if she had found anything else. Neither did Vik.

"I needed to find something that would help me date this site," Dr. Kirkemo said. "So I called in reinforcements. So far, all we have found that can give us a time frame is a small silver ornament, very feminine, very delicate. We have sent it to the university where it can be dated based on the use and the design. If that and the age of one of the young trees coincide, that will provide an acceptable estimate of when this village was occupied."

"How long will that take?" Marti asked.

"We might know as soon as tomorrow."

Marti looked at Vik. He asked the question she was reluctant to ask.

"Any more bodies?"

"Bones," Dr. Kirkemo answered. "They will have to be sorted. It looks more like a mass grave than a burial site. The bodies were not laid out in the Potawatomi way. We can tell that one head was severed; also there are two rib cages sufficiently intact to see knife or sword thrusts. We think we have disinterred everyone, but will dig wider, just in case. And because of the way the bodies were interred, a lot more excavating will have to be done. My primary task is to identify the perimeters of the village. Secondary is to determine when the Potawatomi lived here. Others will take care of the rest."

"So," Vik said as they walked back to their vehicle, "someone had to know this was here. My guess is Josiah. And there has to be a reason—"

"A compelling reason, Vik."

"A compelling reason why nobody wanted anyone to know. That's what stops me. So Harry Buckner happened to find something. Even if it was another skull, what's the big deal? We're talking money here, big money. This won't interfere with the sale of the property. If the developers don't want to build a house on a burial site, they'll put in a retention pond or a swimming pool."

"Maybe we're looking at this like normal people."

"No, we're looking at this like homicide cops. We've heard every reason and non-reason for killing someone. We have investigated homicides that made perfect sense to the person who committed them and homicides that were senseless to everyone involved. This still doesn't make sense and it still isn't senseless."

"Unless you listen to Paul and the others and understand that Harry Buckner wasn't a real person to them and neither was Larissa Linski."

"True," Vik agreed. "But even with that we're left with people who are not mentally imbalanced . . ."

Marti wasn't sure she agreed with that. "At least not obviously imbalanced."

"Not imbalanced to the extent that they would kill without sufficient motive."

"Vik, we just finished reading about eight totally illogical accidents. These are the same people. Members of the same family. And those children . . ." Her voice faltered as she thought of the small bashed-in skulls. "Someone sure as hell was crazy to do that."

Vik walked ahead of her. Something wasn't clicking with him, and his instincts were as good as hers. He needed to think something through. She lagged behind until he stopped walking and let her catch up.

"The victims of the accidents were all males and all related," he said. "I don't think that has anything to do with this except to give them the mind-set that they could kill and make it look like another accident, which is what they attempted to do. I don't think Larissa Linski's life or Harry Buckner's life meant a tinker's damn to any of them. They wouldn't kill strangers unless there was a reason, and we haven't found a good-enough reason yet."

Marti didn't have an argument for that.

There was a message from the accountant who handled the Smiths' financial affairs when Marti got back to the office.

"Buckner life insurance policy overlooked. Proceed with funeral arrangements." Marti returned the call. "We don't make funeral arrangements," she said.

"You don't?" The female accountant did not sound pleased. "Then I suppose we'll have to arrange to have someone handle that. Since there is no family, or friends, a simple burial should be easy enough to arrange."

Marti thought about Harry Buckner's monthly contributions to MADD. She thought about a young girl named Zoe whom Harry had loved. Zoe was the only person who had meant anything to him. "What I think you should do in the interest of . . . discretion," she said, "is send Harry back to Idaho and arrange to have him buried near his daughter. I think that would be the appropriate thing to do."

There was a moment of silence before the accountant said, "Yes, I think you're right."

"And if there is any money left over from that insurance policy, a generous donation to MADD would be a thoughtful remembrance."

"I'll see that everything is taken care of."

Marti winked at Vik when she hung up. For the second time in two days, he smiled.

Josiah continued to seclude himself from the rest of the family. He was up and about and not feeling as sore from his fall, but he still had to sit down and get up carefully. He didn't want anyone to think something might be wrong with him. Besides, even on a good day, the less he saw of them the better. He had heard from his attorney again. He would sign the final papers Wednesday afternoon. And he had made arrangements for a flight to Florida on Sunday. He didn't want his sons, or anyone else, to know about any of this a minute sooner than necessary. He still hadn't told them that their share of the sale was going into the trust. They had probably decided how they were going to spend it by now.

Too bad they couldn't take as much interest in what was happening at the dig site in the woods. He had been watching from his window off and on all day, but he couldn't see the site among the trees from anywhere in the house. There was no word from the police as to what was going on, and as much as he wanted to know, he was not going to ask either one of those detectives. He could ask Richard to make a call to their superiors, but suspected any inquiry would be relayed to them. When he began to feel a little light-headed from lack of sleep he decided to take a nap before Cook brought his dinner.

17

TUESDAY, JULY 9

Marti was eating an apple fritter when Anne Devney called. It was seven-forty A.M. and she was only on her second cup of coffee.

"I called to schedule our appointments," Devney said.

"What appointments?" Marti asked. "We'll be there today at four o'clock."

"Well, since you seem to be having so much difficulty with availability, I thought I'd better get on your calendar for the rest of this week, and next week as well."

Marti wasn't sure if Devney as being sarcastic or if she was just into control. What didn't this woman understand?

"Jessenovik and I are working a homicide case, Anne. Our calendar is controlled by that. And homicides tend to be full of surprises."

"That's one of the things that concerns me," Devney said. "You are not giving the Gonzales case any priority at all."

"Maybe that's because he's already been found guilty of a homicide and he was on death row until his sentence was commuted by the governor. There is also the possibility that as long as he remains incarcerated he might not kill anyone else."

"Officer MacAlister, what you don't seem to understand is that the attorney general's office has determined that this case will be reviewed ASAP—which means as expeditiously as possible. I didn't make that decision, but I have been assigned to handle it. As an officer of the law, you are required to assist me."

"As an officer of the law, I am required to serve and protect my community. I am doing that by trying to prevent any further deaths at the hands of an unknown perpetrator. That is my priority and I must do that as expeditiously as possible."

"Then it would seem we have a conflict," Devney said. "I think I can handle that. See you this afternoon."

There was a click and the phone went dead. Marti slammed down the receiver. Vik didn't ask any questions.

"What's with this sudden popularity?" Cowboy drawled. "Not only do you two get to hobnob with the richest folks in the county, but you're on the attorney general's most-wanted list, and you've even had your own close encounters with our state capital's criminal community."

"Some people have all the luck," Slim agreed. "The biggest thing we've had since last weekend is a three-way at the Tip Top Club. Two hookers and a pimp got into a fight." He sauntered over, looked down at the cast on her lower arm. "And we didn't even get any souvenirs. An orange cast would have been nice," he said. "Or maybe hot-pink. White isn't in anymore."

When Marti pulled out a stack of file folders without answering and Vik got a cup of coffee without saying anything either, Slim commented, "Damn, the Dyspeptic Duo are decidedly discontent this morning."

"Unusually uncommunicative," Cowboy agreed.

"Absolutely antisocial."

When that didn't get a response, Cowboy gave the rest of his coffee to the spider plant. He snapped off a few dangling offspring, tossed them on Vik's desk and said, "Wouldn't want you to lose your concentration worrying about these little guys increasing and multiplying. I did leave a few in case you need to vent any frustrations."

That said, Cowboy announced their departure.

"I hope the coffeepot isn't empty," Marti said, without looking up.

"Was that an attempt to show a little appreciation?" Cowboy asked.

"Damned shame what you've got to do around here to get some attention," Slim added.

They were laughing as they went out the door.

"Alone at last," Marti said.

Lieutenant Dirkowitz called a half hour later and scheduled a noon meeting. The next time the phone rang it was ten-fifteen.

"You've got visitors," the desk sergeant said.

"Anyone named Anne Devney?"

"No."

"How about Howard G. Milford?"

"Who?"

"Never mind." Milford was the attorney general. "Just send them up."

There was a knock on the door a few minutes later, and a uniform pushed it open. "Someone to see you."

A young man and an older man came in.

"I'm sorry," the young man apologized. He had a deep tan and thick dark hair with a cut that tapered at the nape of his neck. "I tried to reach you by phone."

"And?" Marti asked.

Vik motioned to the chair by her desk and the older man sat down. His face was round, his hairline receding. His nose was too big for his face. He was clutching two manila envelopes. His hands had veins as thick as cord. Momma would have called them the map of a hard life.

"I'm Ethan Dana," the young man said. Vik brought over another chair.

When both men were seated, Dana said, "This is Tommy's grandfather, Medwe Nozhagum. He is also one of the elders of our tribe, the Strolling Potawatomi. He knows how Tommy should be brought home. He has some of the papers that you asked for. And he can stay in Kenosha with friends for a few days in case you need to talk with him."

Mr. Nozhagum handed Marti the envelopes. She thanked him and put them on her desk, then looked at Ethan Dana. "If you know for certain that this is your cousin Tommy, then you know why he was here."

Dana looked away.

"You will answer her," Mr. Nozhagum said. His voice was deep and raspy. He spoke with quiet authority.

Dana nodded, then cleared his throat. "Tommy came here looking for someone. Said they owed him from way back and he was going to collect."

"Was this a legitimate debt?"

"To Tommy it was."

"Meaning?" Marti asked.

When Dana didn't answer, Mr. Nozhagum said, "Speak."

"Tommy's been in jail a few times."

"What for?"

"I'm not sure. He traveled a lot. Sometimes we got letters or calls from jail."

"Was he in Madison before he came here?"

"Yes. He came back in January of last year. Enrolled in a Native American Studies program at a junior college not far from the reservation. Said he spent as much time as he could with his grandfather."

"Why was that?" Marti asked Mr. Nozhagum.

"Healing," he said.

"Tommy came to Madison the end of June," Dana went on, apparently accustomed to the older man's brevity. "He waited tables and spent a lot of time in the university library and on my office computer."

"Why did he come here?" she asked again.

"I don't know anything more than I told you."

"Why didn't you report him missing?"

"Because whenever he took off and didn't come back we'd hear from him sooner or later."

"Had he ever been gone this long without contacting you?"

Dana shook his head. "No, and I might have got worried, but I got married last November. We're expecting a baby in a couple of months. I'm working and taking grad classes."

Mr. Nozhagum said, "The machine."

"Oh, right," Dana said. "Tommy was getting oral histories from the elders and tape-recording passages from books that couldn't be taken out of the library."

"Can you access any of that?"

"I don't know. I'll look for his tape recorder and see if there are any tapes around. If he left any files on my computer, I'll print a copy for you."

"If you find anything, please fax it or overnight it as soon as you can." Marti looked down at the manila envelopes. Part of her hoped they could make a positive ID, part of her hoped that this was not Tommy Strongwind, that he would soon be returning to his people.

After Ethan Dana and Mr. Nozhagum left, Marti said, "So, one Potawatomi is found dead on the bluffs, and now more Potawatomi are found dead at the Smith place. I suppose that could be a coincidence, but I don't think so."

"They were all homicide victims," Vik said. "That eliminates the coincidence theory for me."

Marti emptied the contents of one envelope on her desk. Medical reports, birth certificate, photographs of an unsmiling young man who looked more like the computer composite than she expected, a handwritten list of four jails and their locations.

Vik walked over to her desk and picked up one of the photographs. "Hard to believe that a computer could come this close to the real thing." He picked up another one. "He doesn't look like an Indian. Dana doesn't either. And the grandfather just looks old. Maybe they looked different when the white man came here. If not, getting rid of them must have had something to do with their lifestyle. Five hundred years and they still had clean water and nothing was in danger of extinction."

Marti opened the second envelope. Letters, postcards, a college transcript. Several newspaper clippings. Three obituaries. She put in a call to Dr. Altenberg, who agreed to drive up and take a look at everything first thing tomorrow morning.

* * *

At eleven fifty-five, they went to their meeting with Lieutenant Dirkowitz.

"This has to be about the Smith case," Marti said as they headed for his office. "What do you think?"

"Dirkowitz runs his own shop."

"This is high-profile, spelled political," Marti reminded him. She had seen officers with higher rank and as much integrity take special handling orders and issue them.

"Let's hope that doesn't make a difference, MacAlister. I like being a cop and I'm lousy at politics."

When Marti and Vik entered Lieutenant Dirkowitz's office he was munching on carrot and celery sticks. Marti thought that was taking weight watching to the extreme but said nothing. When he offered to share, she declined.

"I can't remember the last time I talked with the attorney general," Dirkowitz said. "It seems he thinks that a five-year-old case of his takes priority over a current case of mine."

Marti hesitated for a moment, then said, "Does it?"

"Hell, no." He reached for a celery stick and bit it in half. After he had chewed it and swallowed, he said, "I also vetoed another suggestion that you be taken off of the Smith case because it requires a full-time investigation and you're only working on it part-time."

Vik looked at Marti and said, "Now that's a coincidence."

For the first time, Marti wondered if there was some hidden agenda in the sudden importance of the Gonzales case.

The lieutenant picked up the last celery stick, looked at it for a moment, then tossed it into the wastebasket. "For the record, if there is anything routine that can be handled with discretion, like the prints and the DNA samples were, run it by me first. Not because it involves the Smiths, but because whatever happens here and becomes known, by association involves Richard Wagner. The senator and I disagree on a number of issues, but even though he's a Republican, he's entitled to be elected based on his record and his platform; not judged in a polling booth because of family issues that he has nothing to do with." He picked up a carrot stick and pointed it at them. "With that one exception, I expect you to handle this case the way you always do."

Marti looked at Vik. He gave her a thumbs-up.

"Way to go, Lieutenant," she said. "Way to go."

"You think so? Just remember, the buck stops here. Make sure it's legal tender if it does. Now, what have you got for me?"

"It looks like we've identified our skeletal remains," Vik said. They filled him in on Ethan Dana's visit.

"What do you think we're dealing with here?" he asked.

"A family involved in a cover-up," Marti answered. She tried to imagine one of the Smiths actually killing someone and could not. "The question is what—and, more important—why. The bones Dr. Kirkemo is digging up are the first thing we've identified that could have a negative impact on the Smiths, assuming that anyone cares."

"There is the lead mine," Vik said.

The lieutenant picked up the defused hand grenade. "What lead mine? They haven't mined lead around here in at least fifty years."

"This would have been in the early 1820's, sir. MacAlister found records of some old stock certificates on the Internet. They were issued in Idbash Smith's name. We were thinking that maybe those Indians were working those mines."

"And? Indians were mining when the French came here."

Marti had forgotten that the lieutenant had majored in history as an undergraduate.

"The yields in those mines were significantly underreported," she explained.

The lieutenant was thoughtful for a few moments. "You might want to look into that. It would have been a federal offense."

"Statute of limitations?" Vik asked.

"If it involved American Indians, that's hard to say. You could spend years trying to unravel treaties and court decisions that involve Indians."

"What about the Strolling Potawatomi?" Marti asked.

The lieutenant smiled. "They're called that because they wandered around for a long time before they joined the other groups within their tribe. Because of that, they were not included by name in a number of treaties." Dirkowitz also had a law degree. "The question becomes if, and at what point, they became included, and based on precedent, that happened when the original treaties and agreements were drawn up."

"If there is no statute of limitation involved, is there anything else about these treaties that we should be aware of in terms of this case?" Marti asked.

"Only if there is an impediment to the sale of the Smiths' property."

Vik frowned. "How would we find out about that?"

"Any attorney familiar with that aspect of the law would have found it by now."

So much for that, Marti thought. Then she wondered how expert the lawyers involved with the sale of the Smith property might be. Whoever it was could be some old guy who had been retained by the family for the past fifty years.

"While we're on the subject," she said, "do you know anything about slavery in this part of the state?"

"On the subject, MacAlister? That's a stretch." Dirkowitz leaned back and grinned. "What do you want to know? And why?"

"Exceptions to the antislavery law, like working the salt mines."

"That happened in the southern part of the state. They had easy access to slaves in Missouri and Tennessee. The amendment to that law was specific to the mining of salt, not lead or galena or anything else. Salt was like gold back then, a major commodity."

"So there were no laws allowing anyone to do anything like that here?"

"No. We were too far north to have easy access to the slave market. If we did, things might have been different."

"We think slaves might have been kept in the Smiths' root cellar," Vik explained.

"There are rumors that the place was a station on the Underground Railroad."

"There are rumors that Idbash Smith helped the Potawatomi escape north."

"Point taken, Jessenovik. The question is, is any of that having any impact on what's going on there now?"

"Nothing that we can prove, sir," Vik admitted. "Unless we can link Tommy Strongwind's death to the Smiths."

"That might explain one death, but it could be a stretch to link Strongwind to Linski and Buckner," Dirkowitz said. "Is there anything else I need to know now?"

"No, sir."

"Any other questions I can answer?"

Marti shook her head.

He dropped the hand grenade on his desk.

"By the way, MacAlister," he said as they were leaving, "is there anything else I should know about this incident in Springfield?"

"Not that I can think of, sir."

"Their chief of police was impressed."

"Thank you, sir."

As they walked back to their office, Vik said, "What if there is an impediment to the sale? We're talking about lawyers. If there is, maybe they didn't miss it, maybe they decided to overlook it. A lot of money is involved. Think we should mention the possibility to the state's attorney?"

"Do you think they have the time to investigate? Where do you even bigin with something like that?" Marti sighed. "I'll call. They'll probably fall out of their chairs laughing, but I'll call."

As they approached the door to their office, she said, "Which of the Smiths do you think is the killer?"

Vik didn't answer right away. When he did he said, "Good question."

"That's what I thought," she agreed.

"You think they hired someone."

"Sounds more likely."

"I know," Vik agreed. "But I can't see them using anyone local. They'd bring somebody in. Do you know how many killers for hire there could be in this country? With their money they could have imported somebody."

Marti sighed again. "Organized-crime heads are control freaks. I'll make a few calls."

Vik looked at her for a moment, but didn't ask what she meant, or whom she was going to call.

Every trip Marti made to Springfield seemed to take longer than the one before. When she and Vik reached Anne Devney's office, Devney was alone.

"The other attorney who was supposed to be here couldn't make it," she explained. "Something unexpected. You two are familiar with that."

"Good," Vik said. "This will be a short meeting."

"We still have seventeen files to go through," Devney reminded him.

"You have seventeen files to go through. As soon as we get to our testimony, we're out of here."

Devney's posture shifted from relaxed to rigid. "We will have to review the appeal process also."

"No," Vik told her. "You will have to review the appeal process."

Marti alternated between irritation and amusement as they maintained their hostility for the next three and a half hours. When Devney suggested dinner, Vik reached for his jacket and did not respond.

"Damned near eight o'clock," Vik said, as they walked to their car. "But I think she set a record. We almost made it through four files."

"Let's stop and get something to eat on the way home." Dark skies and nearly deserted streets made her think back to Thursday night.

"Beats trying to find a restaurant around here," Vik agreed.

The three blocks surrounding the capital building consisted of office buildings, businesses, and historic Lincoln places. There were apartment buildings on the perimeter and then the usual urban sprawl. All of the streets were one-way, whether north-south or east-west. Marti zigzagged her way to a main street that would get them back to the Interstate. A car pulled up behind her as she stopped for a traffic light. It turned when she did. She slowed, watching for the street she needed to turn right on. Behind her the car lights went out.

"Oh, shit," she said and speeded up. "Mars light. Now. Drive-by."

She saw an alley and swung into it. The car followed, but did not have enough room to pull alongside.

The Mars light began flashing. She speeded up. Leaned on the horn. Reached the end of the alley and turned, tires squealing. The other car turned in the opposite direction. She was going the wrong way down a one-way street. Vik turned off the flashing light.

"What the hell was that all about?"

She explained.

"You sure you're not just jumpy because of the other night?"

"Could be," she admitted. "But they had their lights on when we stopped. They didn't cut them off until after we turned."

"Are we going to report it?"

"Did you get a license plate number? See their faces?"

"No lights," Vik reminded her.

She was certain it wasn't her imagination, but she couldn't be positive someone in the car wanted to shoot them.

"Tinted glass," Vik said. "Illegal. And the car was old. Chevy, maybe. Or a Ninety-Eight."

"Let's just go home."

Marti didn't realize how tired she was until she pulled into the driveway. Trouble was inside and the alarms had been set. Bigfoot, their hundred-and-seventy-pound Heinz 57, met her at the kitchen door. While she was petting him, Trouble came in. Marti petted her too and gave both of them treats. The two dogs weren't the best of friends but they seemed to understand that they each had a different job. Trouble protected. Bigfoot provided comfort and friendship. In their his way, each dog was affectionate. Trouble, always calm but always alert, was dominant.

Marti could hear the boys upstairs. It was late but they didn't have to get up early in the morning. They were probably working on their Potawatomi project. She thought about spending some time with them, went to the refrigerator and found some cold chicken, then made a cup of tea. Upstairs, she watched as Ben and Theo and Mike did something with seashells.

"We had mussels with supper," Mike said. "And clams and oysters."

"Yuck," Theo said.

Marti settled into one of the beanbags. When Ben shook her awake, the boys were already in bed.

18

Isaiah was sitting up and eating Cream of Wheat and toast for breakfast when Omari came in.

"Boy, you didn't tell me you were coming back!"

"I wanted to surprise you. How are you feeling?"

"Tired," Isaiah admitted. "But I'm out of Intensive Care and I'm eating." They had moved him to the Cardiac Care unit. He was not allowed out of bed, and still hooked up to machines and an IV. But they were letting him eat, he could turn off the lights, and he had a TV, not that there was much he wanted to watch.

Omari put his briefcase on the bed and snapped it open. "Uncle Floyd and I talked with your doctor. He gave me thirty minutes to go over this with you—provided you don't get excited and make the alarm on the screen with the squiggles go off." He pulled out a photocopy. "I'll talk. You eat."

"Think you're in charge now, boy?" Isaiah asked. He smiled so Omari would know he was teasing. Omari had always been a quiet, well-behaved boy. Did what he was told. Never a trouble to anyone. Isaiah liked the change he could see in him now. He stirred the Cream of Wheat and tasted it. It was still warm. He didn't mind cold toast but he did prefer his cooked cereal hot. "Tell me what you've got, boy."

Omari grinned. "It can wait. I wouldn't want to interrupt a big breakfast like that."

"Just tell me." Isaiah ate quickly as he listened.

"Yes, sir." Without looking at the photocopied document, he

said, "Edward Thatcher was born in 1868. He married Mellie Bishop in 1889. Edward's parents were Samuel Thatcher and Cynthia, no last name. Samuel's father, who would have been Edward's grandfather, was also named Samuel Thatcher; Edward's grandmother was named Dessa Thatcher."

"Both of them were named Thatcher?"

"Right."

"Then Samuel Senior, and his wife Dessa, had to have been owned by the same master. Makes sense. And it could help us. What else you got for me?"

"You've got to stop interrupting and listen, Grandpa, or you're going to get all tired out. Now, Samuel Senior and Dessa were both born in Jefferson City, Missouri."

"It says that? It actually says that? Let me see."

"Eat your toast, then I'll show you."

"Talk," Isaiah said. As he spread jelly on the cold toast, he wished they would allow him to have butter.

"Samuel Junior was born in Little Fort, Illinois, in 1835. He died in 1878, when his son Edward was ten years old. Here."

Isaiah looked at the copy of Edward's marriage application without touching it. Tears came to his eyes and he brushed them away. "You go see if I can have a little more coffee, boy."

He wiped at his eyes, then looked down at the Xeroxed copy and touched each name with his finger as he said them aloud. Then he said each name again.

"Decaf," Omari said when he returned. "Want sweetener or cream substitute?"

Isaiah shook his head. "Adding that stuff is enough to make you stop drinking it." He tapped the paper. "I think what we've got here is that Samuel Senior and Dessa were runaways who made it to Illinois. Then their baby, Samuel Junior, was born; he married Cynthia, who had been a slave too, and they were Edward's parents."

"Does that mean we've found him?" Omari asked. "The Jacksons said I still have a lot more work to do."

"I've got to think on this awhile. There's not going to be a birth certificate or any record of a black child being born in 1835. Could be something if he fought in the Civil War. Someone had to tell Edward what his history was, who his people were. But, knowing what we do, yes, I think we have found the right Samuel Thatcher."

"Yes!"

"Now what we need to know is what happened to Samuel and Dessa when they reached Little Fort. There might be some kind of record somewhere if we knew what happened next."

"Well, there is something else, but the Jacksons can't exactly prove any of it."

"What? Tell me."

Omari explained about the possible connection to Idbash Smith.

"So," Isaiah said. "If we can't find any record of Samuel and Dessa reaching Wisconsin, they might never have made it, but their child survived somehow."

Omari nodded.

"Better to know," Isaiah said. "Even if that is what happened." He felt too weak to push the tray table away. He was so tired. We're almost there, he thought as he closed his eyes.

"You go back, go back today, boy. You're too close to stop now. Find out if Samuel and Dessa met up with this Smith, and if they did, what happened to them. We could have other relatives out there, kinfolk we don't even know about."

Omari moved the table, adjusted his pillow, pulled the covers up to his chin. "You rest now," he said. "I'll leave quick as I can and call as soon as I find out something. And Grandpa, I think we came from Ethiopia, too."

"You did good, boy," Isaiah told him. "You did real good, boy. Real good. Your daddy is going to be pleased with you, your Uncle Floyd, too."

Josiah stood at the window and wondered what was happening at the place where the Indian village had been. They must have found something by now. Idbash's map showed the circumference of the village and the center, where he had ordered Buckner to dig. Idbash had not been pleased with the Indians who lived there. According to his journal, he could not "abide this insurrection by a people so docile and trusting that they were now being forced from their land. They will return to the lead mines," he wrote, "every one of them, or they will die." Another entry said, "They chose now to become stubborn. Their elders complain that too many have the falling sickness. It is true that a goodly number of them can no longer move their limbs and will soon die. This is the cause of much of their unrest, but not one among them is willing to put down those who sicken." A final entry said, "Not even shooting those nigras convinced them. Now I will require even more nigras. They go to the mines without complaint, but they get the breathing sickness much more quickly. I tell them that once they get sick I will settle up with them for their wages and help them continue north. Instead we just take them to the veined-out places in the mines."

Josiah felt the back of his head begin to throb. He thought it might be from lack of sleep but it seemed like a peculiar place to get a headache. If it persisted, he might even see a doctor, but he expected that all of his "headaches" would soon be gone. He had spoken with his attorney yesterday. They would sign the papers for the land sale that afternoon.

He had already purchased a home in Boca Raton. He would fly there this Sunday. Cook would follow in a week to look after him and the house. Paul and Franklin could fight over who got the summer place in Michigan and the condos in Colorado and Arizona. It would require that they speak to each other and perhaps behave like civilized men. It was that or attorney fees and perhaps years in court.

It would not have pleased Idbash to know that after all he had done to acquire this land, twenty acres adjacent to the forest preserve, twenty-five acres along the river, this house and ten acres of the land that surrounded it, would be given away.

Josiah had agreed to the land donations because Paul and

Franklin were against it. Richard didn't care one way or the other, even though the trust for maintaining the house could become a considerable drain, which would impact his share the most because he had the most heirs. Kat Malloy had seen the potential for vote-garnering and favor-currying and kickbacks right away. Between her political connections and Eileen's realty and contractor connections, they would recover a significant portion of the loss they were taking on the sale.

Kat and Eileen. Was that how the land developer got so much inside information about Idbash's mine and land deals? No, that wasn't possible. Not only did neither know anything, but they were too greedy to do anything that would reduce their share. Even though Kat wasn't included in the trust, and Eileen wasn't named either, both women, as well as Jessica, would receive a cash settlement. A payoff, Franklin said. Josiah suspected that the only reason Eileen hadn't divorced Franklin was because he had no way to access the trust fund.

No, the developer found out exactly the way he said he did. Competition, curiosity, persistent research, and a brother who happened to be a Harvard law professor. Needless to say, the developer would only tell him enough of what he found out to ensure that the cost of the land was to his advantage. Josiah couldn't fault the man for that. He would have done the same thing.

Marti and Vik arrived at the coroner's facility at 7:51 A.M. Dr. Cyprian was waiting for them. The office area was dark, the glare of the overhead lights and white walls sudden as they walked into one of the labs. The skeletal remains were in the autopsy room, arranged on a stainless-steel table.

Dr. Altenberg arrived at eight-ten. Coffee wasn't ready yet. When Dr. Cyprian offered to share a thermos of coffee with her, Altenberg declined.

"No need. I filled two travel cups before I left home and had a couple of Danish while I listened to Verdi and played stop-and-go in rush-hour traffic." She began going through the contents of the envelope with Tommy Strongwind's medical records. Some papers she tossed aside with a glance. She read others and made notes. After she had gone through everything twice, she said, "Let's take another look at the remains. We'll need a couple of X rays."

While that was being done, Altenberg examined the skull. "We don't have either of the index fingers," she said. "Too bad. One had been broken. And there are no dental records here. He did have several fillings."

"We'll request information from the jails where he was held," Marti said. "Sometimes they have to see a dentist while they're locked up."

"Don't forget this." She pointed to the bump on the bone where his ear would have been. "This indicates Gardner's Syndrome, a hereditary disease. You need to talk with someone in the family. If anyone had thyroid and or colon cancer, that would be a significant indicator. Autopsy reports would be more conclusive, but the medical history should suffice."

Marti made a note to ask Mr. Nozhagum right away.

When Dr. Cyprian returned with the X rays just taken, the two doctors compared them with the medical notes.

"Contact this hospital," Altenberg said. "Get copies of their X rays. This looks like a match."

She consulted with Dr. Cyprian for a few minutes, then said, "Matching the dental work, and the fractures, will be sufficient. But if you can confirm the familial cancer, that would confirm it. A very small percentage of the population has Gardner's Syndrome." She handed Marti the paperwork. "And thanks for inviting me back. I don't get to follow up on these caseso very often." She looked at the clock. "Driving back to the city will take longer than getting here did. I need to get moving."

When Marti reached Mr. Nozhagum, he confirmed several cases of cancer, but didn't know what kind. He did give her the name of a doctor she could talk with. She got the doctor's answering service and he returned her call about ten minutes later. "Five of the Strongwinds have died of colon cancer so far. Gardner's Syndrome. Everyone in the family needs to be followed up so we can catch the cancer in time, but it's difficult to get people to do that. I never saw anyone named Tommy, but from what you've told me, he did have it. And genetically it's passed on by the male."

By the time Marti had poured a cup of Cowboy's coffee and snagged a chocolate-covered doughnut, she was talking in lists.

". . . and the state's attorney I talked with about the lead mining and land deeds, he actually sounded excited. Said it's the most interesting thing he's come across since law school, except for prosecuting a capital crime."

Vik helped himself to another jelly-filled. "It takes all kinds. Researching anything sounds about as exciting as working that dig site."

"Tedious," Marti agreed. She preferred caffeine fixes and the occasional adrenaline rush.

She checked the handwritten list of jails Tommy Strongwind had been in: Tacoma, Washington; Great Falls, Montana; Willow City, North Dakota; and Minneapolis, Minnesota. She called each in turn.

"Misdemeanors," she told Vik. "Fighting, public drunkenness, petty theft, nothing major. He got a tooth pulled while he was jailed in Tacoma, and they had to replace two fillings in Willow City. They're faxing the paperwork directly to Dr. Cyprian, with the X rays to follow by overnight mail."

She hesitated, picked up the manila envelope with Strongwind's personal correspondence, hesitated again and then pulled everything out. Marti couldn't put the obituaries and newspaper clippings in any context. Tommy wasn't mentioned in any of them and she couldn't figure out their importance.

He had sent six letters, four postcards and three birthday cards to his cousin Ethan. Marti arranged them by type, with the most recent postmarks last. Then she began reading. Each birthday card had a reference to some childhood event that was illustrated by the picture on the front. "Remember when we tried to tape and glue knives to our shoes so we could ice skate?"

The postcards made similar references. "No lake trout here but the salmon are bigger," from Washington State. "Beats the hell out of drag racing on the rez"—a snow-covered ski slope in Montana.

She opened the letters last. They were short, none more than a page.

"Sorry, I did it again. Can't seem to keep my mouth shut or my hands in my pockets."

"Getting married, huh? Church, I bet. Me, I'd have a drumming ceremony. Maybe someday you'll go back to the old ways."

"A kid! You, Ethan, a father? Tell Grandpa."

The one sent from the jail in Minneapolis said, "When I come home this time it's back to the rez for good. I finally got far enough away to miss being home."

She felt as if she had eavesdropped on a very personal conversation as she returned everything to the manila envelope.

Dr. Kirkemo called to say that her phase of the excavation would be completed by the end of the day. They drove out to talk with her before she left. Usually, the workers were relaxed and talkative. Today there was little conversation and everyone seemed intent on what they were doing. Vik was right—too much monotony.

"We've found more silver ornaments," Dr. Kirkemo said. "And a few utensils and tools. Even some toys. The archaeologist doing the dating has narrowed it to the early nineteenth century. The German silver precludes anything earlier than 1800. Their removal was completed in 1836."

Marti felt her jaws tighten as she thought of the small skulls. "What about lead deposits?" she asked. "Can they still tell if any of them worked in lead mines?"

"What's that about lead?" Dr. Kirkemo asked.

"Extraordinary," she exclaimed after Marti explained. "Wait until everyone hears about this!"

"We were not going to remove the bones. They belong to the Potawatomi. But now we'll have to ask for a representative sampling."

"How many bodies were buried there?" Vik asked.

"We're estimating forty."

"Two children, for sure," Marti said.

"Two small children. I'm sure there are more, but older. There are defense wounds on the bones of the hands and arms. And, in a few instances, bullet wounds."

Vik exhaled. "Damn."

"What happens now?" Marti asked.

"The proper government authorities have been notified. The digging will continue until everything is recovered. We've also spoken with a local tribal elder. The Potawatomi will determine what to do with their dead. Maybe a ghost feast and a religion or drum dance and burial. Their rituals are centuries-old and I'm not sure how things like not knowing the victims' names impact what they do."

"A ghost feast," Marti repeated.

"Explaining that can get a little complicated, but basically someone represents the deceased, a Feast of the Dead is prepared, and everybody eats. For some tribes it's a way of remembering the person who has died. Other tribes have a more formal belief in reincarnation or rebirth. They all believe in some kind of spirit life."

"There are rumors of a ghost on this property," Marti said.

Dr. Kirkemo nodded. "Could be."

"Nobody believes in ghosts," Vik said.

"Nor have I ever seen one," Dr. Kirkemo agreed. "However, a person's belief system is a very powerful thing. And I never question that."

Before they returned to the precinct they drove over to the site near the river where Linski's body had been found. Everything had been filled in and the area had been sodded. If Marti didn't know where the holes had been, she wouldn't be able to find them now. The barn was next. Two-by-fours secured the door or window from which Harry Buckner had fallen or been pushed. The doors at ground level were open. The backhoe was inside the barn, but the rider mower was gone.

"Look's like he's been replaced," Vik said.

Promptly at one o'clock, Josiah's attorney and the attorneys for the developers arrived along with the president of the architectural firm and the contractors who would be in charge of building the homes. Thanks to Kat and Eileen, in addition to the sale of the land, the Smith estate would also receive a percentage from the sale of each house. Cook showed everyone into the library, then left. Josiah had made sure that everyone else would be away for the day.

"Here are the contracts, Josiah," his attorney told him. "We'll go over each page."

It seemed to Josiah that there were dozens of legal-sized sheets of paper with typing on both sides. Several times he lost track of what his attorney was saying but he didn't ask for clarification. He just wanted to get this over with. With the exception of his lawyer, he didn't think anyone present knew about the accidents. He had kept the news releases to a minimum and the exact locations weren't mentioned. They didn't know about the excavating either. But he wanted them away from here as quickly as possible.

"Now," his lawyer concluded, "since we are all in agreement, let's begin signing."

Josiah tried not to seem eager as he took his turn. No matter what the status of the land, he would have legal documents and two checks in hand. The developers could worry if any claims were made by the government or the Indians. He didn't see any need to concern himself with the colored. Fugitives couldn't make any claims.

The attorneys passed the documents around. There were

multiple places to sign or initial. By the time Josiah signed his name for the last time, he was getting cramps in his hand. He sent for Cook and they celebrated with a round of drinks.

Everyone was smiling as they left. Josiah's attorney remained behind. He had handled the family's business since his father retired and postponed his own retirement to take care of this, even though he had had a small stroke last winter.

"This is the end of it," Josiah said.

"Yes, this is it."

"Are there any possible obstacles now?"

His lawyer leaned forward, a concerned expression on his face. "Josiah, you have been so anxious to have this deal completed. It isn't your health, is it?"

"No, no, I'm fine. We've just had the land so long and the parcels were added on so randomly."

"Yes, but within a very short period of time, and also a very long time ago. All of your documents were examined by both sides and found to be in order. Barring some unforeseen impediment—and I can't think of one that we've overlooked—everything is fine. We're home free."

Home free, Josiah thought. Nothing had been overlooked, at least nothing the lawyers were aware of; both he and the developer had been selective about that. Now that their discretion had been rewarded, he would board that flight to Florida Sunday afternoon and never look back.

"Josiah?"

"Oh, yes, sorry. I was thinking . . ."

"I know. And this is quite a sum of money to be thinking about, even though we could have gone with someone else and received considerably more."

"And given considerably more to the government. And of all of the plans and designs, I did like what this developer wants to do the best."

"Good. Good. There is one more thing, though. You're going to have to let me know when you want to schedule a photo session."

"Photos?"

"Yes, of course. The newspapers. You're making a very generous gift of land to three county organizations."

"No, please. Handle that as quietly as possible." That would be all that he needed, something to draw attention to the family. Better to let Kat Malloy use it to Richard's advantage. Sometimes Josiah wished that Richard were his son. He was the only one of his generation to make something of himself. "There won't be anything about selling the land in the newspaper? You said . . ."

"Yes. It's your land. Your decision. And with all of the fuss about land development these days, everyone agreed we should be discreet. Of course sooner or later someone will notice the houses going up." He paused. "Yes, you're right. We'll say nothing about the land gifts now. Then when the 'green people' begin their hue and cry about losing skunk and opossum habitats and accelerating the extinction of the spotted tree toad, we will announce the land gifts.

"As you saw in the contracts, Josiah, they did make a few changes and the homes will be built on smaller parcels of land. They will be meeting the minimum criteria for lot sizes. This will increase the population impact on community resources. More houses means more money for you, but we did have to sweeten the pot for the additional city services they will require. Even so, when everything nets out, everyone will see a considerable profit."

Josiah nodded. He felt so tired. It was over. At last it was over. He felt as if he were breaking a promise. Idbash had intended that this land remain in the family forever, but he had buried too many secrets here. Now those secrets had to be obliterated. He had had no other choice than to do what he did.

The office was quiet except for the clang of a chain against the flagpole outside their window. Marti hoped that the wind had picked up because it was going to rain, which meant that it might cool down for a few hours at least. She looked out the window. The only clouds she could see were thin, wispy, and white. The clanging stopped as abruptly as it had begun. She got another cup of coffee and pulled out the Linski and Buckner files. She read through her notes and all of the reports.

"A medal," she said as she looked at Linski's property report from the coroner's office.

Vik looked up.

"She had a medal and some change in her pocket. Don't you wear a medal around your neck?"

"Maybe the chain got broken."

She kept reading until she came to "religious affiliation." "I don't think Christian Scientists wear medals."

"They are small," Vik said.

Marti put in a call to Larissa's mother.

"Oh, that," Mrs. Linski said. "Yes. Larissa always kept some little memento from places she visited."

Marti recalled Mrs. Linski telling her that.

"I don't know what it is, but it can't be anything important or Larissa wouldn't have kept it."

"Can you describe it to me?"

"Sure, just let me get it."

When Mrs. Linski returned to the phone, Marti had a pencil and a piece of paper ready.

"This is made of metal and it's really old. There are numbers and letters stamped on it. Draw a triangle with one-inch sides. Put a hole at the top point. Now, in the center, put the number 83-2962. Above that, print in capital letters JCMO. Below that number in lower-case letters write 'smi.' "

"That's it?' Marti asked.

"That's it. I hope this doesn't mean that I have to give it to you. Can I keep it?"

"For now," Marti said. "I have no idea of what it is. Until I find out, I can't make any promises."

"When I got back home, there was a letter from Larissa waiting for me. She did that sometimes, when she had something difficult to tell me. She had decided that she still wanted to be an anthropologist, but that she wanted to do something similar to what she was doing there. Not just identify or record what had happened, but find some way to restore places to the way they had been or, as she put it, the way they once were and should be again. So that site was a very special place to her. And that makes this a very special memento to me."

"I understand," Marti said. "If we do need this, I'll see to it that you get it back."

Marti showed the drawing to Vik. "Odd, isn't it?"

They played with the letters for a while without coming up with anything.

"Time to bring in the experts again," she said. "These cases have sure expanded my definition of evidence."

Dr. Altenberg and Dr. Kirkemo both suggested that she fax what she had drawn. Neither of them had any idea of what it could be. While she was at it, she called Gordon McIntosh. He had left for the day. Marti sent him a fax, too.

That done, she continued reading through the documents in the folders.

A short time later, Vik said, "If Linski found this thing you drew a picture of where she was digging, I don't see how anyone could figure out something this small had been there unless there was more than one. But if there was, what did she do with the others, and why didn't she put them in her reports?"

Marti told him what Linski's mother had said. "Maybe she didn't want to find anything."

"But she did. And that was her job. That's what they were paying her for."

"I know, and she was probably responsible and all of that, but she was young. And, based on her decision to restore things to the way they were, she might have seen this as an obstacle to that and decided this was not that important. According to her mother, she seemed to have found her mission in life. Maybe sending this to her was symbolic of that."

"Mission," Vik scoffed. "Finding other people's garbage in piles of dirt is not a mission, MacAlister."

"Artifacts, Vik, artifacts."

"Garbage," Vik repeated. "What do you do with a porcupine quill, a buffalo hoof, and a clam shell? You throw them away."

"They were mussel shells."

"MacAlister, they are sifting through a garbage heap."

"And a graveyard," she said.

"Only because they found the garbage first."

"Well, Larissa wasn't supposed to find anything."

"And you think she decided that this, whatever it is, should not have been found."

"Exactly. Why risk something you care about for an old piece of metal that's probably worthless?"

"Because that's your job," Vik said.

"But when we do our job, we have to think, evaluate, make decisions. All Larissa was told to do was look, and if you find, tell. Instead, she made a decision."

Vik considered that, then said, "If she had followed orders, we wouldn't have this. Nickel bet it turns out to mean nothing."

"Nickel bet that twenty years from now, you won't be lying awake at night wondering what in the hell something relatively small could have been."

Ben was on duty. Instead of driving home, Marti went by the fire station. The trucks and the ambulance were inside. Ben was watching a baseball game with Allan and a couple of the other guys. He gave her a look that said, "Want to talk?" Marti shook her head and sat beside him. He put his arm around her and said, "Long night." She nodded. She leaned against his shoulder and didn't wake up until the alarm went off. It was just an ambulance call, no fire. As she drove home alone, she thought about the drawing she had tucked into her purse. It wasn't a medal, but what was it?

19

Marti was still puzzling over the letters and numbers on the drawing she had made of Larissa's memento of her trip here when Gordon McIntosh called. "Where did you find a slave tag?" he asked.

"A what?"

"A slave tag. That drawing you sent—"

"You've got to be kidding. How do you know what it is?"

"I know because I didn't go off on some exotic Egyptian or Middle East dig. I went to Alabama and Mississippi and Louisiana. I dug up a lot of slave artifacts. That's a slave tag."

Slaves had been kept in the root cellar. "What else can you tell me about it?"

"What would you like to know?"

"What the letters and numbers mean."

"Piece of cake," Gordon told her. "JCMO is Jefferson City, Missouri. The numbers are the slave owner's numeric code to keep track of his slaves. I'm not sure where you would find records of that. And, 'smi' in small letters indicates the slave's job or trade. In this case I'm guessing 'smith,' as in blacksmith."

"Why did slaves have these?"

"The tag allowed them to travel within certain boundaries without an overseer's supervision. It meant that they were considered trustworthy. Although why any sane person would expect someone who was treated the way slaves were treated to be trustworthy is beyond me."

"This is a long way from Missouri," Marti said.

"MacAlister, you found this at the Smith place, didn't you?"

"Maybe. You're positive that this is a slave tag?"

"I know what it is. I've found a few."

Marti looked at the drawing. At first she tried to think about who number 83-2962 might have been; if it was a man or a woman. Based on what Gordon had told her, it wouldn't have been a child. Because of the discoveries made at the Potawatomi site, she didn't want to think too much about the root cellar, but she had to.

Slaves, runaway slaves, were free labor. What if they weren't being hidden there until they could continue north, but detained until they could be taken to the lead mines? Was this tag overlooked by someone, or did someone leave it there deliberately, in the hope that someone would find it and know they had been there? She shared what Gordon had told her and what she suspected with Vik.

"We can't prove where that came from," he said. "We can connect it with Linski, but she didn't leave us any record of its existence. At least with Buckner we've got circumstantial evidence, but with this . . ." He shook his head. "Damned shame. We know someone killed her and this probably was why." He snapped a pencil in half, then another. "And we can't lean on the Smiths yet. Not until we've got more than this." He thought for a moment. "Makes you wonder what was on that shelf in the barn."

Marti stared at the phone. "I haven't heard anything on a possible hit. Maybe we should take a trip into the city this evening. Let me make a couple of appointments and we'll talk to a few people. I don't think they would do any local recruiting for something like that, too risky. You okay with being away from Mildred?"

"I'll have supper with her, bring her some flowers."

"Flowers, Jessenovik?"

"She likes fresh-cut flowers." He didn't seem embarrassed by the question, but then, they had been partners for a long time now. "She likes the bunches with different kinds. I used to worry that she'd think she was really sick if I brought them home, but now I just do it."

It was mid-afternoon when Mr. Nozhagum came in with another elderly man. Marti offered them coffee, and when they accepted poured the last of Cowboy's morning batch into Styrofoam cups.

Neither of the men wanted sugar or cream. They tasted it, smiled, and nodded. Marti decided to let Cowboy know they liked it. Unlike Slim, he could accept a compliment without swaggering.

Marti assumed that Mr. Nozhagum had come because of Tommy Strongwind.

"We come from the place of the bones," he said instead. "We do not think they should be moved but we would like to talk with the people who own that place and we are told we cannot."

"You've been to the dig site where we think the village was? How are you involved in that?"

Mr. Nozgahum nodded toward the other man. "The doctor from the university came to talk with my friend."

"Do you think this has something to do with Tommy's death?" Maybe these two could provide a connection.

"I don't know," Mr. Nozhagum told her.

The other man said, "We are here because there are things we need to find out before we can move them. Tommy has already been moved. He is Strolling Potawatomi and we know what to do when we take him home."

Both men seemed sad.

"You can take Tommy as soon as we are sure that this is him," Marti promised. "As for the others, it's complicated. The government had to be notified. Is that a problem for you?"

"Only if they say we cannot have our dead," the second man said. His skin was like copper, his face narrow and lined, his eyes dark with prominent brows, his nose long.

Marti could not stop herself from thinking that unlike Mr. Nozhagum, he looked like an American Indian. She wasn't pleased with herself for making that comparison.

"We also need to know what happened there and who they are," Mr. Nozhagum said.

"The spirits of these dead are troubled and they cannot rest until the proper drumming or dance has been done," the other man said. "The burial ceremonies cannot be held until we know how they died and if they were Prairie Band Potawatomi or Strolling Potawatomi like us, or maybe even members of the Pokagon or Huron bands."

"How will you find out?" Marti asked. "This happened a long time ago."

"The land tells us that it was in the time before the removal," the man explained. "All tribes have elders who can tell the stories of those who came before and what happened during those times and what is rumored about those times. We just have to keep asking until we find the one who knows about this."

"These people were murdered," Mr. Nozhagum said. "We are not a vengeful people, and it is late to seek justice, but the woman who found them thinks the bones might tell their stories. So we have given permission for them to be photographed, and let her choose those she needs to take away and study. The rest of the bones must stay where they are until those they take now are returned. You can see to that?"

"Yes," Marti assured him. "Nothing will be removed from that site without your permission and nothing will be done with those remains without your consent."

"Thank you," Mr. Nozhagum said. "There is one thing, though. My grandson."

When Marti didn't reply, he said, "My brother did the drum dance after Tommy was born. Before he died, Tommy came to me to learn and understand his clan history. Ethan and Tommy have been like brothers from the time they were born. They left the reservation because they did not want to be Neshnabek, or, as you know us, Potawatomi. Tommy returned. Perhaps now he will help Ethan find his way back."

211

Vik cleared his throat. The two men turned to looked at him. "But you don't know why Tommy came here?"

Mr. Nozhagum shook his head. "No. Ethan does not know either. Or so he says."

After Mr. Nozhagum and his friend had left, Marti marveled that those two old men could sit down with young men like Ethan and Tommy and tell them things about their people that had happened maybe two hundred, even three or four hundred years ago. She had no idea of where to go to get information like that about her family.

She looked down at her drawing of the slave tag again. She thought about the Underground Railroad and runaway slaves and root-cellar hiding places. What questions should she ask about that? Whom should she ask? She had called the North American Indian Center when she had questions about the Potawatomi. She knew of no equivalent place to call to ask about African-American slaves. She called the DuSable Museum, the Harold Washington Library and the Newberry Library. She asked one question. Could anyone give her any information about an Underground Railroad conductor in what was now Lake County or Lincoln Prairie by the name of Idbash Smith? The three people she spoke with promised to look into it and call her back.

When Marti's stomach gave a long loud rumble, she realized they had been in the office all day without even a lunch break. She suggested a sandwich at the Barrister since Vik planned to go home and have supper with Mildred before he accompanied her into the city. They walked. It had been about eighty degrees when she left home that morning. It felt closer to a hundred degrees now. Even the petunias looked wilted and they were well-watered and growing in concrete planters that were shaded by trees. The streets around the precinct were never crowded. They were deserted now. Marti's blouse was sticking to her back by the time they walked the short distance to the pub. The

212

air-conditioning hit her as soon as she walked through the door. A too-late-for-lunch and too-early-for-dinner crowd sat at the bar and filled most of the tables and booths. A waitress brought frosty glasses of iced tea garnished with thick slices of lemon almost as soon as they sat down.

Instead of going home, Marti stopped at the softball field where Joanna's game was in progress. It was the fifth inning and Joanna's team was still in the game, down by only one run. The shortstop made an error in the sixth inning and they lost by two, but Marti had watched enough softball games to know that the team was making significant improvements. After the game, she hung around long enough to congratulate the girls and listened as the coach told her how much Joanna was contributing to the team. Joanna took the coach's praise in stride.

"Last year my team only lost two games, Ma," Joanna said as she walked Marti to her car. "I got so used to winning I forgot how good it feels."

"I am so proud of you," Marti told her, and gave her a big hug.

The bus from Grand Rapids arrived in Chicago forty minutes late. Omari had intended to try to reach the Jacksons as soon as he arrived, but now he didn't have time. He got into a cab, pulled the slip of paper with the address out of his pocket and read it aloud. The driver asked him to repeat it, then said, "It's a long ride. Lots of money. Forty dollars, maybe."

"That's okay." His father and his Uncle Floyd had slipped him some extra money. "I need to be on this corner in fifteen minutes."

"Twenty minutes, maybe. Twenty-five. We can't do it in fifteen."

Omari had not seen much of Chicago. The cabdriver got on one of the expressways and as Omari watched from the window, the tall buildings that crowded the skyline were soon behind him. The pink-streaked sky became dark. Crowded streets gave way to wider, less populated avenues with three-story apartment buildings and chain-link fences and flower boxes. When the cabby pulled over near a corner on a street not unlike the street the Jacksons lived on, Omari was glad to be in a place that seemed familiar and not much different from the street he lived on in Grand Rapids.

He stood near the corner with his suitcase and waited for a silver Expedition to pull up. He was ten minutes late but he didn't think that mattered. The gentleman he had spoken with, Josiah Smith, seemed anxious to meet with him, but explained that although he could not on such short notice, another family member could. Mr. Smith said he had many documents that had belonged to his grandfather, Idbash, and that once he had narrowed that down to what Omari needed, he would be pleased to share that information with him if he could.

Omari looked about for a telephone, but didn't see one. He had tried several times to call the Jacksons, to share the good news with them, but also to see if there were any names that they wanted to add to Samuel's. He looked about as he waited. The street was almost deserted. There was little traffic and he saw only a woman walking a dog about half a block away. The city still surprised him. When he thought of Chicago, he thought of the el train and car chases and smoke-filled bars with hookers standing outside and flagging cars. Seeing it like this was so different that he wasn't worried or afraid at all.

He was thinking of how happy Grandpa had been that morning, and how tired and gray he looked, when two men came from behind him, one on each side. Before he could speak, he felt a sharp pain in his side, then another.

Post-rush-hour traffic was light as Marti drove into the city. She exited on Cicero, which was north of the Dan Ryan/Kennedy Expressway junction, and proceeded west past Milwaukee Avenue. It was a quiet neighborhood. Not many trees, but little patches of grass in front of brick bungalows and window boxes filled with flowers.

A Hispanic woman wearing an apron admitted them. They

followed her down the hall to a screened-in porch. The man sitting there rose to greet them.

"Detective MacAlister. Long time no see." He was six inches shorter than she was, and wore Bermuda shorts and sandals and spoke with just a hint of Italy in his voice. His hairline had continued to recede since the last time she saw him. From the size of his waist, he was still eating too much pasta. "Sit down, sit down."

They sat in wicker chairs with thick cushions and he sat across from them on a sofa. "So, once a cop, always a cop, huh? Things must be a lot quieter, though, that far north."

The woman returned carrying a tray with a pitcher of iced tea and some glasses. Marti knew the woman was his wife, but she could not remember her name.

"It is sweet tea," the wife said. "I will bring ice now." When she returned she put a silver ice bucket on the table.

The man waited until she had left the room again. He spread his hands out, palms up and said, "So."

Marti poured herself a glass of tea, and poured one for Vik, then she explained what she needed to know.

"A small thing, snuffing somebody," the man said. "But not something you want an amateur to think he can get away with. Be chaos out there if that happened. Got to keep things like that under control. If there is such a person and we find out who it is, are you going to be needing to talk to him, or can we just . . ."

"I'll need to talk to him, have him finger his contacts."

"Ah, well, the boys will go along with that if I ask them too."

"Thanks, Paisan," Marti said. She finished her tea. Vik hadn't touched his.

"What the hell was that all about?" he asked as soon as they were outside.

Marti mentioned a name. "Ever hear of him?"

"That wasn't—"

"No, that was just one of his assistants."

"Damn, Marti."

"Trust me," Marti said. "If the Smiths put out a contract or a hired a hit, he'll know before morning."

"What will we owe him for that information?"

"This isn't television, Vik. It doesn't work that way. This guy is just another snitch. The only difference is that he's a little higher up on the food chain."

"Where are we off to now?" Vik asked when they were back in the car.

"To see Don Corleone," Marti teased.

Vik swore in Polish.

"This is just a friend. Jessenovik. Just a friend."

"Right, like the last guy."

"Just wait until tomorrow," she said. "Seeing Gonzales in prison is big time, not this."

The thought of being in an enclosed space without a weapon where hundreds of felons were confined made her stomach churn.

Vik didn't say much as she drove over to Hyde Park. She found a parking space and they walked a half a block to a rehabbed row house not far from the University of Chicago Hospital campus.

Angie Hutton, a slender woman with dark hair pulled back in a ponytail, opened the door.

"Marti, come on in." She looked Vik over. "This is the new partner, huh?" She didn't seem impressed.

They followed her down to the basement where the White Sox were losing on a fifty-two-inch television screen. The sound was turned off.

"Beer?" Hutton asked. "Who's driving?"

Marti declined and so did Vik. They each had a Coke instead.

"So, what's this about a hit?"

Marti explained again.

"You talk to Paisan?"

"Just left there."

"They'll give it up if they know something. Self-preservation.

Of course, if it's a cowboy, they might want him first. The Smith family, huh? That's interesting."

"You've heard of them?" Marti asked.

"Well, it's not like they publicize their activities, but one of them has a ghost job with the state gaming board that has to conflict with being on the state lottery board and the president of a bank with international affiliates. We've been working on building a case for almost a year now."

"The things people will do for money. Especially those who already have too much."

"And with the wife on the real estate board that controls everything that is built, torn down, or rehabbed for the city, you can bet the deal they've worked out to develop their land is a blockbuster. Everyone from the guy who builds the houses to the guy who installs the plumbing will be kicking in something for the honor of doing business with the city."

"Have you heard any rumors about one of them putting out a contract?"

"Nothing. Not even a rumor. The Smiths? Why would they?" Angie asked.

"I wish I knew."

"What about the senator?" Marti asked.

"Oh, yes, Richard Wagner. Sure you won't have a beer?" When Marti and Vik declined again, Angie Hutton got herself a bottle of Killian's Irish Red. "The politicians are all in each other's pockets and we've got the new stadium project, we want to expand O'Hare, we don't want another airport in Peotone, and then there is the matter of who gets the tenth casino license. Big issues. Big money. The senator is in and out of town a lot. Nice wife, smiles for the camera at state and local functions, doesn't object when Kat Malloy travels with him to Washington."

"Kat Malloy?"

"His mistress, also known as the power behind the throne. If you can't see him, you see her. The two of them are grooming his oldest son to be his successor. Rumor has it they've got their eye on the attorney general's office next time around. Junior's working his way through the ranks. He's on the appellate court right now."

Before they left, Hutton said, "I've whispered in the right ears and I've got my ear to the ground. The possibilities on this one are interesting, to say the least."

As soon as they got outside, Vik said, "Cop friend of yours?"

"Not exactly," Marti answered. "FBI."

Vik whistled.

"Angie Hutton heads the fraud division here. You wouldn't believe what comes across her desk. She knows something about damned near everything that goes on in the city and everybody who has anything to do with the action."

Vik was silent as they headed back to the Dan Ryan. As they passed the China Town exit, he said, "There's not much excitement for you working in Lincoln Prairie, is there?"

"No," she agreed. "But I get to work my cases from beginning to end. I'm not constantly mentally fatigued or physically exhausted. I don't worry about burnout. I have time for my family. My kids don't complain that they never see me. Most of the time, I'm not too tired for my husband. Sometimes I get to do something to help somebody. And I work with a partner who is still married to his childhood sweetheart and, after twenty-five years on the force, still believes there is good in the world."

Vik didn't have any comeback for that, but he was smiling again.

20

When Marti woke up, so many things came to mind that she knew it was just a way to avoid thinking about that afternoon's prison visit with Gonzales. She left the house before anyone was up and arrived at the precinct right behind Vik. They were just in time for roll call. Vik seemed distracted. He didn't laugh at the sergeant's joke or acknowledge Lupe's greeting when she waved at him from across the room. He didn't even want a slice of Momma's banana bread when they reached the office.

"What's wrong with Mildred, Jessenovik?"

"Muscle spasms," he said. "In her legs."

"When is she going to see the doctor?"

"This morning."

"Go with her. I'll call if I need you."

"Helen is going to take her."

"Maybe you should go too."

Vik didn't answer right away. "She gets more upset if I go. Thinks there's something we're not telling." He picked up some paper clips that were scattered on his desk, put them in a drawer, then said, "The remissions keep getting shorter. I'm going to call the doctor before we drive downstate."

"Why don't you take her out to dinner when we get back?"

"Good idea," he agreed.

Dr. Cyprian called to let her know that they had made a positive identification on Tommy Strongwind based on medical reports and dental X rays. Marti thought of Tommy's cousin, Ethan Dana, and of the grandfather who was now guarding other Potawatomi bones. Tommy was a Strolling Potawatomi. At least they would know which burial rite to perform.

By the time Cowboy made coffee and left with Slim for pretrial meetings with the state's attorney, a uniform had delivered fourteen single-spaced pages of computer printouts faxed in by Ethan Dana.

"Too bad it's not this easy to get information on African-American slaves," Marti complained. Each page had the date August 17 of last year at the bottom. Marti read through them. There was no obvious organization, just sections of conversation that seemed verbatim, notes, questions—some answered—random thoughts, ideas, passages from books that were footnoted. Nothing cohesive. She read through them twice and figured out Tommy had been documenting his and Ethan Dana's family's history.

It began with relocation. Not all of Ethan and Tommy's clan had traveled west. A Potawatomi woman named Naawe had traveled with a slave woman named Dessa and her child, Samuel, from Lake Michigami, now Lake Michigan, to Lake Superior, where they all settled. Naawe was great-great-grandmother to Ethan's mother and Tommy's mother.

The connection between Naawe and Dessa was not further explained, except for a notation that Samuel was named for his father and had married Cynthia. Samuel Junior and Cynthia had five children. Only the youngest and only male child, Edward, was named.

Tommy did have a reason for coming here, but Marti didn't know what it was. She read through everything twice, but found no connection to the Smiths. She tapped her finger on the faxed sheets and wondered if this was the extent of Tommy's files, then put in a call to Ethan Dana. He was not at home.

"Did you call the doctor?" she asked Vik before they left to meet with Devney and Gonzales.

"They made some changes in her medication, gave her something for depression." Vik sounded depressed, too.

"It's noon now. We should be back by six. Spend some time with her this evening."

"Time. Right." He sighed.

"This doesn't look much like a prison," Vik said, as they approached the red brick building.

"Except for the observation towers and the razor wire along the fence," Marti agreed.

"They really keep the grounds up."

"Trustees," Marti explained. She pulled into the parking lot.

Once inside, they signed in. Vik gave her an uneasy look as they relinquished their weapons.

"Now what?" he asked.

"Now we wait until they call our names and then we get searched. I hope you don't have any contraband in your shoes. Oh, and they stamp your hand."

Marti hated being searched. She felt more like a prisoner than a guest.

When Vik rejoined her, he didn't look too comfortable either. "They let me keep twenty dollars," he told her.

They went through a series of interlocking glass doors with guards on the other side of the windows watching them. The doors closed behind them, sealing them in before the next set of doors opened. By the time they reached a room where they could see the visiting area, Vik was sweating. Anne Devney was waiting for them.

"So, this shouldn't take more than half an hour," she said.

"Good," Vik answered. He walked closer to the glass wall. "Looks like a McDonald's. They even have a place over there where you can buy stuff. Microwave, I bet." When he began rambling on about the trip down here, Marti knew he was as twitchy as she was.

"See that one-way mirror, in that wall where the pop machines are? Guards watching."

That seemed to reassure him. The mirror went the entire length of the visitors' room.

"What's taking so long?" he asked a few minutes later.

"They're bringing him in," she explained. "He gets a full strip and body-cavity search coming and going."

While they sat in the waiting area, it seemed that every prisoner in the room got something to eat. There was a line at the counter. Trustees dispensed microwaved plastic-wrapped food and collected money. Some of the inmates had two or three cans of pop. Marti knew that everyone was allowed to bring in and spend that twenty dollars, but even so, she couldn't remember seeing prisoners sitting at tables crowded with so much food. Recent budget cuts must have affected the quality or quantity of prison meals.

Ten minutes later they were admitted. The tables were plastic with attached seats. Vik walked to a table nearest the wall and sat with his back to the one-way mirror. Marti sat beside him. It was a good place to be. They had a full view of the entire room. About half of the tables were occupied. Two visitors were in the small glass room in one corner that was reserved for mentally ill prisoners. There was a glass-enclosed, walled-in outdoor area where children could play with toys. Several men were in there, playing with their children. A guard observed them.

"Nice, isn't it," Devney said. "Not all correctional facilities have a playroom."

Vik looked at her as if she had said something obscene.

Five minutes later Gonzales, a short, husky Hispanic, entered the air-locked, glassed-in prisoners' entrance. He stood there while one door locked behind him and another opened, then walked toward them. A lot of men worked out with weights while they were in jail. From the amount of weight Gonzales had gained, Marti guessed that he had lain around and watched television. He didn't bother to bathe often, either. When he came to the table, Anne Devney gave him her twenty dollars.

He bought three burritos, three cans of pop and pocketed the change.

"So," Gonzales said, sitting across from them. He spoke to Devney. "You still think you can get me out of here."

Based on that comment, Marti assumed Devney had talked with him before.

"We're still working on it," Devney said. "There appear to be some irregularities."

That was the first Marti had heard about that.

Gonzales grinned. He had either lost his upper front teeth or someone had knocked them out.

"Need to get out of here, man," he said. He opened a can of pop and took a long swallow. "Too damned many booty hunters."

"What's the matter?" Vik asked. "You got a problem with being somebody's girlfriend?'

"Hey, look, man. You just do like you're supposed to. Get me the hell out of here."

"My job was putting you in here."

"Just a minute," Devney intervened.

"No, no," Gonzales said, talking loud. "I didn't come here to take no shit from no asshole cops!"

With that, he threw a burrito and hit Vik in the chest. Then he threw the can of pop at the one-way mirror. Within seconds, food was coming at them from all directions.

"Down!" Marti yelled. "Floor!"

An alarm went off.

Within seconds, someone was on top of her. She smelled sweat. Gonzales. She scooted forward, gripped the base of a seat. Heard a crack.

"My head! You bitch!"

She twisted away from him, felt a sharp pain in her shoulder.

"Knife!" she yelled. "Knife." She thrust out her arm. Pain. Above her cast. More pain. Her shoulder.

Gonzales yelled. "Help!" he grunted.

She was free. She scooted farther under the table. Saw Vik's shoes. Gonzales was slumped against the wall. Guards were everywhere. Her blouse was sticking to her back, felt warm, wet. Her left arm and shoulder throbbed.

"Good thing he hit your deltoid and your triceps brachii," the prison doctor told her.

"What the hell are they?" Vik asked.

"Just muscles," the doctor explained. He spoke to Marti. "Both puncture wounds are deep. You'll be sore for a while. I'll give you enough pills for the pain to get you through the night. See your doctor first thing tomorrow. You'll need to have the bandages changed, but I don't think they'll have to replace the cast."

Marti looked down. There were nicks in the plaster from the shiv. From the looks of it, the cast might even have provided some protection. Vik drove back to Lincoln Prairie.

"That was planned," she said. "They were ready for us. And somebody paid a lot to get them to do it. When something like that goes down, the entire prison goes on lockdown and everyone directly involved is thrown into solitary." Her arm and her shoulder hurt like hell. She took one of the tablets the doctor had given her and slept until she got home.

Instead of taking Mildred out to dinner, Vik ordered a picnic supper from a restaurant and he and Mildred went to Bowman Park. It would be dark soon, but after being shut up in that prison, he needed open spaces and fresh air for a while. He tried not to think about what it had been like. People shouting. Food flying. He had lost sight of Marti. It wasn't until he heard her yell "Knife" that he realized Gonzales was on top of her, pinning her down. She said "Knife" again as he grabbed him. Two quick punches in the gut and Gonzales went down. When Gonzales tried to get up, he shoved him—hard. He hit the wall. The doctor said he had a concussion. Too bad it wasn't a broken neck. The whole thing had lasted less than two minutes. It had seemed like an hour. According to the guard, the trustees working behind the counter must have passed Gonzales the shiv. None of the other inmates had a weapon. Someone had set them up. He didn't think Gonzales would tell who it was. Lieutenant Dirkowitz was demanding a full investigation.

"Matthew? Marti is going to be all right?"

"She's fine. Deep cuts but no major damage. She'll be sore for a couple of days."

Mildred was having difficulty walking but was able to walk with her cane.

"I have to sit in the shade, Matthew," she said as he took her arm.

He knew how much she used to enjoy the warmth of the sun and wondered if bringing her here had been a good idea.

"Is it too hot outside for you?" he asked. They spoke in Polish.

"No, it's the humidity. But it's cooler here, closer to the lake."

"Let me know if you're not okay."

When Mildred was seated on the bench, he returned to the van, got out a lawn chair with thick cushions, made sure she was comfortable in that, made another trip and brought back the food.

"I remember when Krista and Stephen played here," she said. "That seems like such a long time ago, but, if I close my eyes, I can remember it as if it were yesterday."

Vik remembered Mildred pushing Krista on a swing, standing at the foot of the slide to catch Stephen, running after both of them, sledding with them in the winter—things she would never be able to do with their grandson.

"Do you mind?" he asked.

"Not being able to play with little Sean? Of course. Sometimes I am so angry. I am not even fifty yet and already I am old."

He looked at her, saw her hair, short and graying, no longer as blond, saw the fine lines etched into her face, saw how much weight she had lost, and the way her breasts sagged.

"I still see you young," he said.

She blinked and looked away.

"What do we do about this? How do I help you?"

She reached out and patted his knee. "This will not go away, Matthew."

"Neither will I. I just don't always know what to do."

"There's not much to do now. Just wait with me."

She sounded as if she was giving up and that frightened him more than anything a doctor could tell him.

"Moje serce," he said. My heart. My heart.

Marti was more worried about how the kids would react to what had happened than she was about being in pain. There was no way to protect them from things like this. Ben agreed that they should have a family meeting.

"Are you okay?" Theo asked.

"Do you have to go back to that prison again?" Mike wanted to know.

Theo inspected the cast again. "Are they still after you?"

"I don't know," she admitted.

"Does this mean you get to stay home?" Mike asked.

"No, but Lupe's going to stick with me and Vik until we get this taken care of. She'll be in uniform. That will force them to think. And nothing has happened while I've been here. I won't be returning to Springfield."

Whatever was going on with Gonzales had been tabled, thanks to his obvious involvement. There were so many layers of bureaucracy in the attorney general's office, she might never know who was behind it, but she suspected the trail led back to Senator Wagner.

Josiah went into the hallway and locked all three locks on the door to his room. He looked toward the top of the stairs again, almost expecting to see the woman there. He took a deep breath of relief when she was not. The lights were off, even the night-lights. The maid must have forgotten to turn them on. He turned just enough to look down to the far end of the long hall. As his eyes adjusted to the moonlight coming in from the window, he could see the benches from an old church placed along the walls, the grandfather clock that had stopped keeping time years ago, the floor lamp with the fringed shade that had belonged to his mother. He listened for the sound of a footstep, or a creaking stair, or even a rattling window, but the silence was absolute, just the way he had wanted it until the woman came inside. He tried not to look behind him as he walked down the hall toward the window. Each time he did, he told himself she would not be there again, sitting on the stairs. Each time she was not, he realized he had been holding his breath. When he reached the end of the hallway, the moonlight seemed brighter. He put the keys to his room in a box of Kleenex that was in plain sight on top of the table that was just beneath the windowsill.

He hesitated, looked toward the staircase with a feeling close to dread. He was alone. He was. Still he hesitated. His part of the house was always quiet. He had insisted on that. He had welcomed this silence when his sons and then his grandchildren were playing and doing whatever children did, which always seemed to be noisy. Now he wondered what he had missed. There were no reverberations of children laughing or parents scolding. There were no echoes of youth; not his, not his children's, not his grandchildren's. All was as he had wanted it. No sound, not even the memory of sounds. He had not known he would miss that now.

The staircase and everything downstairs were dark as well. The night-lights along the steps had not been turned on. Josiah hesitated at the top of the stairs. He had become so accustomed to the dimness of the night lighting that he became uneasy now. Or was she the one causing his unease? She had become as real to him in her absence as she had been when he could see her. He glanced up, noticed something about the ceiling that he could not quite make out, something different. He didn't want to turn on a light at this hour, but in the morning he would have another look.

When he reached the cellar, even with the lights on, many things remained in shadow. Belowground, it always smelled damp. A green mold covered the base of the north wall, and if he looked he would find clusters of tiny mushrooms growing from the crevices of the rough-hewn stone walls. He went to the far southwest corner where the skeletons were, and began dragging canvas bags to the bottom of the stairs. He would have to get these out of here tomorrow night.

The bags were heavy. His arms were aching by the time he pulled the three with the bones of the coloreds to the stairs. There were two more bags, Indians. Whoever the woman mourned, they would all be put into the same grave. Exhausted, he decided to leave the bags with the manacles where they were; let someone else wonder what they had been used for, where they had been found. He hadn't picked out a burial place yet. He was keeping track of the obituaries in more rural areas where he would have easy access to a new grave. He would decide in the morning. There always seemed to be quite a few funerals on Saturday.

He wondered how he would manage to get the bags up the stairs and then into the SUV. He hadn't driven a car in years, had never driven anything the size of a small truck, but his license was current. He was panting as he stood at the foot of the cellar stairs and looked up. It was just a short distance to the kitchen door. It would be quiet, dark, just as it was now. Cook and the maid did not have rooms close enough to be disturbed. He would have to drive the SUV away from the house without turning on the lights. He could do this. He would have to.

When Josiah returned to the kitchen he felt exhausted. He was so tired from not being able to sleep at night, that he had started dozing off toward dawn. Sleeping during the day would have helped, but he found that difficult because he was too concerned about the digging going on in the woods. Now that he was weary enough to sleep for the next twenty-four hours, he realized that he was so concerned about the woman coming inside that he didn't want to sleep at all, at least not until he was in Florida and certain that the woman had remained here. He thought about making a cup of coffee, but all he wanted to do was get back to his room and lie down. He took a can of Coke from the refrigerator instead and gulped down half of it, paused, then drank the rest. He had a microwave upstairs and instant coffee if he needed it.

His legs hurt as he made his way along the first-floor corridor to the stairs. Twenty-four steps and he could get into his bed. He had counted these steps when he was a boy. He could run up to his room then. Now, even when he wasn't tired, he wished for an elevator. He would have installed one of those seats that went up and down but he didn't want anyone to know that climbing stairs was becoming difficult. He grasped the banister and took one step at a time, pausing on each. Just as he reached the landing he saw her. She was standing at the far end of the hall. She was near the table where his keys were. There was no way he could get into his room. Maybe if he spoke to her . . . Could she hear him?

"Listen to me," he said. "I don't know why you come here. Can you tell me what it is that you want?"

"My children," she said. "The bones of my dead sons."

She moved toward him.

He took a step back. There was nothing behind him. His foot missed the step. He was falling.

21

Marti went to Joanna's game Saturday morning. She had had a good nights' sleep, thanks to the pain medication. It was wearing off now, and she felt sore and stiff—in fact, her shoulder hurt like hell—but she was not going to allow this to make any difference in her life. Her only restrictions would be those imposed by bandages and the cast.

Joanna's team had made so many mistakes at the beginning of the season that sometimes it had almost hurt to watch them play. Now that they were improving, there was something more satisfying about watching them than there had been when Joanna was on teams that won most of the time. Marti sat at the top of the bleachers. It was hot in the sun. The girls had to fight for the win. They were tied at six all when the first baseman and shortstop came through to prevent a go-ahead run. Then Joanna hit one over the fence. All the parents waited until the girls had hugged each other and jumped up and down and pumped their fists before going to the bullpen to congratulate them.

"Did you see that, Ma?" Joanna said. "We did it! It was our game to lose and we came through."

Before Marti could answer, Joanna ran over to the girls. "Yes!!" she yelled, slapping high fives. "Yes! Way to go!"

It was after eleven when Marti arrived at the precinct. Her shoulder hurt so bad that she wanted to go home, take some pain meds and sleep for two or three days. Instead, she took four Tylenol capsules, asked God for a little relief, and called

Gonzales a few appropriate cuss words. That would have to do until she had time to go to the doctor.

Vik was on the computer. He didn't look up when she came in, just mumbled something that sounded like "urrr" when she said good morning. She poured some coffee, refilled Vik's cup, and brought him a jelly-filled doughnut.

"Thanks."

He didn't ask how her arm felt. She didn't need to ask how things were with Mildred.

She was looking through the logs completed by the uniforms assigned to the two entrances at the Smith place when a call came in. Vik answered, listened, then groaned.

"The Smith place," he said when he hung up.

"Again? Who's dead now?"

"Josiah,"

"What?"

"Josiah," Vik repeated.

"Damn. What happened? Stroke? Heart attack?"

"You'll never guess."

"Another accident."

He looked at her for a moment. Dark pouches were under his eyes again.

"You okay?" he asked. "I really think you need to stay on this case, but if you're in too much pain . . ."

"I'm okay."

"Neither of us is okay, MacAlister. The question is can we function. I think I can, but I didn't get stabbed yesterday. Lupe can fill in for you if she has too."

"No. You're right. I've got to stay with this." Lupe hadn't put the time into the case that she had, and now Josiah was dead. There was no time to bring Lupe up to speed. Without suffi-cient information, Lupe could miss a critical piece of evidence, or just not correctly interpret something that was said. They could blow the whole case with a personnel change—not that they had much of a case.

"You're talking yourself into making this trip to the Smith place," Vik asked.

"Something like that," she admitted.

"Can you make it without a pain pill for a couple of hours?"

"Maybe—if I take four Tylenol every twenty minutes."

"I'll make a quick stop so you can pick up a day's supply."

When they arrived at the Smith place, a van from a local funeral home was parked out front. Marti and Vik followed the maid to a long narrow room with many windows. The maid stopped just inside the double doors and pointed to the stairwell. Josiah was lying on his back at the foot of the stairs. One leg was at an angle that could only be achieved if it was snapped at the knee. His left arm was stretched above his head, with his hand palm-up. His right was arm was flung out and almost touching the newel post. His eyes were open. His mouth gaped as if he had stopped breathing mid-scream.

Whatever had been in his stomach was now a puddle touching his face. He was wearing pajamas and a bathrobe. The carpet and his pajama bottoms were damp with urine. There was a noticeable odor of bodily waste but it wasn't overwhelming. Marti could see something dark on the fingers and palm of his left hand. It looked like dirt, but she would have to wait for the evidence techs to find out what it was.

She turned to look at the man and woman standing to one side. They were wearing black slacks and short-sleeved white shirts. They looked to be in their mid-twenties.

"You two are the mortician's assistants?"

The young man nodded.

"You should not have come unless you were called by a hospice worker. Did you go near the body?"

"When they called they said he was eighty-five and had died of natural causes."

"Has anyone called the coroner's office?"

"Dispatch," Vik said. "Where's the family?" he wanted to know.

"We haven't seen or spoken with anyone but her." The young man indicated the maid.

Vik turned to her. "You found him?"

She nodded. "Mr. Josiah must have turned off the lights."

"What lights?"

"At night there's a little light on both sides of each stair."

Marti could see that no lights were on.

"Are you the one who notified the family?" Vik asked the maid.

Another nod.

"And?" he prodded.

"They said they would take care of it, that I was to stay out of here and just answer the door."

"What time did you find him?"

"Eight-thirty this morning."

Vik turned to the young man. "What time did you receive the call?"

"About eleven o'clock."

"I told them," the maid said. "I told them right away."

"Told who?"

"Mr. Franklin."

"Why not Mr. Paul?"

Marti sat down in the nearest chair. It was time for more Tylenol, but this was not the time to go off in search of a glass of water.

"I . . . he . . ." the maid stuttered. "Mr. Franklin . . . I . . . I . . ."

Vik waited. The maid's face got flushed. "I . . ." She looked away.

"Why didn't you go to Mr. Paul?"

"I didn't think he would come."

"Did Mr. Franklin come?"

"No. His wife did."

Again Vik waited. Again the woman's face became flushed.

"Miss Eileen came down and took a look at him."

"She didn't touch him?"

"No, sir."

"Did you?"

The maid trembled. "He was dead, sir. He was dead."

"How did you know that?"

"Didn't you know he was dead when you looked at him?"

"Where's Cook?

"In the kitchen, sir. Mr. Franklin told me to have her prepare breakfast and not tell her there was anything wrong with Mr. Josiah."

The bell rang and the maid admitted Dr. Cyprian. When the evidence techs arrived, Vik directed them upstairs. Then he walked over to Marti. "Are you doing okay?"

She nodded. The Tylenol wasn't doing much for the pain, but she was getting used to it.

"It does look like an accident," he said. "Luck of the Smiths."

As she waited to get to the body, Marti also waited for one of the Smiths to put in an appearance. It had been a long time since she had seen a family who seemed this indifferent.

Dr. Cyprian stood, called to the evidence techs and walked over to Marti and Vik. "Rigor mortis is almost complete," he said.

Marti checked her watch. "That means he's been dead anywhere from ten to fourteen hours.

"Give or take a few hours," Dr. Cyprian agreed. "I'm not going to be able to tell you anything else until the autopsy. I'll see you tomorrow morning at six."

"Could you make that tonight?" Marti asked. She wasn't sure how she was going to manage it, but if this wasn't an accident, they had already lost too much time.

"Normal people call nine-one-one," Vik said. "Not the funeral home. Maybe they needed to buy a little time."

One of the evidence techs came over. "One door upstairs is locked. Three locks, two of them dead bolts. Maid says it's the deceased male's bedroom. We can't find the keys."

Marti turned to Vik. "Let's just make sure nobody goes up

there for now. See who has the keys when we question the family."

"Three locks," Vik said. "I wonder who he wanted to keep out."

By the time the technician's had processed the scene, and Marti had shot three rolls of film, and the body had been removed, it was ten past three. Marti walked to the top step and checked the carpet. No tears, nothing. She stood with her back to the steps because Josiah had landed on his back. All she could see was the far end of the hall. There was a long, wide window. Wooden benches with kneeling angels carved at each end were placed at intervals along the walls. This was the center wing. There were no doors upstairs to connect it with the north or south wings where Paul and Franklin lived.

Before they went downstairs to speak with the family, then Cook, Marti said, "When this call came in, I was reading the logs turned in by the uniforms watching the two entrances. The only unusual activity took place on Wednesday. Two cars with drivers picked up the wives, returned them about five in the evening. Paul and Franklin went out and returned at about the same time, but drove their own cars. A little before one, six cars arrived, everyone stayed for about two hours and left."

Vik thought about that, then said, "What else?"

"On Tuesday, Franklin was gone for the day. On Thursday Paul was. Neither of them drove. The wives made several half-day trips. They use a limo service, had several different drivers."

"No night trips?"

"Nothing. But we are reasonably certain that they took something from two of those dig sites. It doesn't sound like they've taken whatever it is off of the property yet, does it?"

"How about deliveries?"

"Three," she said; then, "Damn. If they weren't what they seemed to be . . ."

"If it's gone, it's gone," Vik said. "Won't be the first time the family stonewalled the cops. Doesn't mean we don't get them anyway."

"Maybe it is still here. We didn't get a search warrant for the house. Even if they weren't smart enough to figure out that we didn't have probable cause, they could have been smart enough to call their lawyer, who would have told them. They might think the house is the safest place to keep whatever it is."

"Maybe," Vik conceded. "But don't take any bets."

"A little pressure, maybe?"

"Can't hurt," Vik agreed.

"Let's let them know the autopsy is today, and that we've found human bones at the dig site, and mention that Mrs. Linski is sending us something that Larissa found."

"And then we wait," Vik said. "If we're lucky, maybe we don't wait long."

The Smiths had assembled in the library again. Marti counted four floor-to-ceiling bookcases. The lower shelves were filled with books. The upper shelves alternated between empty and bric-a-brac. Marti noted that there were no photographs. The maid came in pushing a cart with a silver service and served coffee to the family. When nobody offered any to her or to Vik, Marti walked over to the nearest bookcase. All of the books were in sets. The covers were shiny and looked to be leather. None were worn. The sets were either in numeric or alphabetical order.

After coffee was served, nobody suggested that they have a seat either.

"We'll need to speak with you individually," Marti advised them.

"Why?" Franklin asked.

"Standard procedure."

After consulting with an attorney, Franklin agreed to the request and volunteered to be first.

His face got flushed when she told him that Paul's wife, Jessica, would be interviewed first.

"Jessica . . ." Paul began. "But she . . .

"Paul," Franklin interrupted. "We have two highly experienced police officers here. Let's allow them to do their job."

Marti could tell by his voice inflections that he was being sarcastic.

They went to what Jessica described as the small sitting room, which had enough chairs and sofas to seat at least two dozen people. Jessica chose a chair by the window. The sun added highlights to her long chestnut hair. She was wearing a short white pleated skirt, a short-sleeved top to match, and a visor.

"When did you find out that your father-in-law was dead?" Marti asked.

"A little after ten this morning."

"Who told you?"

"Franklin. He said that the old man had taken a fall down the stairs."

"Did he say anything else?"

"Just that Josiah was unquestionably dead."

Marti waited. She was not in the mood to coax every word from the woman's mouth.

"Oh, and when Paul started to go to Josiah's wing, Franklin said not to bother, that he would handle everything."

"Have you seen your father-in-law?"

"Today? No. Why would I want to see him dead? Having to see him when he was alive was bad enough."

"Did Josiah discuss anything about the dig sites with you?"

"No. Why would he?"

"He didn't tell you that we've found Indian remains?"

Marti remained passive as Jessica stared at her, wide-eyed. "You mean there really was someone buried out there?"

Marti nodded.

"Well, I'll be damned. What exactly did you find?"

"A variety of things that tell us Indians lived there."

Jessica hesitated, "But you said remains. Human remains? Or just dishes and things?"

"Both," Marti said.

The corners of her mouth turned up. Marti thought it was more of a sneer than a smile. "My, my. I wonder what the developers will do about that."

She didn't seem too concerned.

Vik escorted Jessica back to the group.

Marti had a glass of water now. She took a few more Tylenol. The interviews were taking her mind off the pain. Vik brought Eileen in. Eileen was wearing sweats and a headband. She wasn't perspiring and didn't look as if she had been out for a run. She walked to a window, adjusted the draperies, then went over to a table and moved the lamp, stood back, moved it again, then walked over and sat in a chair not far from where Vik was standing. She leaned forward, as if she was anxious to leave. Marti repeated the questions she had asked Jessica.

"The maid told us," she said. "She didn't seem upset. Franklin told her that she was to stay downstairs and wait by the door until someone came for him."

"What exactly did the maid say?"

"That Mr. Josiah was lying on the floor and he didn't look alive anymore."

"Then what?"

"Then I went down and took a look at him and the maid was right. I went back upstairs, told Franklin that his father was dead, and he told Paul. About an hour later Franklin called the undertaker."

"Why did he wait so long?"

"He didn't want to deal with it on an empty stomach and didn't do anything until Cook fixed his breakfast."

"But you did tell Cook?"

"Eventually. We thought she was fond of the old man, thought she would get upset. She's been with the family for forty years. Her grandmother came here as Cook straight from Ireland, then her mother was Cook. She's training her niece to be Cook when she retires."

Four generations, Marti thought, and all just called Cook.

She wondered what it was like never to be called by your name by the people you worked for.

"What was her reaction when you told her Josiah was dead?"

Eileen didn't answer right away. She seemed thoughtful for a moment, then said, "I was braced for hysterics. Instead, Cook just blinked a few times, and said, "Yes, ma'am." Josiah was just her employer, and it isn't like he ever gave her any reason to like him. Still, you expect something when a person's been in your employ for that length of time. All those years and no appreciation. It's amazing."

"It does make you think."

"It certainly does," Eileen agreed. "Paid vacations, holidays, sick time. Josiah was very generous with her."

"Sometimes it doesn't pay to be generous."

This time Eileen looked at her as if she suspected sarcasm. Marti smiled.

Vik escorted Eileen back to the group and returned a few minutes later with Franklin. It was the first time Marti had seen Franklin when he wasn't sitting down. He was at least six inches taller than his brother Paul, and at least thirty pounds heavier. He sat where Jessica had sat. The sunlight and his hair, dyed a dark brown, made his skin look sallow.

"Now that you've spoken with my wife, I cannot see any need for further conversation. However, with Lincoln Prairie's finest on the case, we must follow the correct procedure, mustn't we?" He leaned back with both arms on the arms of the chair and crossed one leg over the other. "So. My father is dead." His voice sounded almost jovial. "He fell down the stairs He was an old man. We all have to go sometime."

"The maid told *you,* not Paul."

"Aha! An astute observation." He uncrossed his legs and leaned forward. "You're not going to believe this," he said, his voice just above a whisper. "Paul and my father never got along."

"Who hired Larissa Linski?" Marti asked.

"I don't know."

"Who contacted the university?"

"Don't know that either."

"Did you know that Larissa Linski found a slave tag?"

"Really? Then I guess this was a station for the Underground Railroad." He stroked his chin. "Interesting. From what little I've heard of Idbash, he never struck me as the type."

Marti wanted to ask what he had heard but went for. "What type?" instead.

"Humanitarian."

Marti thought of two small skulls. "What do you know about the digs?"

"As little as possible."

"Why?"

"I just wanted to keep clear of everything. My father was very attached to this property. If he regretted selling it later, I didn't want him blaming me." He cared, Marti thought. At least enough to want the old man's approval.

Paul was last. Marti asked him what she had asked the others. She expected him to be the most talkative, but he was not, answering mostly in monosyllables. He sounded tired.

"You did not know there were two additional dig sites until we found them?" she repeated.

"No."

"But you were at the first site."

"Yes."

"Why did you know about that one and not the other two?"

"I'm not sure." He looked up at her. "I never knew any more than the old man wanted me to. That usually wasn't much."

Marti wondered what would happen if he did receive some useful information.

"In order to expedite things and have the body released, they'll be conducting the autopsy today," she told him. When he didn't seem interested in that, she added, "And we need the keys to his room."

"Keys?"

"Yes."

"If the door was locked, he must have had them with him."

"No. He didn't."

"Then I have no idea."

When Marti and Vik met with Cook, she was in the sitting room by the kitchen preparing tea. As Marti watched, she filled a metal ball, put it into a pot shaped like a marmalade cat with its tail as the handle, poured in boiling water and covered the pot with a tea cozy. The cream pitcher and sugar bowl matched the teapot. The cups Cook took off the shelf were decorated with kittens and balls of yarn.

"Do you have a cat?" Marti asked.

"Animals aren't allowed." She invited them to sit down. "It just needs a few minutes to steep." She reached into her pocket. "You'll be wanting these," she said as she handed Marti a set of keys. "They fit the locks on Mr. Josiah's bedroom door."

Marti looked down at the keys and then at Cook, whose expression was stern but not hostile.

"Are you giving us permission to search his room?" Marti asked.

"I'm not family."

"But he did give you these keys."

"Yes, ma'am. He told me not to give them to anyone in the family."

"Well," Marti said. "That excludes us."

Vik put in a call for the evidence techs to return.

"What's your name, ma'am?" he asked.

"Maigread." She brought the pot of tea to the table and poured. "Maigread Clancy."

"Miss Clancy . . ." Vik began.

"Cook is fine." She put a paper doily on a plate and arranged some cookies on it. "Not a proper tea, but I've not had a proper schedule today, so I've not made any scones."

"Miss Clancy," Vik repeated. "Josiah Smith is dead. You worked for him for a long time. Is there anything that we should know that you can tell us?"

Cook began pouring tea. "Mr. Josiah would not have lost his footing and toppled down those stairs just because those night-lights were not on. He could walk this entire house without any lights and go about the property without a flashlight. He had no need for either."

"But he did fall down the stairs."

"That he did. And I don't know that anyone would push him. But the maid did not forget to turn on those night-lights along the stairs, although the poor girl is convinced that she must have. And Mr. Josiah did sign the papers selling the property on Wednesday. Half the proceeds at least would have been his, had he lived."

Marti caught Vik's eye as she reached for the sugar. Miss Clancy knew a lot to be just a cook.

"I'm not much of a tea drinker, Miss Clancy," Vik said. "What would you suggest?"

"Just a minute." She got a demitasse cup and a slice of lemon. "If we're going to make a proper tea drinker of you, then you're going to have to know which way you like it. Try it with nothing first."

After sipping various samples, Vik settled on tea with cream.

"Ah," Miss Clancy said, smiling. "Exactly the way I like mine, along with just a bit of sugar."

Vik helped himself to some cookies. "Do you make everything from scratch every day?"

Miss Clancy frowned. "They won't eat leftovers, not one of them, told not to as children. So I cook plenty of food and snacks for all of them. Whatever is left over, I freeze. Then on Tuesday, someone from my church picks it all up for the soup kitchen."

"Mr. Smith allowed that?"

"Mister Josiah would not have cared much. Good for his soul, it was, though, now that he's dead. He did something to help someone else, even if he didn't intend to. It's the others who would have objected. Very concerned they are about what comes out of their pockets."

The maid came in and announced that the evidence techs wanted to see them. Vik waited until she had left, then said, "I'll have a uniform keep everyone else downstairs. We might not want them to know we can get into his room, or where the keys came from."

Miss Clancy looked at him for a moment. "Thank you," she said.

"And thank you, ma'am. I never thought I would ever enjoy a cup of tea."

As they walked to the hallway, Marti smiled at him and gave his arm a squeeze. Cook knew more than she was telling. She was a shrewd woman who wouldn't be fooled by pretense. Vik had just earned her trust.

Upstairs, Marti took one look at the benches and asked Vik to find her something more comfortable. Twenty minutes later one of the technicians motioned them into Josiah's room.

"Finished already?" Vik asked.

"No. We might be here for a while, but I want you to see this."

Marti and Vik followed him as far as a chandelier that hung from the ceiling.

"See that?" He pointed to the ceiling.

"It looks like a cigarette case with a little round circle attached," Vik said.

"Someone installed a sensor," Marti guessed. "For smoke? Or carbon monoxide?"

"It's a laser beam," the technician corrected.

"And?" Vik asked.

"It could be there for any number of reasons," the technician said. "But, given that the person who slept in this room also installed three locks, fell down a flight of stairs, and is dead— I'm thinking hologram."

"That's where you see something that isn't there," Marti said.

"Close," the technician agreed. "The light shines through photographic film and projects a three-dimensional image that looks totally real."

"Be damned," Vik said. "Did you check the hallway for one of these?"

"We can see small holes at each end of the hall where there are light fixtures and these could have been installed. They're gone now but the wiring could still be in place."

"And anyone with half a brain could do it with the wires for the lights already there," Vik said.

"And you know this, Jessenovik?"

"It didn't take Steven ten minutes to replace a ceiling light with a ceiling light that had an attached fan. He used the wires that were already there."

"We need to talk about this," Marti told him. She spoke to the technician. "Good job. A real good job."

Back in the hallway, they found the holes the technician had noted.

"So," Vik said. "We've got probable cause to search the place."

Marti heard the hesitancy in his voice. "But?"

"So we find something." Vik said. "We confront the Smiths and nobody knows anything. Josiah did it. He's dead."

"We sit on it."

"For now."

"Then we're assuming there are no more outsiders. Nobody else they need to kill."

"If we get lucky, they'll turn on each other."

They returned to Josiah's room.

"Can you guys take some pictures of this and finish up to-morrow?" Marti asked.

"That's what you want?"

"Trust us," Marti said.

They locked the door on their way out.

Downstairs, they found Cook in the kitchen stuffing chicken breasts. Vik motioned her into the sitting room. "Are you safe here?" he asked in a low voice.

She nodded.

"Do you want the keys back?"

"No."

"Good. We'll be back in the morning."

"Officers"—she gave Vik a large Baggie filled with cookies—"thank you."

Franklin stopped them on their way out. "May I ask why you had those technicians return?"

"Sure," Marti said. "The coroner's office called to say that there was something on Mr. Smith's hand. They were just checking to see if they could see anything on the stairway or in the upstairs hall."

"And?"

"I didn't ask."

"What about the door to his room?"

"We've taken photographs of it."

"You're not going to open it?"

"Not yet."

He gave them a wide smile.

As they walked to their car, Vik said, "Nothing like putting one over on the cops."

"He was gloating, wasn't he," Marti agreed.

When Marti got back to the precinct there were voice messages from the people she had contacted at both libraries and the DuSable Museum, along with faxes. There were lists of reference materials and, more important, names and phone numbers of area people involved with African-American genealogy. She had a little over an hour before Josiah Smith's autopsy. She gave part of the phone list to Vik and called Lupe Torres, who agreed to come in to help.

As she called, she was surprised by the number of people who were aware that Idbash Smith had been a conductor on the Underground Railroad. Vik mentioned the same thing. Nobody was able to tell either of them much more than that. After half a dozen people had suggested she contact the genealogy group at the Charles V. Woodson Regional Library, Marti called. Their president was not at home, but she left a message.

They were ten minutes late for Josiah's autopsy, but Dr. Cyprian had waited. The body was losing its rigor. There was bruising. His leg had been broken at the knee, both hips were broken as well. His upper body had sustained fewer injuries. According to Dr. Cyprian, Josiah was in good health for a man his age. There were significant changes to his heart, but no surprises until Dr. Cyprian examined his brain. "Several tumors," he said. "We'll have to biopsy them to be certain, but cancerous growths tend to look angry, and these do."

After the autopsy, Marti and Vik walked back to the precinct.

"How's the shoulder?" Vik asked

"Better," she said. "Or maybe I'm just getting used to it." The autopsy had taken her mind off it.

"You're getting cranky," Vik said.

She hadn't noticed.

Lupe was on the phone when they reached the office. She handed Marti a note.

"Call Gretchen Jackson. Speak with her or her son, Carlton."

Marti dialed the number and identified herself to the woman who answered.

"Yes, Detective MacAlister." The woman spoke in the modulated tones of someone in broadcasting. "I'm a member of the genealogy group at Woodson. You left a message with our president and he suggested I call you. You have questions about Idbash Smith. My son and I are interested in him also."

"Why?"

"The Des Plaines River was part of a northern route for the Underground Railroad. Over the years, we've been able to document slaves who traveled it to reach safe houses in Wisconsin. However, it became apparent from the records kept by some of the conductors that not everyone who made it as far as what is now Lake County continued on to freedom. My son and I have documented slaves journeying as far as southern Illinois who were taking the river route to Wisconsin, Idbash Smith was a conductor. A significant number of those who disap-

246

peared were scheduled to stop at his station before continuing on to Wisconsin."

"I'd like to see your documentation," Marti said. She wasn't sure how important this was to her case in terms of a possible motive for Larissa Linski's death, but once she had a specific suspect, a preponderance of evidence might be sufficient to establish motive and guilt.

"I think you should talk with a young man who just spent a few days with us. Omari's grandfather has spent nineteen years tracing his family back to slavery, and we've established a link to Mr. Smith."

Marti wrote down the name and phone number. When she called, the man who answered identified himself as Omari's father and told her that his son had returned to Chicago on Thursday. He hadn't phoned home yet, but they were expecting to hear from him anytime now. Marti called Mrs. Jackson. She had not heard from Omari. Marti spoke with Omari's father again. She didn't want to alarm him, not yet, and just asked if Omari had mentioned an Idbash Smith.

"Omari came home Thursday morning. He visited my brother in the hospital, then made a few phone calls. Then he caught the next bus to Chicago. The man he spoke with—wait a minute. I've got everything written down right here. He called a Senator Wagner, spoke with someone named Kat Malloy, she gave him this phone number"—he read it off—"then he spoke with Josiah Smith. Mr. Smith wasn't able to see him, but he did arrange for another family member to meet him here."

He gave her an address on the north side. She was familiar with the neighborhood. Quiet, gentrified, not far from troublesome elements, but relatively safe. She put in a call to the local district. Yes, there had been a mugging near that address on Thursday night. Yes, the victim's name was Omari. The desk sergeant gave her the name of the hospital he had been taken too. It took her a few minutes to get through to someone at the hospital who would give her patient information. Omari was still there. He had not regained consciousness. Marti put in a call to his father.

She hated cellars. This had to be one of the worst. Damp, moldy, cobwebs, spiders. And it smelled. Someone needed to get rid of all of those cardboard boxes and the junk that was stacked on the shelves. They were lucky they didn't have any rats. For a moment, she wondered if there was anything valuable down here, but she wasn't curious enough to care.

She expected to find the bags where they had left them. Instead, all but two had been dragged to the stairs. Josiah was going to get rid of them himself. The nerve of that old bastard. First he didn't tell anyone when the property was sold; now this. What had he been planning next, a one-way trip to Switzerland to live with his bank account?

The bags with the chains and manacles were in a far corner. Of course, he hadn't moved those. She hefted one. It was heavy but she could manage it. She dragged it to the steps, then carried it upstairs and returned for the other one. She was hardly out of breath when she lifted the bags of bones. She would drive to the city tonight, toss them into a Dumpster.

When all of the bags were stacked by the kitchen door, she opened it, pulled them outside. The sky was dark, the moon partially obscured by clouds. All of the lights were out in the main house. There were only a few lights on in the wings. She opened the back of the SUV, stowed the bags, and climbed into the front seat.

Lights came on, blinding her. She ducked down, opened the door and took off running.

"Subject running," a uniform called.

"Call for additional backup," Vik yelled.

Marti ran ahead of him toward the SUV. As she ran, she unholstered her weapon. She could see three uniforms in pursuit. She could not see the subject. There was a stand of oak trees. As she ran past the SUV, the trees seemed to close in on

248

her. Behind her, she could hear Vik breathing hard. Ahead, she heard the dull thud of footsteps. She tripped on a root, grabbed at a tree trunk with her left hand, and felt a sudden sharp pain from her wrist to her back. Rough bark scratched her palm.

"Where the hell are we going? Damn." She had trouble finding her way around here during the day.

Someone called, "Over here." She turned in that direction.

"No," Vik said. "Follow me."

Instead of running, he walked fast. "Can't let him hear us," he whispered. "Let him think we're with the others."

"Why?"

"So he'll stay away from them and head for the front gate."

At least he knew where he was going. The pain in her left arm was constant. She couldn't ignore it. She would have to act in spite of it.

As they walked, Marti became uneasy. The voices of the other officers got farther away. A scrabbling sound made her jump. An owl hooted.

Vik stopped. She bumped into him.

"Skunk," he whispered. A shadow with white stripes waddled across their path. Two shorter sets of stripes followed.

The clouds moved away from the moon. Marti ducked into the shadow of a tree. She listened. Nothing. Vik shrugged. They kept walking. The path was narrow, the dirt hard. Leaves rustled. Two small red eyes stared at her. She moved away. The trees were dense. She had no idea of where she was.

There was a noise ahead. Someone panting. They stopped. Vik motioned to her to fan out. She moved to his left. Guns pointed, they inched forward. Ahead Marti could see someone bent over. She could hear shallow gasps.

"Police!" Vik shouted.

The subject dropped and fired.

Marti ducked behind a tree. She couldn't see Vik.

Another shot. Marti aimed in that direction.

Vik returned fire.

The figure stayed low and ran.

Marti fired. The kick made the pain shoot across both shoulders. She heard nothing. Clouds scudded across the moon. In the sudden darkness, she was momentarily blinded. When her eyes adjusted, she inched her way toward where she had last seen Vik. He came toward her.

She pointed to where she had last seen the subject. They stayed apart as they walked in that direction. She did not see any movement. She did not hear the jagged breathing.

She stopped. Waited. Listened. Something to her left caught her eye. She turned, looked, blinked. Looked again. A woman in a long white garment stood in the shadows. She beckoned. Marti moved in that direction. As she approached, the woman disappeared. She heard the breathing again. She stopped. It was to her right. She aimed in that direction but didn't move. The breathing didn't get closer. It didn't move farther away. She motioned to Vik and made her way toward the sound. The subject, wearing dark clothes, was leaning against a tree. A winter hat covered his face and head. The gun was pointing down.

Marti's finger tightened on the trigger. "Police!" she said. She watched the gun. "Do not move."

Vik came out from the cover of the trees. He stood opposite Marti on the other side of the subject.

"Drop the gun," Marti ordered. "Now move away from the gun and the tree."

When the subject was lying facedown on the ground, Vik cuffed him. Then he pulled off the hat. "I'll be damned." He sounded surprised.

Marti moved closer. "Eileen! Nice to see you again."

Vik didn't mention seeing the woman in the white dress. Marti didn't say anything about it either, just in case she was the only one who had seen her. She thought of the rumors of ghosts. No way, she thought, but it did make her wonder.

"Come see what we've got," a uniform said.

Marti looked where he was pointing, saw Vik standing by

half a dozen canvas bags aligned on the grass. He opened one, took a closer look and said, "Damn."

Marti's knees almost buckled as she watched him. Her adrenaline flow was ebbing. The muscles in her legs were screaming. Her shoulder and arm hurt like hell. The muscles in her back felt as if they were about to go into spasms. All she wanted to do was go home.

She walked over to where Vik stood. "More bones?" she asked. "Or artifacts?"

"Bones," Vik told her. "And manacles, collars, and chains."

"Indian restraints?" She thought of the slave tag. "Or were they used on runaway slaves?"

"We'll have to consult with the experts yet again."

Cook was standing in the doorway. Marti and Vik walked over to her.

"Will you be okay here, Miss Clancy?" Vik asked.

"I'll be fine. Nobody else here knows how to cook."

They all laughed.

"I have something else for you," Miss Clancy said. "It's in an upstairs storage closet. You'll need help carrying it down."

Vik brought down a strongbox. A uniform carried a wooden chest with designs carved on the top and sides.

"Mr. Josiah said nobody in the family was to have this. I think he might be wanting you to have it now."

Marti looked at the box and the chest. Miss Clancy handed her two keys.

"Thank you," she said. She smiled, acknowledging the woman's trust.

Turning to Vik, she said, "This is going to be a very long night." She yawned, then said, "Now that we've got a suspect in custody, let's wake up the state's attorney too, get subpoenas for the limo company's and the telephone company's records, and a search warrant for the house." It was after four in the morning when she went to bed. She skipped the bathtub, even though the muscles in her legs were screaming for moist heat, set the alarm for eight, took two painkillers and tried to ignore the pain while they took effect. The last thing she thought about was the woman she had seen in the woods. If Vik didn't mention it, neither would she. One thing was for sure: it hadn't been a hologram.

22

Marti and Vik met with Lieu-
tenant Dirkowitz at eight o'clock. Vik didn't seem too happy
about not going to Mass with Mildred. Then again, Marti
thought, he didn't seem that happy when he did. The lieutenant
surprised them with doughnuts and bottles of orange juice as
well as hot coffee and fresh fruit. Marti poured coffee for both
of them while Vik snagged the only jelly-filled.

"I hear you two finally got a little exercise last night," the
lieutenant said. He looked at Marti. "Busy week, MacAlister—
a mugging, a possible drive-by and a prison riot."

"Food fight," she said.

"The whole issue with Hector Gonzales looks questionable.
I'm not sure how far we can go with it, and I don't think any
heads will roll, but I'm not the only one making noise. You two
have earned a lot of respect around here."

Vik brightened at that. "Thank you, sir."

The lieutenant peeled a banana. "So, how are you feeling,
MacAlister?"

"Not bad at the moment. It gets worse."

"Try to make it through the day, and then get some rest," he
advised. "I'd like to tell you to go home, but I need you. We
do have Josiah Smith's daughter-in-law in custody, but the only
thing we can charge her with is firing at you."

They hadn't talked with Eileen. She demanded to have an
attorney present and one had not arrived yet.

The lieutenant finished off the banana and picked up the

defused hand grenade. "So, we've got bags of bones and restraints, two homicides that we know of, a houseful of suspects and no proof."

"That about sums it up, sir," Vik agreed.

"How did Cyprian rule on Josiah Smith's death?"

"We know that he fell, but the question is why," Marti said. She explained about the laser beam and possible holograms.

Dirkowitz shook his head. "This is one hell of a mess."

Marti helped herself to a Bismarck. "The Smiths are going to alibi for each other as far as Linski and Buckner are concerned. I've got Lupe looking at telephone records, limo service records, and checking out anything they've said that can be verified; but for the most part it's a matter of Paul and Franklin saying they were with their wives, and the wives agreeing."

"We've got enough on Idbash to get the death penalty," Vik said. "Damned shame he died in 1870. Just when you think you've met the ultimate killer, you come across someone who's worse. The state's attorney has a law expert looking at those old maps and documents that the cook turned over to us. Too bad nobody found out what Idbash was up to in time to hang him."

"I'd choose a confession from one of them over finding an impediment to the land sale," Marti said. "An impediment could lead to a motive, but the pathway to a homicide charge could be long and obscure." And would probably lead to the Internet, research, or experts. She didn't care if she never had to use them again.

The sergeant stopped them as they returned to their office. Eileen Smith's attorney had arrived and was consulting with his client. During their walk to the county jail, they agreed that since the Smiths didn't like it when Marti took the initiative, Vik would talk with Eileen first. He would try to establish some rapport or ease the animosity, and perhaps lower her guard.

They met in a small room. Most of the space was taken up by the table. A deputy brought in a fifth chair for the stenographer, who had a tape recorder.

Vik handled the introductions. Marti knew the attorney, David Greeley. He worked in the criminal division of a large Chicago law firm. His hair was graying at the temples now, and he had put on a little weight, but she still remembered their two courtroom confrontations years ago. Greeley's handshake was firm. His eyes had a wary look that suggested he might remember her, too.

"I understand I'll be here until tomorrow," Eileen said. "It's not a mansion, but what the hell."

Marti's immediate thought was, she thinks she's gotten away with something. She glanced at the lawyer. He too seemed relaxed.

Vik went through the obligatory introductions for the tape—who was present, that Eileen understood her rights as explained.

"So, Mrs. Smith," he began.

"Just call me Eileen." She smiled but her eyes, more gray than blue today, made Marti think of steel.

"Why did you have the skeletal remains and the manacles, chains and collars in your possession?"

"My father-in-law had just passed away and he had asked me to make sure the bags in the cellar were taken to a landfill if he died."

"Did you know what was in the bags?"

"No."

"Did you look in the bags?"

"No."

"Why did you do this at night?"

"You and the other officers were at the house all day."

"So you did understand that this was to be done in secret."

Marti scored one for Vik when Eileen paused to think about that. She looked at the lawyer. He remained impassive and didn't interrupt.

"I might have been under that impression," Eileen admitted.

"Why?"

"The bags were in the cellar. He didn't want anyone else in the family to know about them."

"And you didn't question that?"

"You didn't live there," she countered.

"Why were you wearing a winter hat with a ski mask?"

Marti scored another one for Vik. He had decided to leave the door open on the question of whether or not she knew what she was doing was illegal. That would give the state's attorney room to work with it.

"I didn't want the guards to see me." She smiled at Vik. "They would have called you."

"Your security guards or the police officers?"

"Either."

"You were carrying a weapon."

"Only because anyone could access the grounds. And I wasn't used to being out there at night."

"And you did fire your weapon after we identified ourselves as police officers."

"That was an accident," she said. "I'm not too familiar with guns. I didn't . . ."

A look passed between her and the attorney and she shut up.

When Vik didn't mention that two shots had been fired at them, Marti scored another point for him. Vik put his hand on the table. He didn't have any more questions. Marti didn't have anything to add.

Between being in a jail and confined in such a small, enclosed space, they were both a little twitchy as they walked into the sunlight.

"You and the lawyer know each other," Vik said.

"We've met a couple of times. Thank God I had a good training officer who made sure I never testified unprepared. He's one of those chew-you-up-and-spit-you-out types in court. No grandstanding, just a steady grind."

"We can handle that," Vik said. "They think they've got us."

"Right now they probably do."

They walked along for a few minutes. "I told Mildred I'd be home for a quick visit since I didn't go to Mass with her. It's almost noon now and this is going to be a long day, so I'm going to take care of that now. Why don't you come, too. She'd like seeing you."

Mildred was sitting on the back porch. Marti was taken aback by how much she had changed. Not just the weight loss or the cane and the walker by her chair, but a more subtle change. Her smile was tentative, wavering. Her voice not as strong. And for the first time that Marti could remember, she wasn't cheerful.

"Look at all the flowers," Marti exclaimed. "The garden is beautiful." She hadn't been out here since last summer. Everything had been grass then. Now there were flowers growing everywhere. Their fragrance sweetened the air and there were so many colors it was like walking into a rainbow.

"Vik had a gardener in last fall and again this spring," Mildred explained. "Now something is in bloom all of the time and the gardener comes back every few weeks and takes care of them."

When Vik sat down beside Mildred, Marti walked down the steps and followed a stone path until Vik called to her. On their way out, Helen handed them a bag. "Sandwiches," she said.

Back in the car, Marti said, "So, how bad is it?"

"It's not that bad, Marti. Could be a lot worse. It's her. She doesn't want to be this way. She's just got to work through it. Nothing is going to change."

"And you?"

"As long as she's here, I don't care."

"Does she know that?"

He was silent for a minute. "She knows. And sometimes that's enough." He paused again. "Memories," he said. "You fall, can't keep your balance, and you remember being able to dance in *The Nutcracker* and go ice skating. But that was then, and this is now."

"It can take a long time to get from where you were to where you are."

"I know," Vik said. "I know."

Omari listened to the strange noises around him. He felt too tired to open his eyes. A wheel squeaked. Someone flushed a toilet. A woman's voice said, "Let's try your left arm this time." The wheel squeaked again. And something was beeping. He felt a hand on his shoulder, then listened as his father prayed. He had never heard Pops pray. Maybe he was dead. He tried to open his eyes but could not. A voice he didn't recognize said, "He's coming out of it."

Lupe was sitting at Slim's desk when Marti and Vik returned to the office, going over the Smiths' telephone calls and limo service for the last three to six months. Marti checked her voice mail. She hadn't heard from Paisan or Angie Hutton, which could only mean there was no hit man out there. The killer lived right in that house. Who was it?

A half hour passed before Lupe called them over. Marti read through what Lupe had highlighted, then called the state's attorney and explained what they had. Within ten minutes he called back. Eileen's attorney was coming from Deerfield to speak with her.

By five-thirty Marti was back in the interview room trying not to feel claustrophobic. Eileen smiled at Vik.

"Let's begin with the telephone calls," Marti said.

Eileen reacted with a scowl.

"Are you familiar with this telephone number?" She read it out loud.

Eileen hesitated, looked at her attorney, nodded when he did.

"Please answer verbally."

"Yes."

"Whose phone number is it?"

"Kat Malloy."

Marti went to the limo reports.

"Where did your livery service take you on May fifteenth of this year?"

Eileen glared at her. Her eyes were steel-blue. The muscles in her shoulders tightened.

She gave Kat Malloy's Chicago address.

"And on June third?"

They had met at a restaurant.

Marti went down the list, repeated the highlighted dates and got the same responses.

"Why did you call and visit with Kat Malloy?"

"Because we had things to talk about."

Her attorney put his hand on her arm. "Eileen," he said. "Cooperate."

Eileen moved her arm away. "We had business to discuss. Family business."

"What did that business involve?"

"The sale of the Smith property."

"Eileen." The attorney interrupted. "We discussed what you would say. Please do not say anything else."

"My father-in-law, Josiah Smith, asked me to assist him in removing some remains and artifacts from his property, which was going to be sold or given away. I tried to do as he asked, but it became complicated when people outside of the family found things that they were not supposed to. I wasn't sure how to proceed, so I asked Kat Malloy what she thought I should do. She said she would handle everything."

"Do you know what she handled?"

Eileen looked at the attorney.

"I prefer not to answer that at this time."

"Then this interview is over."

As Marti stood up, the lawyer spoke again. "Give her an answer."

"When people outside of the family found things they should not have, or gained information they should not have, Kat took care of that."

"What are the names of these people?"

"Larissa Linski and Harry. I don't know his last name."

"How did she take care of them?"

The lawyer nodded.

"She went to the dig site, dug down to the root cellar and loosened two boulders. The next morning, the girl saw the hole, went down, and while she was down there, Kat pushed the stones on her."

"And Harry Buckner?"

"He found a collar, figured out what it was, and wanted money. She pushed him out of the barn window during the storm."

"Why did you speak with Kat Malloy six times on Thursday, July eleventh?"

The attorney raised his hand to silence her. "I think you have told them enough."

They got an arrest warrant for Kat Malloy and headed for the city.

As they drove, Marti thought about the strength it had taken for Eileen to get those bags upstairs and into the SUV. She had tried lifting the bag with the manacles; it was heavy. "You know, Jessenovik, I don't know how big this Kat Malloy is, or if she works out or whatever, but it would have taken a lot of endurance to dig down to that root cellar and a lot of strength to loosen those rocks. Kat could have done that and made the fieldstones fall on Linski, or we could have been talking with Linski's killer."

Because Kat Malloy lived in a three-story condo, two Chicago cops were posted at the rear and two at the front. Another two remained in a vehicle parked in front of Malloy's car.

One of the Chicago cops posted in front was grinning. "A senator's girlfriend."

"You can have the bust," Marti said. "We just want the action. We've been working this one for almost a month."

The Chicago cop touched his fingers to his cap and sauntered toward his partner.

260

The front door and first-floor windows had burglar bars. Marti and Vik unholstered their weapons. Vik rang the bell. A petite redhead, not more than five feet two, opened the door and looked up at them from the other side of a security chain. Marti noticed a scattering of freckles and deep brown eyes. Kat Malloy had to be close to forty and she was attractive. Marti had expected someone younger, and prettier, and certainly bigger. There was no way that the woman facing them now could have done what Eileen said she did.

They identified themselves as police officers.

"We'd like to speak with you, ma'am," Vik said.

"So speak."

"We thought maybe you would prefer to talk inside."

"You're kidding."

"No, ma'am. Do you see that man standing on that corner over there? The guy waiting for a bus?"

"And?"

"We tried to keep this from getting out, ma'am. Didn't want the news people to get hold of it because of the senator and all."

"Let me see your stars."

They took out their badges.

"You're not cops."

"We're from Lincoln Prairie, ma'am. If you want to talk with a Chicago cop, there are two of them standing right there and two more in the car parked in front of yours. Of course, that would get that man at the bus stop's attention."

She let them in. She was wearing a short loose-fitting dressing gown, belted at the waist.

"Ma'am," Vik said. "We have a warrant for your arrest."

Her face remained impassive as she said, "What are the charges?"

"Accessory to homicide, ma'am."

"Says who?"

"Says your accomplice, Eileen Smith."

"I don't believe you."

261

Marti holstered her weapon and pulled out the telephone and limo reports. "Care to sit down?"

They followed Kat into the living room. Everything was white, even the tables. Picasso-like abstracts flashed bright from the walls, complementing strange-looking sculptures with impossible to describe shapes and forms.

Kat sat on a a love seat. Marti sat across from her. Vik stood behind Kat, weapon at hand.

Marti asked the same questions she had asked Eileen Smith. Predictably, Kat Malloy placed the blame on Eileen.

As Marti merged with traffic on the Dan Ryan Expressway the next day she said, "Not bad, Jessenovik, two confessions. Even if they are blaming each other, it beats the hell out of circumstantial evidence. Their lawyers and that state's attorney will sort out who takes the fall for what. They won't get away with murder, even if we never know the exact truth."

She exited on the north side and drove down the street where the assault on Omari had occurred before heading to the hospital.

"Damned shame," Vik said. "All of this. When I was a kid I saw this Indian in the grocery store and he was wearing an army uniform. His hair was rubber-banded at the nape of his neck and hung halfway down his back. And nobody wore their hair long then. When I asked my father about it, he said it was because his people did not believe in cutting their hair. It wasn't until I was in college that I realized I had interpreted that as a sign of respect for Indian people. The reality of what we really did to them was a real kick in the ass."

"And this Omari," he went on. "The first funeral I ever attended was for the kid down the street. Another uniform, war this time, Korea. That kid had taught me how to ride my bike, patch the tires. My father showed him how to put a worm on a hook. We'd catch a mess of fish, bring them home, gut them and have them for supper. And there he was one day, nineteen, and in a casket. The funeral service wasn't anything like Mass.

It was the first time I understood that we were different. Me and my family were the only white people there. All of us were there because someone important to us had died. That was all that mattered to any of us that day. Joseph had died. I was never going to see Joseph again."

The hospital was just ahead. When Marti inquired about Omari, she was directed to the brain injury ward and expected the worst. Instead, a young man was sitting in the bed and talking on the telephone.

When he looked at her, she said, "You're all right."

"They tell me I slept for three days, but I feel just fine. I think I have to stay for another three or four days, though, at least."

After they identified themselves, Marti asked him what had happened. He didn't remember. She gave him her card. "There's someone I think you should meet, and when you're discharged from here, I'll arrange it."

"Who?"

"His name is Ethan Dana; his mother's great-great-grandmother was called Naawe. She and a slave woman named Dessa escaped to Wisconsin in 1835, with Dessa's newborn son, Samuel Thatcher."

"Samuel," Omari said. "I have found Samuel." Grinning, he reached for the phone.

23

A sheriff's deputy led the way to a small interview room. Marti and Vik had walked the three blocks from the precinct to the county jail in ninety-five degree heat. Inside the jail it was much cooler. Kat Malloy was talking with her attorney when they walked in. As soon as she saw them, she shut up.

Marti took the chair nearest the wall, out of Malloy's line of vision. Vik sat across from the petite redhead. Following her arrest, Senator Wagner had issued a three-sentence statement referring to her as a former senior staff member no longer in his employ.

Malloy turned to look at Marti. Her expression was neither hostile nor welcoming. She folded her arms and her jaw jutted out as she looked away. Marti thought of the senator's dismissive public comments after a ten-year relationship with her. She wondered if Malloy would try to get even. Then realized that politics being what it was, she already had.

Vik began the questioning. "You are aware that preliminary DNA testing as well as your palm print place you at the site of two homicides that took place on the Smith estate."

When she nodded, Vik said, "We need you to speak. This is being recorded and videotaped."

"Yes," Malloy said in a subdued voice.

"Were you at the scene of these crimes?"

"Yes."

"What happened at the Linski site?"

Malloy looked at her attorney. She looked to be in her early thirties, was tall and slender, and wore her shoulder-length brown hair in a simple but attractive style. Marti's first impression was that she seemed earnest, willing to cooperate, but she did not trust that impression. Malloy had become powerful in her own right during the years she had spent with the senator. She was not the kind of woman who would entrust her life to anyone who wasn't damned good.

"What happened at the Linski site?" Vik repeated.

The attorney nodded to her client and Malloy said, "Three holes had been dug there. Three in a row. Eileen went into the one at the east end. She dug down—until she came to a cellar with walls made of stones. She loosened two of them. The next day when we went back, the girl was down there. Eileen dislodged the stones. They fell on the girl."

"What happened at the barn?"

"I went there while the place was empty and found the slave collar. I should have let Eileen do it but she had to have her hair and nails done that day. I don't know what happened after that."

"Why did the two of you do this?"

"My client was not directly involved in either death," the attorney interjected. "Nor does she have anything else to say at this time. She will cooperate as appropriate."

Vik nodded to the video technician. This interview was over. There would be more. Since neither woman was admitting responsibilities for the murders, they would keep them short, specific, and review the transcripts and tapes many times.

Fifteen minutes later, they were interviewing Eileen Smith again. They had decided that they didn't know enough about Josiah Smith's death yet to ask either woman any questions about that. Eileen's attorney was present; Franklin had not visited her at all. According to the guard, she had called him repeatedly, stomping her feet and cursing because he had refused to come to the phone.

"What happened Sunday, June twenty-third, at the site where Linski was digging?" Marti asked.

"I don't know."

"What happened Saturday, June twenty-second, at the site where Linski was digging?"

"I don't know," Eileen repeated.

"Did you at any time go to that site?"

"No. I did not."

Neither Marti nor Vik intended to mention one woman to the other by name. They would convey what they wanted to about what each woman told them, during questioning. The women's lawyers would be communicating back and forth. That would be enough to keep the women accusing each other, and the more they accused each other, the more information they would be giving out. Even though what they communicated would be controlled by their attorneys, it was a no-lose situation for Marti and Vik.

"When did you go to the barn?" Marti asked.

"I've never been there."

"Were you there on June thirtieth?"

"No!"

"How long have you lived on the Smith estate?"

"Twenty-three years."

"And you never went to the barn."

"No."

Marti took out the three slave tags that they had found in a desk drawer in Eileen's sitting room.

Eileen gasped. Her hand went to her throat as she stared at them. There was a confused expression on her attorney's face.

"Damn," Eileen said. "I forgot. Josiah gave them to me."

Marti nodded to the video technician.

Vik drove to the Smith place. Marti's shoulder and arm were much better, but began hurting again when she used them.

"Let's let Paul and Franklin cool their heels someplace else while we have tea with Miss Clancy," Vik suggested.

When they returned to the sitting room near the kitchen, Marti settled back and relaxed. The pale yellow walls and chintz curtains made the room welcoming and cozy. She caught Vik looking at her and returned his smile.

Miss Clancy put on the teakettle, then rinsed the marmalade-cat teapot with warm water. She searched among boxes of tea, pausing to look at one, then another.

"Darjeeling," she suggested. "It tastes best without milk, but let's try it. I enjoy a cup of it this time of day. One of the things I like best about teas is that there are so many different kinds and so many ways to enjoy it. Come back again and we'll try a fruit herbal."

Marti watched Vik while Miss Clancy spoke. She was sure he wouldn't frown, but his eyes didn't squint a little either. He was enjoying this.

Miss Clancy prepared a plate of ham sandwiches, served on tiny rolls spread with butter. She went to the kitchen and returned with little squares of cake.

"Not a proper tea," she explained. "I've not baked yet today."

"And I haven't eaten since breakfast," Vik told her, helping himself to a sandwich.

Miss Clancy waited until Vik had helped himself to another sandwich, then asked, "Did Mr. Josiah really fall down those stairs?"

"Hard to say, right now."

"Mr. Josiah was always a gentleman," Miss Clancy said. "He was always polite. He never asked me to do anything that I did not feel was included in my responsibilities. He trusted me with many things that cooks are not often trusted with. I could order whatever I pleased, sign for deliveries, sign any other invoice that came to this house. Not once in forty years did he ever question anything I put my name to."

Too bad he wouldn't let her have a cat, Marti thought.

"And I was to go with him to Florida."

"Florida?" Vik asked.

"Yes." She lowered her voice. "The others didn't know, but

he was moving there, you see. Had already bought a house. He would have left this past Sunday, had he lived. Gave me an airplane ticket, he did. I was to leave this coming Saturday."

Vik thought for a few moments, then told her about the laser beam.

"We think they could have created some three-dimensional object that frightened him."

"Poor man," Miss Clancy said. "But that explains it. He fell, he did, or he said he fell. Hurt himself too, but nothing serious. Whatever it was, it happened in his room. He had another lock put on the door, gave me the keys. Didn't want anyone to know. Kept to himself and away from the others from then until he died. Didn't look like he got any sleep, though. What does this laser thing look like? How does it work?"

After Vik explained, Miss Clancy said, "Miss Eileen."

Marti was eating one of the cake squares. She paused in mid-bite.

"See that?" Miss Clancy pointed to the lamp by her chair. Except for the cats playing with yarn that were painted on the globe-shaped base, it seemed ordinary.

"I had that made special. One day it wouldn't work. Miss Eileen took it apart, did something with the wires, and fixed it. When I told Mr. Josiah, he said, "And I thought she wasn't good for anything." After she fixed this—it was a couple of years ago—I asked her to fix the toaster and a light switch in one of the bathrooms, and she did."

Marti and Vik exchanged looks. Marti didn't say anything. Vik asked if he could have the last sandwich.

"You just help yourself. I'll just make a few more and you can have some to take with you as well. The ham is imported from somewhere. I buy it by the case, so I have a lot for the freezer."

Marti recalled what she had said about feeding the poor.

"And this tea will be needing some warming up."

"Do you know Kat Malloy?" Vik asked as she refilled his cup.

"That one," Miss Clancy said. "I knew there would be trouble around here as soon as she showed up again."

"Showed up?"

"Yes, last Christmas. And her and Miss Eileen thick as thieves ever since."

"You've been reading the papers," Vik said.

"Yes, and nothing that I've read so far surprised me. Bad news, that Kat Malloy. Clever, but too much in love with Richard Wagner. Never came here, she did, unless she needed Josiah to give money or do something to help him."

Vik accepted another sandwich. "You wouldn't happen to know exactly when Miss Malloy came here?"

"Of course I do. Keep a calendar. I have to. With all the deliveries, all the limousines. It's the only way I can keep track when the bills come."

Miss Clancy opened a drawer, handed Vik a thick ledger. Vik paged through it and smiled. When she went to turn the heat on under the kettle again, Vik gave Marti a thumbs-up.

Before they went home, they returned to the site of the Potawatomi village. Mr. Nozhagum and friend were there. A Porta Potty and a camper had been provided for them by Paul, as well as wooden deck chairs with thick cushions for the seats and backs. A table had the remains of a picnic and tall glasses of lemonade.

Ethan Dana was there too, sitting beneath a tree talking with Omari, who had been released from the hospital that morning. An elderly woman sat with them. She was elegant, almost regal, in a summery white dress, sandals, and a wide-brimmed straw hat. A younger man who looked a lot like the woman was there too. A breeze stirred the oak leaves. The sun filtered through the branches. As Marti watched them, scenes from Scott Fitzgerald's novels came to mind.

Mildred was sitting in the kitchen when Vik got home. She was alone, with just a dim light on.

"Are you all right?"

"Come sit beside me."

He pulled up a chair.

"I think the medicine the doctor gave me for the depression is beginning to work."

"That's good."

"It is good, Matthew. It was like I had a blanket pulled over my head. Everything was dark. Today, my leg got numb. Instead of the darkness, I thought, it's felt like this before, and it will again. And that was all. I didn't think about dying. I didn't wonder how long it would be before I could not walk at all. I didn't want to stay in bed all day. I sat outside this morning," she went on, "while it was warm but not yet hot. I did not complain to God because I cannot sit in the sun anymore, or tolerate the humidity. I sat beneath the tree and enjoyed all of those flowers. Do you know the butterflies come now, Matthew? All different kinds. And, you know what, I thought to myself, this is what my life has been like all these years. Like a beautiful garden. And now I don't even have to do my own weeding."

He touched her face, stroked her hair. "Moje Cerce," he whispered. "My heart."

"Moje cerce," she said, and smiled.

Marti brought Trouble inside when she got home and set the alarm. Bigfoot padded in and Goblin came out from her hiding place in the pantry. Marti could hear the boys overhead. She patted the dogs, gave them a treat, and found one of Goblin's catnip mice. Then she went upstairs. The Potawatomi project had progressed to the demonstration stage. Ben, Momma, and Joanna were watching as Theo and Mike floated their birch-bark canoes in a pan of water.

"How would you like to go to a real Potawatomi ceremony?" Marti asked.

"Like they have at the powwow every year?" Mike asked.

"I don't think so. It's a funeral."

"Has this got anything to do with those skeletal remains?" Joanna asked.

"We've all been invited to the burial ceremony on their reservation."

"A reservation!" Mike exclaimed.

"It doesn't have a casino, does it?" Theo asked.

"No. It's somewhere north of Madison. And a real reservation, no casino. My friend, Mr. Nozhagum, is a Strolling Potawatomi. He thought you might like to have these." She opened her purse and took out a buffalo-hoof rattle, a silver brooch, and a small leather bag decorated with beads.

The boys looked at them, but didn't touch anything.

"They're real, aren't they," Theo said.

"And old," Mike added.

Neither boy touched them.

"They're yours," Marti told them.

"We have to do something special with them," Theo said.

"And take real good care of them," Mike added.

The boys walked about the room, then cleared off a shelf. They were almost reverent as they arranged the artifacts.

"And guess what!" Mike grinned. "We're going to work on our family's genealogy next. The whole troop."

It was Momma's turn to smile. "They've got me walking around with a tape recorder telling it everything I can remember."

They all went down to the den. Marti felt exhausted and a familiar ache was beginning again, but she wanted to be with her family more than she wanted to get the heating pad and go to bed. Besides, everyone was still making a fuss over her. Theo and Mike took her shoes off and put on her slippers. Joanna went upstairs to make some tea. Momma checked the bandages and brought her some Tylenol. Ben plopped down on the sofa and said, "I've got the best job of all, comfort detail. All I've got to do is sit here, hold your hand, and tell you how much I love you."

"And I love you." Marti took his hand in hers and squeezed it. "I can't imagine what my life would be like without you. To think there was a time when I didn't think I would ever be happy again. Now I just enjoy it and thank God that we all have each other."

Franklin was in Josiah's room looking out the window when he saw it. There was a light of some kind moving among the trees. Eileen must have rigged up a hologram out there, although he couldn't imagine how. When clouds obscured the moon, the light became brighter and more defined. It looked like a woman. Curious, Franklin hesitated for a few moments, then went downstairs and outside.

The night was warm. The day's humidity lingered. The light was smaller. It seemed to be moving away from him. He rushed toward it, entered the grove of trees, lost sight of it for a moment, then saw it again. A tree branch brushed against his face. He pushed away another. He couldn't remember the last time he had walked here. The trees were much denser than he remembered.

An owl hooted. He looked up, saw a bat in silhouette as its flight path crossed that of the moon. When he looked at the light again, it was much closer. He could see that it was a woman. She raised her arm and beckoned to him. As he hurried toward her, he tripped over a tree root and fell forward.

The call came in at ten-fifteen the next morning. Marti listened. Franklin Smith's body had been found in the hole dug at the apple orchard site. Apparently, he had tripped over a tree root, fell in, and broke his neck. When she hung up, Marti looked at Vik and said, "You're not going to believe this."